unseen

By Amber Lynn Natusch

Unborn

The Caged Series
Caged
Haunted
Framed
Scarred
Fractured
Tarnished (novella)

Light and Shadow Trilogy
Tempted by Evil

Undertow (a novel)

unseen

AMBER LYNN NATUSCH

47NORTH

Text copyright © 2015 Amber Lynn Natusch
All rights reserved.

Published by 47North, Seattle

www.apub.com

Amazon, the Amazon logo, and 47North are trademarks of Amazon.com, Inc., or its affiliates.

ISBN-13: 9781477821374
ISBN-10: 1477821376

Cover design by Stewart A. Williams
Cover photo by Dannielle Gleim Damm

Library of Congress Control Number: 2014952351

Printed in the United States of America

*To my fans who have been patiently
(and sometimes not so patiently)
waiting for this book.*

You make me smile.

Whispers in the darkness,

From shadows on the wall,

telling of his wicked fate,

now echo through the hall.

The dead will soon be rising;

the mighty one doth pall.

The dead will soon be rising

to see his kingdom fall.

PROLOGUE

I had wanted to return home, but not like this—not to this.

This was no longer my home.

My dark companion and I entered the Great Hall, the epicenter of the Underworld, to find chaos awaiting us. Though one unfamiliar with the Underworld may have believed the havoc to be normal in a place such as this, it was anything but. My unease beset me immediately. I knew my father would never have allowed such upheaval. Not in the Great Hall.

The implications were grim.

With a tightening chest, I searched for him amid the near-rioting souls of the damned, desperate to catch a glimpse of the one who had raised me, cared for me—protected me. But I saw nothing; no one stood apart from the frenzying mass, whose screams were nearly deafening.

I had been gone for only a matter of days, but somehow, in that scant amount of time, all order appeared to have been lost. I could think of only one scenario in which that could have occurred, and it did not involve Hades being alive. With that realization in mind, I broke free of Oz's grasp and darted foolhardily into the mob, calling for my father.

No reply rose over the ruckus of the damned.

In an attempt to steer my thoughts in a more rational direction, I reminded myself where else my father was likely to be. If Hades was not in the Great Hall, then he would be in his chambers, far down the hallway that extended from the opposite side of the room. He would often retreat there to strategize, emerging only once he had devised a plan to counter a given situation. Upheaval of this magnitude, to my knowledge, was unprecedented in the Underworld. Surely he would be preparing to address it?

Provided he had not already met an unenviable fate.

My efforts to navigate the crowd were nearly futile; my body was tossed amongst the tormented beings. I wanted to let my wings erupt from my back, to spread them wide and take flight, but there was no room. My haste to find Hades had eliminated that option. So I struggled onward. With no way to see beyond the masses, I continued calling for my father, even though I knew that the cacophony reverberating throughout the stone-walled room would drown out my cries. But still I tried, my frustration mounting as I did.

And then I screamed.

The sound was shrill and sharp, and it cut through the room like a knife, leaving nothing but silence in its wake. I scanned the room to find it full of tortured souls, standing still and silent, their eyes fixed upon me. I continued my frantic search for my father amid this mute sea of pale, blank faces, crashing through them with a rising urgency, all the while shouting his name.

Then I heard mine in return.

It was faint and distant, but I knew his voice when I heard it. Father was alive. I forced my way through the frozen crowd, headed in the direction from which I had heard him calling. He cried my name over and over again, a growing sadness tainting his every cry. Finally, I pushed through the edge of the mob to find him standing in the hallway I had been destined for, his face peaked and slack.

"Father?" I said softly; his appearance caused me to falter.

"I have failed you, my princess."

A tear fell from his eye when he looked upon me.

"Father, what is wrong?" I asked, taking a step closer. His behavior was disarming.

"You should not have come here," he continued, his voice detached and distant.

"But I needed to see you. . . . I need your help, Father."

It was then that his eyes narrowed as they focused upon me with the shrewdness I had always known them to hold.

"If you have returned here, then I cannot help you, Khara. Even I cannot release the souls of the Underworld."

I looked at him in confusion.

"I do not understand."

His eyes softened, pity and regret filling them slowly.

"I would do anything for you, my princess, you know this. But I cannot let you leave," he whispered, leaning in closer. "Your soul belongs to me."

//////////////////////////////////////

1

"Well, this trip just got astronomically more interesting," Oz purred when he walked up behind me, my insides warming at the sound of his voice. Where Oz was concerned, my body continually betrayed me. It was most distressing.

Ever since he had been attacked, left for dead, and ultimately tainted by the souls I had taken into myself when I eliminated the threat that had stalked me in Detroit—the Soul Stealer that sought to make me Dark—Oz had seemed different, and yet also not. From the moment he leapt off the couch in my brothers' living room, his new, black wings erupting from his back, something in him called to me. He was not a dreaded Dark One as I had expected. A Dark One like those Father had long warned me of. There was an intensity in him that drew me to him most inexplicably. I tried to deny it. I tried to fight it.

Regardless, the call was ever present.

I did not bother to turn around to see the look of smug satisfaction on his face. This, his signature expression, had never wavered from his face since the moment we stole away from my brothers' home, fleeing under cover of night. Instead of looking to Oz, I studied my father's expression, which bled from disbelief to rage in a heartbeat when he caught sight of Oz. Then confusion settled in.

"You know this one?" he asked me, his eyes never leaving Oz's ominous form.

"I do. He is how I returned."

My response to his question garnered his immediate attention.

"He brought you here?"

"Of course. How else would I have come? Deimos did not bring me, nor did my usual escort, Aery—"

"You are not dead," he whispered before lunging toward me and crushing me in his arms. The gesture reminded me of Kierson. "I thought I would have felt you pass, but I have been distracted. . . . Things have been—" He cut himself off before explaining further, ever wary of Oz's presence.

Once the initial surprise of his overt display of affection dissipated, I realized what he had said. Then I realized why he had said it. His earlier words had not been a threat to detain me in the Underworld. He thought that I had died in the world above and I had come to him as so many others had—to be his eternal prisoner. What surprised me was that if I had come below in that way, then he should have felt my presence when I entered the Underworld. He always felt the arrivals of the newly departed.

Though I sometimes withheld my affections from Kierson, I showed them to my father. The Soul Stealer may have stolen my happiest memories of Hades during the attack in Detroit, but he could not steal the residual feelings they left behind. I loved Hades in my own way. That was not something that would change. In a rare act, I allowed my arms to wrap gently around his back, squeezing him lightly in return. Kierson had taught me much about love in my time with him. And the rapid changes in my own emotions since meeting my family and birthing my own wings seemed to further fuel my expression of his lessons in loving.

"I am not dead," I said. The continued quiet in the hall allowed me to speak softly; I no longer needed to shout to be heard above the riotous noise. "I am far more resilient than you give me credit for, Father."

"When you were taken—" He clipped his thought short, pausing for a moment. "I could not go to you. I could not find you. I dispatched all those I could to look for you, but they failed. Some remain on Earth, still searching for you."

"I have brothers," I told him, uncertain why I shared that information so disjointedly. It was as if the boys had taught me nothing about remaining reserved until security was ensured. My excitement had overridden my awareness, a mistake that often proved costly in my father's realm.

My mind wandered back to the night when Oz had whispered those ancient words to me on the rooftop of the Victorian; something deep within me had changed. His utterance had awoken a side of me that I had long thought disappeared. Emotions had forever been foreign to me, virtually absent from my being. But there was a stirring the night when I met my brothers, which intensified slowly until the night Oz thrust me over the roof's ledge. As soon as my wings emerged, life as I had known it changed.

Hades pulled me away from himself quickly, his eyes darting around the room while he reviewed the congregation of damned that continued to stare at us, unmoving. He did not comment on the bizarre scene.

"Come with me," he said, ushering me down the hall toward his chambers. I followed his directive, as I always had.

"Father," I started cautiously. "What of the Great Hall?"

"I will take care of it."

"But why were all those souls—"

Hades stopped abruptly and turned to face Oz, who had been following us. My father did little to contain his irritation.

"Your services are not required any longer. You can leave," he said curtly, turning and continuing on without awaiting Oz's reply. It mattered not. Oz never bothered to give him one. He sauntered behind us as though he had not been dismissed. When Hades realized this, his irritation grew to outright anger. "You. May. Go." He clipped his words, making them sharper and harsher.

Oz eyed him curiously for a moment, seemingly amused by my father. He then turned his assessing eyes to me, as though he was trying to gauge my thoughts. But he would learn nothing from my expression. I took confidence in the knowledge that my visage remained just as steady—just as indifferent—as it always had in the Underworld. When it came to Oz, however, even though I managed to maintain a façade of tempered indifference, my body warred against it.

"Though I appreciate the gesture, I think I'll be staying. I have a vested interest in Khara. Leaving her alone here is not part of my plan."

"Your interest in her is not as vested as mine," Hades retorted quickly, pulling me to his side and away from the towering dark angel.

"I would not be so certain of that," Oz replied, his voice low and his tone cautionary. It was plain that he would be staying, regardless of Father's wishes. And it was strange to witness such a struggle for power between the two of them. It was an intriguing sight, indeed.

"He knows my brothers, Father," I explained, hoping to refocus the conversation onto the topic of importance. "He was there. He lives with them," I started, realizing the tense I had used was no longer correct. "He lived with them. They were the ones who found me where I was left by my abductor. They took me in and cared for me. Trained me. Kept me safe."

"This one, too?" Father asked, eyeing Oz with a dubious glare.

I was unsure how to answer him.

"He played a role."

"Yes," Father sneered. "I am quite certain he did."

Perhaps Oz's reputation preceded him, even in the Underworld.

"Shall we . . ." I said, staring down the hall to Hades' room. He followed my gaze and then ushered me in that direction, Oz tight on our heels.

"Perhaps we can find some time alone to discuss the entity that is stalking behind us," Father whispered to me as we walked.

"There is little to discuss."

He scoffed in response.

"I highly doubt that, Khara."

With no further remarks, we—Oz included—made our way into his private room, and he closed the stately doors behind us. I had sought refuge in his room before, so I was familiar with it, but Oz was not. He surveyed the cavernous domain, taking in every nook and corner, assessing it as though in preparation for battle. If he had come there in hopes of one, he would soon learn it unwise to challenge my father in his realm, Dark One or otherwise. Father may have been wary of Oz—of all Dark Ones—but he would not step down from a challenge, even if it might prove one he would ultimately lose. That knowledge made me further suspicious of their behavior in the hallway. It had been a standoff of sorts but did not escalate there, almost as if they were testing the waters, seeing how much latitude they had with one another. It was an unprecedented scene as far as I was concerned. I had seen my father's orders refused on only one occasion, maybe two. The fates of the defiant were unenviable.

But those that had challenged him had never been Dark Ones.

Just as my curiosity about the duo began to heighten, I heard Hades call to me.

"Khara?" he asked as though he had been trying to gain my attention for eons.

"Yes, Father?"

"I feel as though I do not know where to begin. . . ." He looked at me from only feet away, a deep sadness filling his eyes. Oz was still familiarizing himself with the room, pacing it slowly, but I knew he was listening. That was surely the reason he had insisted on accompanying us in the first place. "I knew of your siblings," Hades admitted, his eyes dropping away from mine for a moment.

"You knew?"

"I knew who you were born of, Khara, and I am perfectly aware of the Petronus Ceteri and those who are in it."

"Why did you not tell me?" I asked, noticing the slightest note of sadness in my own voice. I had always known my father to be a strategist. But what advantage he had seen in not telling me of my family was beyond my comprehension.

"My princess, please understand that I did not do this to hurt you. I did it to keep you from being hurt. Potentially," he offered in his defense. When I said nothing, he continued. "It seemed cruel to dangle a life in front of you that you could never have. Though I may torment those I reign over, I would never intentionally do the same to you. You have been kept hidden for a reason. To jeopardize your safety by telling you something that could have broken the covenant would have been foolishness on my part. It was a risk I would not take . . . even if it now means your resentment of my actions."

I ruminated on his explanation for a while before replying. The sincerity in his tone was undeniable. He had done what he thought was best for me. I could not ask for more than that from him.

"I understand," I said plainly. "But what I do not understand is why, after all this time, I was taken from the Underworld. Have you any knowledge of why that occurred? That was the primary question that my brothers and I were unable to answer in my time with them. Though there were others."

His lips pressed firmly together and his brow furrowed. Everything about his expression told me that he was weighing his response. And that told me that he very likely knew why the Dark One had come for me. I hoped that meant he knew other things as well.

"The covenant that bound you to both Demeter and me was broken. Once that happened, you were returned to Earth, and Persephone was brought back to me, where she will remain."

"When the Dark One absconded with me, I heard you say you had feared that day would come. Why did you say this? How could you have known such a thing?"

His eyes narrowed.

"Because when something so important rests solely on the virtue of those bound to it, it is certain to fail. I knew who I was getting into bed with. It was only a matter of time before a misstep happened." He moved toward me, extending his hand for me to take, which I immediately did. "And one did. Now, the only question is why."

"And who," Oz called from the far side of the room. "If it fell apart because of a weak link in the chain, then you should be curious who that weak link was, should you not?"

"Your participation is not needed in this discussion," Hades said, turning his attention to Oz.

"Maybe not. Or maybe it is. I just find it interesting that you're not doing all you can to discover who it was that breached your magical contract."

"I do not care for what your words imply, Dark One," Hades warned.

"I am merely noting that, if it were I who had had something of great value stolen while under my care and protection, I would not rest until I knew whose death to seek in retribution."

"Do not mistake my tact in this matter for an attempt at misdirection. I can assure you that the party responsible for this disruption is never far from my mind."

"Then you know who it is," Oz pressed while he moved to stand behind me. Close behind me.

Hades said nothing, only stared over me at Oz. When he was done silently warring with him, his eyes returned to mine.

"We will soon know more, I am certain," he assured me, giving my hand a light squeeze. "In the meantime, I want to know more about what happened to you. I was so worried."

"It has been an eventful few days," I told him, pulling my hand away from his. "The Dark One who took me left me in Detroit, which is a city of veritable squalor filled with seedy supernaturals and copious amounts of evil. However, within minutes of my arrival, one of my brothers—a high-ranking member of the PC—found me, as I mentioned before. It was rather serendipitous, though he initially tried to kill me." Hades' dark eyes quickly turned to bottomless pits of rage at my words. My explanation was doing little to portray my siblings in a favorable light. "It was not his fault. He had mistaken me for something else. Once he realized both who and what I was, he took me to meet the others, and from that point on they all worked to protect me while sorting out precisely what had happened to me and why."

"And what did they come up with?"

"Nothing but conjecture, though I imagine you already know the answers."

His eyes softened yet again.

"There were things I could not tell you, Khara, though not because I did not wish to."

"The binding covenant," I stated plainly. "It kept you from sharing certain details and information."

"Precisely."

"And now that it is broken?"

"I can share what I know, though I fear that, in light of what you have already learned from your time above, what I am able to share will offer you little."

"Why was I given to Demeter?"

"The exact reasons are not known to me. That was before my involvement with you, Khara. I never asked Demeter why you were left in her care, and she never volunteered the information."

"You do not know my mother, then?"

"I know of your mother by reputation alone. That is all."

"You have never met her?"

"No."

"What can you tell me about her?" I asked, my voice carrying the sudden frustration I felt.

"Her name is Celia. She used to reign in the world of the Light Ones. She was fierce but merciful. Tales of her skill as a warrior have long been told. Many have come to the Underworld by her sword."

Celia . . . I rolled her name over in my mind. It was familiar to me. Oz had said it once on the rooftop of the Victorian. He had spoken to her as if she could hear him.

"You use the past tense when you speak of her," I observed. "Is she no longer these things?"

"I have not heard her name spoken for centuries," Father hedged, his expression faltering for a moment. "Not since the time surrounding your birth." There was an apology in his stare, though I could not yet gather why.

"You know what you need to about her," Oz cut in gruffly, his body brushing against my back. My mind and body had conflicting responses to his proximity.

"Which is little more than nothing."

"Precisely."

"Was she Dark?" I asked, addressing the room. I cared not whom the answer came from. Though I knew deep down that she must have been, I wanted the confirmation. I needed it.

Oz became still behind me. I could no longer feel his breath in my hair.

Father, however, exhaled heavily, preparing to speak.

"There were rumors—speculation about how the Queen of the Light had been . . . *tainted*," he started. I felt Oz's chest rumble against my back. "Persephone alluded to Ares having courted Celia, luring her to a life she was not intended to live. After that, her name was never mentioned in connection with the Light. And only a few months after that, you would have been born."

"And then?"

"I have heard no mention of her since."

I absorbed the weight of his unspoken words.

"You think she is dead."

"That is my belief—"

"My brother, Sean, said that Celia—our mother—had sent him a message, warning him that I was in danger."

"Khara," he said in a tone meant to placate me, "you, above all others, should know that the dead can send word to the living."

"He said she came to someone he trusted implicitly in a dream. That is not how the dead communicate."

"That is not how the *damned* communicate, my princess. You know not of how the saved return to those they once loved."

"But if she had been Dark and she was eliminated, she would be here," I contested, the slightest hint of anger polluting my tone.

"Perhaps," Hades replied with a shrug. "Dark Ones cannot be slain easily, for I have none residing with me. And since they are far from being saved, they would not go elsewhere." His piteous eyes bore through mine, willing me to see the truth he was convinced of. "I do not believe that your mother ever was Dark, Khara. I believe that unfounded story was used to cover up her disappearance from the Light while Ares held her captive. And, once finished with her, Ares did what he does so elegantly."

"Which is?"

"Tie up loose ends."

Again he reached for me, taking my hand in his to draw me closer. The moment my weight shifted toward him, Oz's hand clamped down on my shoulder, holding me where I stood. Hades' eyes flashed with rage when they locked with Oz's, but then calmed when they fell back to mine.

"Your mother has returned to her home, though in a different form. She is in the care of her kind now. You should find peace in that."

"You should not attest to things you cannot possibly know," Oz warned, pushing himself in front of me to stand defiantly before my father. "Celia is not dead. She is far from it. And there are other places to go upon death, Soul Keeper. Places far more dire than even here. I am confident you know this."

Hades' whole body tensed. The name with which Oz addressed him had insulted him.

"How could you possibly know where she is, fallen one? They do not allow your kind in the realm of the Light. Especially not when you are what you have allowed yourself to become. You are a disgrace to the Light. A stain on their pristine wings."

I did not need to see the look on Oz's face to know the satisfaction he felt when he delivered his rebuttal.

"Luckily, I do not need to return to my former home to confirm she is not there. Your daughter is living proof that she is not yet dead." Without further ado, Oz turned me around abruptly, tearing the back of my shirt open with his hands. "These," he said, harshly outlining my markings, "contain some very surprising and damning evidence that contradicts your contention. I have seen what they contain— what lies beneath is far from a shade of pure white."

"He speaks the truth, Father," I said, still facing away from him.

"No," Hades stated defiantly. "If you have indeed taken after your mother and have been gifted with wings, they are wings of the Light. They have to be."

"Show him, Khara," Oz demanded while his eyes remained fixed on my father's. "Show him he's wrong."

I looked over my shoulder, my eyes darting between the two imposing figures. It was clear that neither would be content until I showed them what my mother had bestowed upon me, blessing or curse that they might prove to be. With no further hesitation, I did as Oz had instructed me. Focusing on the extension of my still-unfamiliar appendages, just as he had taught me, I forced them through my raw and healing wounds. He said it would take time for the openings in my back to scar over, which would make the emergence less painful. I looked forward to that occurrence.

The burning that I had felt when they had initially sprung forth returned, unwelcome though it was. I masked my pain with a placid expression while my wings spread fully behind me, their collective breadth spanning more than ten feet. I glanced behind me to confirm their shade. My gaze took in the mottled-gray color I expected. The black was gone. It had been ever since I saved Oz.

Saved him or condemned him.

Carefully, I turned to face Hades, whose facial expression conveyed his disbelief. His hand drifted up to trace a feather of one of my wings. Judging by his reaction when he saw me observing his gentle act, he had been unaware that his hand had risen to do so.

"What are these?" he whispered to himself.

"Aside from the obvious, no clue," Oz answered. "She is an enigma. I have never seen anything like her."

"The Light have not claimed you?" Hades asked, his eyebrows drawing together. He looked utterly befuddled.

"No one has come for me," I answered plainly.

My reply was met with a low rumbling from Oz.

"I came for you."

A sound in the hall snapped my father from his disbelief and Oz from his growing anger at my oversight. Panic overtook Hades instantly.

"Put them away!" Hades ordered, pointing at my wings while he reached for the lock on the door. "Put them away immediately and do not release them again while you are here. Do you understand me?"

I tried to do as he bade me, but withdrawing the vast gray wings back inside me was challenging at best. At worst, it was an exercise in futility. While I struggled to put them back from whence they came, Oz stormed the door and my father, defiantly spreading his own dark appendages. He had not bothered to hide them upon entering the Underworld, and why would he? He was both feared and respected because of them. To discard such an advantage would have been lunacy.

"Make them go," Oz growled, his voice low while he leaned his ear to the door, his dominating form crowding Hades. Father looked as if he were going to tear Oz apart, piece by piece. Feather by feather.

By the time the great door buckled under the weight of the one trying to open it, I had almost succeeded in withdrawing the wings that would so clearly give me away. Focusing on the task before me, I pushed through the excruciating pain and retracted the last of them through the openings along my shoulder blades, leaving no trace of my newfound appendages, except for the healing scars. Oz's lessons in how to do so had paid off. With a gasp, I stood up straight, swallowing what remained of the burning pain in my back.

"Hades?" a woman's voice called. I turned to face the door, doing my best to situate the remnants of my tattered shirt behind me as I did. My wings would have certainly given me away, but my markings could have easily aroused suspicion in anyone curious enough to notice. And the Underworld was full of darkly curious creatures. "What is the meaning of this door being locked? And please do explain why things have suddenly gone so silent around here."

When I nodded to Hades that it was safe to open the door, he did so in a flash while Oz made his way back to my side.

"My love, I am so sorry. We were just discussing private matters. You surely understand," he gushed, sweeping the door wide open for the one I still could not see. A moment later, in walked a stunning woman, her dark hair intricately woven far down her back and adorned with gold. She wore lengths of red silk, wrapped about her in the ways of old. Whoever she was, she had not modernized over the centuries. She was a vision of the greater times, when Mount Olympus still reigned. Her dark, heavily rimmed eyes fell on Oz as she looked about the room, and a wicked smile marred her otherwise studied expression. Then they landed on me.

Her smile fell instantly.

"You," she said softly, though there was little warmth in her tone. "Who are you?"

"Persephone," Hades called, rushing to her side. With a calming hand on the small of her back, he introduced me. "This is your adopted sister, Khara."

At the mention of my name, her expression softened slightly.

"And here I thought you had finally decided to become a bit more *adventurous* in the bedroom. . . . I would have never forgiven you if you had done so without me."

Again, her eyes fell heavily on Oz, who stood stoically under a gaze that promised more than it should have, especially in my father's presence. I had long heard rumors that his wife was unfaithful, taking up with whomever she could whenever possible, but I assumed they were false. My father adored Persephone. I could not imagine him being so in love with someone who was allegedly a flagrant whore.

"So, *sister*," she said, reaffixing her gaze upon me and stepping toward me elegantly. There was a sense of grandeur about her, a regal quality that was befitting of her position. "Let me look at you." She swept her arms wide, and I turned for her slowly. "She is stunning. Her eyes—so green. I have only once seen a pair so vibrant."

"She is special," Hades added, a hint of a proud smile tugging at his lips.

"Indeed," Persephone purred. "But what on Earth has happened to her clothing? You allow her to dress like a human, and a poor one at that? Tattered clothing? Really, Hades. I think you could provide better for her, could you not?"

"She dresses as she chooses. And as for the state of her shirt," he began cautiously, "the Dark One is to blame for that."

Persephone's eyes widened with pleasure, taking in every inch of Oz. She seemed delighted by his alleged deviant nature.

"And who, pray tell, is this Dark One, sister? A friend of yours?" Her hooded eyes remained fixed on Oz, his bare chest accentuated by the dancing firelight in the room. While she took him in, his wings twitched. He appeared irritated by her. One look at his face confirmed that suspicion in an instant.

"He is unimportant, and he is also leaving," Hades cut in, not allowing Oz or me the opportunity to answer Persephone.

She smiled widely at his interruption.

"Now, now, dear. No need to be so testy," she drawled, turning her body to press against him. Taking his hand in hers, she continued to stare at Oz in all his winged glory. "He is Khara's friend, no? We should be a tad more hospitable, do you not agree?"

Hades looked down at her, and she turned her chin up toward him, wearing a pleading look on her face. Hades' emotions played out in his countenance. He did not agree, that was plain, but he seemed unwilling to go against his wife's wishes, however ill-conceived they might be.

"He is still here. Is that not hospitality in and of itself?" he countered. Her amusement with his reply was evidenced by the sparkle in her dark eyes.

"So generous," she purred, slowly pulling away from him to look back to Oz and me. "Now, I came looking for Hades because I was ever so curious about the Great Hall, which is now full of unmoving souls. I could not help but wonder how that came to be." Her eyes fell heavily on me. "Might you two have something to do with that?"

"That was my doing, love," Hades cut in. "I had called forth various souls whom I thought could be of use in the search for Khara—souls that might have had an understanding of where the Dark One would have taken her. I left them unsupervised for only minutes, wanting to get Deimos to question them with me; then I heard the ruckus brewing and Khara calling for me once it was silenced."

"Silenced? How curious. Tell me, will you leave them to stand there paralyzed for eternity?" Persephone gently pressed.

"No. I shall get Deimos to dispatch them to their rightful fields now."

Persephone turned to face my father, pulling lightly on his arm to force his face closer to hers. She kissed him lightly on the cheek, then whispered in his ear.

"Where has he gone?" he asked her, pulling away from her with surprise. Her eyes fell on me heavily, and Hades' followed.

"Back above to find her."

Hades pressed his lips together in a look of utter frustration.

"That complicates things," he began. Persephone pulled him close again, speaking softly into his ear. He nodded once in agreement with whatever she had said and then headed toward the door. "I shall go and address the situation in the Great Hall," he said, stopping by the exit to address me. "I will dine with you later, my princess. We have much to talk about."

I inclined my head in a show of respect to my father. Oz did not move. Once the door closed behind him, Persephone turned back toward us, a wicked smile on her face.

"Now," she said, clasping her hands in front of her. "Shall we get to know one another better? I have heard so much about you, sister.

But I would like to observe you myself and draw my own conclusions. I do so hate to be misinformed."

She approached me, keeping her eyes focused intently on me. Their depth was mesmerizing. It was only when Oz stepped in front of me, blocking her from my view, that I came back to myself.

"I think Khara is otherwise engaged for the night," Oz rumbled, his tone a warning.

"Aw, pity that," Persephone replied. I could hear the pout she feigned in her voice. She bent down so that she could peek beneath Oz's outstretched wings. "I will come find you later then, sister."

Without awaiting my response, she disappeared behind the ominous veil of Oz's black wings and walked out of the room, the sound of her soft footfalls accompanying her departure. Once they faded, Oz turned and faced me, his deep brown eyes searching mine.

"I think it's time for you to give me a tour of this place, starting with your room."

A rush of blood surged through me at his words. I quickly stifled it.

"You do not trust her?" I questioned.

"No," he replied firmly. "Persephone is many things, but trustworthy is hardly one of them."

"Do you trust anyone?" I countered, knowing that during the time I had originally become familiar with him—when he was simply fallen, not Dark—he was wary of virtually everyone surrounding him. Everyone but me. I seemed to provide him with an unending source of amusement and intrigue.

He quirked a brow at me, an amused smile spreading across his face.

"It's as if you don't know me at all," he said softly, leaning closer to me. "Don't worry. You will. Eventually you'll know me all too well."

An awkward pause extended between us while his face hovered near mine, an invitation—a precipice he dared me to jump from. When I dropped my gaze from his, he laughed, turning to leave the room without any further discussion.

"You coming, new girl?" he asked over his shoulder, stopping to straddle the threshold of the doorway as he did. "Leaving me to explore on my own would be ill-advised."

Indeed, it would.

I headed toward the doorway and pushed past him to exit into the hallway. Although the opening was massive, Oz seemed to dwarf it inexplicably. Even with his wings tucked in tightly behind him, they were formidable in size. Their bulk left little room in the door-way, which forced me to push against his chest when I slid past. His eyes were forever on me when I did. The immense weight of his stare was nearly paralyzing.

Once I stepped into the hallway, I could breathe more easily. I turned to walk down the high-ceilinged yet narrow stone corridor, knowing that Oz would follow. My Dark shadow was he.

"This wing of the Underworld is for those that reside here to serve my father," I explained, not bothering to turn and look at him. "Or those that have been 'assigned' to this place as punishment but are not deceased."

While we continued onward, we passed wooden doors along the way to the rooms of those that inhabited this part of my father's king-dom. The hall was winding, and it seemed to extend forever. There was an end, though, and it was where my room was located, right next to the library.

"This is the room I took when I would spend my six months here," I said, opening the door and entering the vast but sparse space.

"Homey," he said mockingly. He brushed past me to case the room and its belongings, of which there were few. "No wonder you liked the basement at the Victorian so much."

"It was familiar," I replied. I watched him pick up a hand mirror off a simple wooden bureau before I made my way over to his side, opening one of the drawers to procure a new top to wear. One that was not shredded in the back. "I prefer things that way."

He looked down over his shoulder, cocking his head curiously at me.

"Your life will never be the same again, new girl. You do understand that, don't you?"

"Perhaps." I grabbed a plain black turtleneck out of the dresser before closing the drawer. The garment was one I often wore in the Underworld. It was soft and tight and warm. I stroked it as I walked away from Oz. It was then that the truth in his words smacked me. I was not cold. I had always been cold when I spent my time below. Now, for the first time ever, I was not.

"No, there is no 'perhaps' about it. Gone are the days of being in the custody of others. You are a warrior, an angel, and a vessel of the dead. Your life as you knew it is no more." He stalked slowly toward me while he spoke, the intensity of his words and the care with which he chose them demanding my attention. And he had it. Even as I pulled the tattered remains of my shirt over my head, I could feel his eyes on my body. "I said this once before, and I maintain its veracity still. You are an impossibility, Khara. There is no other like you. There never will be. The circumstances that brought you into this world will never again be duplicated. Your uniqueness brings you power—a power you must decrypt, study, and master. It will be your ticket to that which tempts you so."

"Precisely what is it that you think I want so ardently? I just told you that I prefer that which is familiar." My voice was far softer than I had intended. His looming presence while I pulled the cashmere sweater over my bare torso did something to me. Something I was loath to admit.

"You forget, new girl. I have seen the truth in your eyes. Your composed and compliant demeanor belies your true desire—*freedom*."

"I can have that now. I am no longer Hades' ward, and I will never have to return to that deplorable motherly figure, Demeter, again."

"You can never be free here," Oz rumbled. I turned to see his narrowed eyes absorb my form. "Which reminds me. I have something I need to do." Without another word, he hurried toward the door, pulling it closed behind him as he disappeared into the hall. Then, suddenly, his head peeked back through the doorway, a mischievous look on his face when he did. "And, new girl? Don't wander far from your room. I'll be back for you soon."

Both his words and the slamming of the door that followed them jarred me out of my confusion. Whatever had possessed Oz to leave so abruptly, I knew that it could not have been good. Exhausted both physically and mentally, I made my way to my bed and sat down on it with a somewhat inelegant thud. I wanted to sleep, but my mind raced furiously, unwilling to yield to the fatigue that plagued it. I did not relish the sensation. Thoughts of the Great Hall and my father's quick dismissal of what had transpired there, Persephone, and Oz ran through my head, mixed in with those of Deimos, my gray wings, and my absent brothers. Being away from them—my newly acquired family—felt indescribably wrong. I may not have realized it while in their presence, but something connected all of us on the most basic of levels. I felt a part of something greater when I was with them. Away from them, I felt a rift in my being—a pestering void.

Casey, Drew, Pierson, and especially Kierson—I missed them. All of them. It surprised me when I heard myself say as much out loud, my voice startling me out of my ruminations.

With my mind finally succumbing to the weariness I felt, it was not long before I found myself reclining on the bed, tired from the long journey home and the unexpected happenings that had transpired upon our arrival. Hades was taking care of those in the Great Hall, and Oz was off doing whatever it was he felt he needed to. Knowing that investigating either matter was futile, I decided to sleep. Fatigue would not benefit me in my endeavor to find out all I wanted to regarding my mother, what I was, and what could be done for Oz.

He would soon be coming back for me, and I would need my wits about me in his presence in order to override the ridiculous inclinations my body had toward him. No matter how strong the attraction I felt, I needed to keep my distance from the Dark One. Centuries of Father's warnings could not be dismissed so easily. Danger followed in the Dark Ones' wake.

And I no longer wished to be cannon fodder.

2

I awoke alone. Oz had not returned, despite his threat to do so. But I did not remain alone for long.

Outside my room, I could hear a man's voice in the hall accompanied by high-pitched laughter that sounded like the tinkling of bells. Trouble was headed my way, regardless of whether or not I desired it. The approaching laughter was a testament to that.

Before I could even exit my bed, the door to my room was slowly opened, and a tiny, familiar face—one I had known for longer than I could recall—poked around the edge of it. She could not contain her enjoyment of the situation, as was evidenced by the pure elation in her expression.

"I wanted to come and see you the second I heard you were back, but I got sidetracked," Aery said, her petite, lithe frame prancing into the room. She looked over her shoulder and shushed someone who remained behind her in the hall before continuing. Despite her size, Aery was an Underworld nymph who warranted respect. I had seen her take on and defeat more than one of Father's warriors. It was part of the reason she was kept in the Underworld. That, and her ability to ferry its inhabitants to the world above and back. "I hope you don't mind," she continued, motioning to whomever she had just silenced, "but I picked up a couple of things for you, you know, as a welcome-back present."

Just as I started across the room toward her, two other familiar faces came into the room—a welcome-back present indeed. Kierson came running at me, scooping me up in his arms the way I had grown accustomed to. Not far behind him was Casey, who wore his signature scowl. Though I tried my best, I could not contain my felicity at their appearance. Balancing my need to return to the Underworld for answers against my increasing desire to stay with my new family had become a source of great tension in my mind during my short time in Detroit. But now, having them in the home I had long known made my decision to return to the Underworld far more sufferable.

"I hope you don't mind, Khara," Aery called from behind us. "I came to your room last night and heard you talking to yourself about your brothers. I just couldn't help myself."

Nymphs were stereotypically a mischievous lot, but Aery took that trait to a new level. She watched my brothers and me reunite with an impish grin on her face.

"How did you know?" I asked her, wriggling free of Kierson's grasp. The disbelief in my voice was plain. If she knew I had brothers and knew who they were, then she also knew who I was born of. That meant the secret that had been tightly kept for centuries was more exposed than I had imagined. First Deimos, now Aery: who else knew of my lineage?

Aery shrugged shyly, clasping her hands behind her back in an attempt to look innocent. It almost worked. When I scowled at her, she dropped her hands to her sides and set her shoulders back, reminding me that she was not the helpless young girl that she appeared to be.

"Deimos . . . when he returned from his search for you, I *might* have overheard him raging in his room one night. His rant may have included a few sordid details pertaining to you."

"Such as?"

"Your 'fucking PC brothers and their fucking meddling,'" she explained, using air quotes as she mimicked Deimos' tone. "He also mentioned Detroit and something not going to plan, so I assumed that was where you had been. There are only a few PC warriors in that city, so I took a chance and hunted them down." She leaned toward me, covering her mouth with the side of her hand as though to keep her next revelation between just her and me. "But don't worry, Khara, your secret is safe with me. The boys read me the riot act when I arrived at your house. And by 'read me the riot act' I mean they basically flipped their shit and tried to kill me." She smiled at my brothers in a taunting manner. "But we straightened all that out rather quickly, didn't we, boys?" Neither brother responded.

"Then we shall not speak of this again," I told her, my warning clear in my tone. She nodded in affirmation, her countenance serious.

"I'm so mad at you," Kierson declared, snatching me back up into one of his monstrous embraces. It was strange to me that what had not so long ago been foreign to me felt so comforting in that moment. I had missed him—probably more than I had even realized. To show him just how much I had, I wrapped my arms around his neck and squeezed him in return.

"I am sorry for how I departed," I apologized softly. "I saw no other way. Not at the time."

"You should have come to us," he continued, a look of sadness plaguing his expression when he pushed me away enough for me to see it. "You should have come to *me*."

"I knew that my actions would hurt you, Kierson. Especially you. But I needed to come home for answers," I explained. "You are always concerned for my safety. My hope was that, by unearthing the truth of my past, there would no longer be a need to fear for me at all. Oz provided the opportunity for me to return. I saw no reason to pass it up."

"Bat. Shit. Crazy," Casey growled, eyeing me as though he would strike at any second.

"It is nice to see you as well, brother," I replied, raising one of my brows slightly while I looked at him over Kierson's shoulder. Casey could not suppress the smile my response elicited from him.

"I can't say I approve of your choice in transportation," he drawled, looking around the room as if searching for the Dark One.

"Sometimes we are not in a position to be choosy."

His smile widened.

"Apparently not."

Kierson reluctantly released me, placing me gently on the ground, and I looked over to Aery, who was still hovering near the doorway. I was uncertain if I would find her pouting in defeat, had her intentions been to start the trouble her kind is notorious for; instead, I found her beaming.

"So I did well?" she chirped, barely able to contain herself. She fidgeted with the scarf that was tied around her waist while her gaze jumped wildly from face to face, seeking approval. "They all wanted to come, but I could manage to bring only these two before you woke up." Her gaze then fell heavily on Kierson, a wicked smile overtaking her countenance. Aery's particular expression was far more familiar to me from my extensive time with the nymph—it was one she wore often. "That one insisted I bring him first," she explained, pointing to my sensitive brother. "I thought he was going to kill the others if they cut in front of him."

"I am not surprised," I replied, stealing a glance up at him. I was rewarded with a playful grin.

"That one," she continued with disdain now tainting her words. "I don't know how you deal with him." She had fixed her eyes upon Casey. "He is barely tolerable. So gloomy with his whole 'I'm scarier than your worst nightmare' shtick. Really, it's been done before. You want scary, hang out around here for a while." She leaned toward him in a conspiratorial manner. "Take notes."

That was the Aery I remembered: flighty one moment, fierce the next. Perhaps Casey had met his match.

Casey said nothing in response, which only furthered Aery's assessment of him.

"I must admit that I am surprised that you came, Casey, instead of Drew," I said.

He shrugged.

"I thought I would come see what all the hype was about." His response was aloof, but, given our previous conversation about being cast out and orphaned by his mother, I knew he had wanted to come to see the life that had been taken from him. The one he felt entitled to. His mother, Hecate, would not be far from Persephone at any given time, and she not far from my father. Casey was certain to encounter her eventually. That reunion was sure to bring about the type of chaos that would entertain Aery for years, should she be fortunate enough to be present for it. It would make for the gossip her kind thrived upon.

"And what is your assessment thus far?" I asked, already knowing what he would say in response.

"It's dark here."

I felt a tugging at the corners of my mouth.

"Then you should feel right at home."

"Okay, okay," Aery shouted, clapping her hands together excitedly. "So, tell me. Where is he? The Dark One? I've heard rumors. I need to see this one for myself." She looked as though she would explode with excitement at the thought of meeting Oz. The concept baffled me.

"He seems to be absent for the moment," I replied.

She thrust her bottom lip forward dramatically, folding her arms across her chest as she did.

"Well, I expect to meet him," she informed me. "No hiding him from me! You know how I feel about brooding immortals."

"I shall do my best to arrange a meeting, then," I told her in placation. There was such a childlike quality to her at times that I could not help but wonder if she was not better suited for the likes of

Kierson. Oz would certainly not entertain the possibility of bedding someone like her.

My face reddened at the thought.

"Khara?" Kierson called.

"Sorry. Yes?"

"We want you to come home," he said solemnly, unveiling his true reason for making the journey to join me in the Underworld. It was not to visit. It was to rescue me. "Drew especially. He totally freaked out when he got that little note you left."

"I am sorry for that, truly. I shall be sure to apologize to him when I return to the Victorian." I felt a small pang of what I had come to know as guilt in my chest. "You did not say why he stayed behind, though. It surely had to be something of great importance if his desire was to come here instead."

"He would have come, but when he told Sean what you had done—and let me tell you, your twin is some kind of pissed off at you and your unannounced trip home, too—Sean freaked out on him." He grimaced at the memory of my twin brother's reaction to the news of my escape to the Underworld. I knew Sean's wrath to be quick and punishing; my chest constricted at the thought of what he might have done to Drew if he had viewed my running off in the night as Drew's fault somehow. "It was *not* a pretty sight."

"I was almost certain Sean was going to flay him alive," Casey added. His appraisal of what occurred did little to assuage the guilt I already felt. "When the nymph showed up unannounced, Sean forbade Drew from leaving. He said he had something for him to do. Something that could redeem him and reinstate him to his position in the PC. Obviously, being the good little soldier that Drew is, he stayed."

"And Pierson stayed because, well, he's Pierson," Kierson said with a shrug, as though his twin's name was explanation enough. Having spent time with Pierson, I understood what he was saying.

"If only he had known of the library the Underworld boasts," I added, no jest in my tone at all. My brothers were both unable to stifle their amusement.

"Talking about me again, I see," Oz said as he walked in the room. He, too, looked amused, though I had no idea why. "And I hardly came here for the books, new girl. I think you should be aware of that by now." He added a flirtatious wink to his sardonic comment for effect. If the response he wished to garner was unadulterated rage from both of my brothers, he elicited it. From Aery, however, he received no less than complete and utter admiration.

Her stance may have even faltered slightly in his presence.

"I see that little about him has changed, other than his fluffy new appendages," Casey sneered, giving little more than a sideways glance at the object of his disdain. "Same old ego-driven asshole."

"No," Oz countered. "Not the same ego-driven asshole. An even bigger one. One that can destroy you far more efficiently than before." That comment got Casey's attention, and he turned his black, hate-filled eyes to the Dark One. "Care to see if I'm right?" Oz challenged.

Before Casey could take the bait, I interceded.

"Aery, could you please take the boys to get something to eat? I'm quite certain that Kierson at least is hungry. Casey, you go too; make sure Kierson doesn't get into any trouble while there. It is not uncommon for possessiveness of food to start a fight amid Father's warriors. Given how much Kierson likes to eat, I fear he might inadvertently create a situation that would require mediation."

"So you want me to babysit?" Casey asked, fixing his dark eyes on mine.

"Yes."

"You know my thoughts on babysitting."

"I do, but, given the likelihood of a skirmish, I thought you would welcome the opportunity to possibly kill something. It seems to do wonders for your mood."

Again, Casey could not contain his amusement.

"Well, when you put it that way . . ." he replied, heading to the door. He brushed past Oz, being sure to knock his shoulder into him on the way. "We're not done," he added, looking behind him at the soulless angel.

"On that we can agree." When Oz responded to Casey's threat, the tone of his voice sounded different than it had before. Darker. More foreboding. He sounded like the Dark One that had come for me the night he had changed into the Oz I now knew him to be. The ease with which he shifted back to that persona was unnerving. It warned of his true nature.

A warning I seemed loath to heed.

I watched Casey, Kierson, and then Aery file out of my bedroom, Aery looking back mischievously at Oz and me before closing the door. Perhaps entrusting the boys to her care was not the most prudent decision I had ever made, but it seemed the lesser evil when the other option was to allow Oz and Casey to fight to the death at the foot of my bed.

"Clever way to get me alone, new girl," Oz drawled, staring at me with a dark heat in his eyes. That, too, I recognized from the night he had changed. Pressed against the large windows of the living room in my brothers' Victorian, he had exuded raw sexual energy and danger. I could not deny the appeal of that heady combination, though I tried. Standing alone with him in my bedroom, no barrier separating us, I now found the draw painful to ignore.

"I wished to get Casey away, not to get you and me alone," I said, correcting his errant observation. I kept my eyes off him while I spoke, focusing them instead on the thick wooden door at the far side of the room. Part of me begged to escape through it.

"Such a waste," he sighed mockingly.

"You did not return last night as you had said you would. What kept you?" My attempt to redirect the conversation was weak at best, but necessary. I needed him to slip back into the Oz I knew him to be. That Oz I could deny—if I focused on doing so.

"I was looking into something." I could hear the faint squeak of my bed when he sat on it.

"And did you find it?"

"No."

"Is that to your betterment or detriment?"

"It's nothing to me at all," he said, shifting his weight on the bed behind me. Without thinking, I turned to see him leaning back on his elbows, his upper body highlighted gloriously in that position. When my eyes finally met his face, the smile I found there let me know that he had accomplished precisely what he had endeavored to.

"Then why go looking for something that is of no consequence to you?"

"Because it is of great consequence to you," he answered, his eyes narrowing. With that, he pushed off the bed and stalked toward me. My breath caught for a moment, signaling just how traitorous my body had become. "Now, we have things to sort out. Answers to get so that we can leave, do we not?"

"*I* have answers to get," I corrected as he walked past me without a beat of hesitation.

"One and the same, new girl. One and the same. But you'll figure that out soon enough. For now, let's go get those answers *you* came for."

He exited the room, turning toward the Great Hall. Not knowing where he was going or who he was after, I felt compelled to follow. Perhaps the Dark One knew far more than I had ever imagined. The thought was not overly surprising. When it came to Oz, expecting the unexpected was an excellent plan.

Perhaps it was also the only plan.

3

Oz led the way through the maze of tunnels as though he was suddenly at home in the Underworld. As though he had been there before. It made me question what he had been up to in the night while I slept. The swagger with which he carried himself was no different than it had been in Detroit, but that day there was an edge to it. An urgency. I wanted to know why.

"You seem rather keen on my getting what I have returned here for. Is there a reason?"

"I have reasons for everything I do, new girl," he tossed over his shoulder. "I thought you'd know that by now."

"Perhaps I should have asked if there was a particular reason."

"There is."

There was finality in his answer, implying that regardless of what the reason was, he would not be sharing it with me.

I found this disagreeable.

Stopping in the middle of the corridor, I held my ground, waiting for him to realize I was no longer trailing him like a compliant minion. The second he did, he turned to stare me down with narrow, disapproving eyes. I had angered the Dark One.

"There was a brief time when I found your indignant behavior amusing. It is amusing no longer."

"And there was a brief time when I found your secrecy and deviousness of no consequence to me. That time, too, has passed."

"What is it you want, new girl? Full disclosure?" He laughed at his own words. "You're never going to get that, and for good reason. It saves time."

"I have all the time in the world, Oz, as do you," I countered, eyeing him acutely. "We are immortal. It is a perk of sorts."

"But immortality is not invincibility, is it? You did not inherit that trait like your twin did," he reminded me. Unfortunately, there was truth in his rebuttal. "Time is your ally only when no one seeks to take it from you, Khara. I would do my best to remember that, if I were you."

"You think I am in jeopardy here," I inferred.

"I know you are in jeopardy everywhere."

"You have thought that ever since you realized what I was in Detroit."

"And I was right, if you remember correctly."

"You were the cause of that danger," I noted, much to his disdain.

"I did all in my power to keep you from harm," he growled, stepping nearer.

"You did, after you were backed into a corner that you could not find another way out of."

"You should be careful, new girl. Assumptions can be very dangerous."

"So can lies."

"I never lied to you."

"Convenient omissions qualify," I argued.

His dark eyes narrowed to angry slits.

"There was nothing convenient about those omissions."

"I am inclined to agree, given that both my brothers and I would have been in far less danger had you just done what you were forced to do in the end anyway and changed me."

"That," he snarled, "was for your own good."

"How so?"

He opened his mouth to defend his actions but then snapped it shut, thinking better of it. With a few cleansing breaths, he was back to his smug, collected self. It was as though our conversation had not just happened. As though I had not just rattled his cage.

"Let's go find your father," he said, turning to head back down the hallway. "Maybe he can give you something to satisfy your curiosity."

"Yes," I agreed, my irritation boiling over into my tone. "Perhaps he will."

We continued on in silence until we came upon my father's door. Before I could knock on it to gain entry, Oz stepped in front of me and intercepted my arm, pulling me close to him. There was tension in his features, his jaw muscles working furiously while he gritted his teeth.

"Let me make something clear to you right now," he rumbled, keeping his voice low enough that only he and I could hear his words. "Whatever you think happened in Detroit, I can assure you there is far more to it than that."

"Regarding your involvement with the Stealers? Your constant and mysterious disappearances from the house when circumstances warranted your presence? Or your sudden ability to birth my wings just before the enemy threatened to take me?"

"Yes," he replied tightly. "All of the above."

I stared at him shrewdly.

"Did you know what would happen when you called forth my wings?"

His grip on my arm tightened.

"No."

No. I contemplated that single word for a moment, absorbing the weighty stare of the one who had uttered it to me. It seemed a concession. An explanation. An apology. A warning. That tiny, simple word carried more meaning than my mind could then comprehend. Too many potential implications could be traced from his response.

And my eyes conveyed that to him.

Before I could say anything to him, footsteps approached from the other side of the door. Oz released me and rushed past, disappearing from sight around the corner in the hallway. I rubbed my arm where he had held it captive, suddenly feeling cold and uncertain. My mind reeled with possibilities.

Oz had not known what would happen when he changed me on the rooftop that night. *I tried to keep you from this fate,* he had said. *I did not wish for it to come to this.* At the time, I had taken his words to mean that he did not want to thrust me into a world that had scorned him. A life that he was loath to return to. But now, that thinking seemed so erroneous. It caused me to question what else I might have been wrong about and how that error in judgment might have harmed more than helped me.

While my father opened the door before me, I came to a painful realization.

Oz was right.

Assumptions were indeed dangerous.

4

"You seem distant, my princess," Hades said softly.

"Sorry, Father," I hastily replied, jarring myself away from the thoughts in my head.

"No need to apologize. Did you come here to see me?"

"I did. May I?"

"Of course," he replied, stepping backward into the room to allow me entrance. "Khara, is something wrong? You just . . . seem so distracted since your return. You are different somehow, barring the obvious." He gestured to my back, acknowledging where my wings should have been.

"Different," I repeated, trying the word on to see if it suited me. "Yes. I am different now."

"How so?"

The question seemed so innocuous. So simple. And yet, I felt ill-equipped to answer it. I walked past him and into his lofty office where he and his minions would meet to plot and debrief each other about Underworld matters. In the center was a massive wooden table that extended for almost the full length of the room. There were countless seats nestled around it. I made my way to one of them and pulled it out, sitting on it somewhat inelegantly before folding my hands neatly in my lap. I looked up to my father while I struggled to find the words necessary to explain that which I barely understood myself.

"I . . . I *feel*," I finally said. For some, that explanation would have left them wanting, but judging by the expression on his face, Hades understood me. Nobody was closer to me than he.

"That is quite a change for you, my princess. Do you not like it?"

"Perhaps not. It vexes me."

"Because it is foreign, or because you do not weather the storm of emotions well?"

"Both, I think."

"Do you not think you will adapt, just as you adapted to life here?" he asked, raising an eyebrow as he came to sit beside me.

"It seems likely, though the journey does not appeal to me."

He chuckled lightly.

"No. I imagine it does not." He reached for a crystal decanter and a tumbler from the center of the table before he poured me a glass of water and placed it before me. Then he took my hand in his, gently demanding my gaze with his stare. "Khara. Emotions are not the enemy. Feeling is not wasted energy. There is a time and place for both. You must learn the art of balancing them."

"Just as you have," I observed.

"Just as I have."

"Forgive me for speaking out of turn, Father, but I am not so certain that in the matter of your wife your emotions are balanced."

"Oh?" he inquired, a certain curiosity coloring his tone. Others would never have thought to question him on such a matter, but I was afforded a latitude that few were. I chose now to push the boundaries.

"That is just how I see it. You may disagree."

"May I?" he asked, tauntingly. He seemed darkly amused by the topic at hand. "I appreciate you allowing me my own opinion in the matter."

"That is not what I meant," I said in my defense before he dismissed my efforts with a wave of his hand.

"I know it is not, Khara. I thought perhaps your sense of sarcasm would have improved with your time in Detroit. At any rate, let me address your concerns. You have undoubtedly fallen victim to the rumors that abound in this place—rumors that my wife is promiscuous. That she despises me. That she is sullen and morose when relegated to her time with me. But that is not the case. Persephone adores both me and the Underworld, of that I can assure you.

"Love is the exception to nearly all rules, my princess. It is an emotion that is not easily balanced. All reason is lost in its presence. Should you endeavor to outmaneuver it, evade it, or deny it, you will fail," he declared, as though he had attempted all three and suffered the same result each time. "You view me as weak when it comes to my love for her, do you not?"

I nodded.

"It is not weakness. It is strength. The willingness to sacrifice all for another is the ultimate act, Khara," he said soberly. "For Persephone, I would do that in an instant."

"And that only supports my claim that the balance you profess to have does not exist."

"And when you, too, know that love one day, all that you have spent a lifetime to master will fall in an instant as well." He gave my hand a light squeeze before releasing it and leaning back in his chair. "Until then, my princess, we shall endeavor to make you comfortable with the swell of emotions crashing inside you."

"They are at their worst when my brothers are near," I offered.

"Of course they are. You are attached to your siblings by blood and magic. It would stand to reason that your connection to them is stronger than to others."

"They also run rampant where Oz is involved."

His brow furrowed while he mulled over my observation. He appeared dismayed by my admission.

"The Dark One has a way about him that inspires *irritation*."

"Most definitely, though I feel more than simple annoyance when he is near," I clarified, my voice trailing slightly at the end. "It is as if he and I have a connection similar to, though different from, that between my brothers and me."

Again Hades was silent for a moment, pondering.

"The Dark have dangerously attractive qualities, Khara. Make no mistake about that," he warned. "Evil is seductive. This is one of its greatest strengths."

"But the connection between us was present when the darkness was not."

He scowled at me in response.

"I think you are mistaken, my princess. Perhaps the dire circumstances you found yourself in while in Detroit have clouded your memory."

"Perhaps. Though maybe it had more to do with the emptiness."

"The emptiness?" he asked, his interest piqued.

"Yes. All victims of the Soul Stealers are left with it, though I suffered only a little and it seemed to abate shortly after Oz joined me."

"You were attacked?" he growled, a storm brewing behind his eyes.

"I was. Oz slew the one that had sought to steal my soul and make me Dark."

"And you were left with this emptiness directly afterward?"

"Yes."

"He saved you, Khara. That is the connection you feel. That and this emptiness you speak of." He stood abruptly, pacing the room for a moment before stopping at my side while I continued to sit. "At any rate, let us no longer speak of the Dark One. He will be gone soon enough."

"Gone?"

"Yes. I have made arrangements."

"For what, exactly?" I pressed, wanting to know what precisely Hades had planned for my ominous counterpart.

"He is a danger, Khara. He may not be easily eliminated, but he *can* be easily distracted."

"Distracted how?" I asked, slowly rising to face my father.

"I do not like the intensity of his gaze when he looks upon you," he said sourly. "I have found something else to occupy his misguided attention."

"I think you misunderstand him," I argued, not liking his interference in the matter.

"I think I understand him far better than you can possibly imagine. You forget that I have had an eternity of dealings with Dark Ones. I believe I have also spent the better part of your time with me warning you of the dangers they pose. Whoever you knew him to be before is gone now. There is no changing that. No turning back time. You need to release any notion of that immediately."

"I am not delusional where Oz is concerned, I can assure you."

He pressed his lips into a tight line.

"I wish your opinion was more convincing, Khara."

Before we could discuss the matter further, a knock came from the door of his office, cutting through the mounting tension.

"Khara?" Casey growled, storming into the room without invitation. His black eyes went wide, then focused on me. Tight lines surrounded them and betrayed the anxiety he felt. "We have a situation."

"What, pray tell, might that be, Casey, son of Hecate?" Hades rumbled, displeased that he had been barged in on so rudely. He did not reprimand my brother's affront directly, though, affording him that leniency. Whether he did this because he knew my brother or for my benefit, I did not know. However, I knew that Casey would not survive another infraction. Hades had been on edge since the moment I had arrived.

Casey's dark eyes shot to my father, then back to me. He refused to answer.

"Father," I said, placing my hand lightly on his arm. "Can we continue this conversation at a later time? I think Casey wishes to speak to me alone."

"Whatever he has to say can be said before me," Hades replied tightly. "Lest he forget who exactly is in charge of the realm he is a guest in. An uninvited guest at that."

Casey's gaze remained on me, as if he was awaiting my cue. I nodded once, knowing that Hades would not concede in the matter. Whatever Casey needed to say would be said in his presence, regardless of whether my brother wished that to be the case or not.

"Deimos is here," he said, unable to withhold the chill in his tone. His resentment for my father's second in command was plain.

And Hades took notice.

"I hardly see that as a situation," he retorted.

Casey's chest rumbled with irritation.

"I was sure you wouldn't." My brother took a step closer to me, his eyes narrowing. "Perhaps we should go home earlier than expected, Khara."

"What is going on here?" Hades asked, stepping in front of me. His expression implored me to answer him.

"Casey is not a fan of your soldier, Father. There is some . . . *history* there. Allow me to take my leave and aid in his predicament, if you will."

With a dubious nod, he agreed, and I stepped around him to join Casey, who all but rushed me out of the room and down the hall, grasping my arm with his hand to quicken my pace.

"I cannot find your bloody fucking chaperone anywhere, but we need him on this one, Khara. We need to get you out of here ASAP."

"I am not leaving," I said, pulling away from him. "I have come here to get answers, and I will stay until I receive them."

"Do you have amnesia? Have you forgotten what that fucker tried to do to you? What he did to Oz?"

I felt my features darken while I stared Casey down.

"Hardly."

"Then wake up, Khara! He's here, and there ain't shit that Kierson or I can do for you. Maybe not even Oz. And I think it's rather apparent that your father has his head up his ass about his right-hand man," he sneered. "What was up with that, anyway? Why didn't you tell him what happened the second you arrived here? Judging by his response, he doesn't know a damn thing about Deimos' master plan."

"That matter is complicated."

"The fuck it is! He should know who he has serving under him—that his trusted inner circle has a traitor in it."

I took a moment before responding, trying to sort out how best to explain why I didn't tell my father about Deimos. I had my reasons. But I was unsure that Casey would understand them.

"Do you trust me?" I asked him, which took him off guard. His dark expression faltered for only a moment. "I, like you, believe in strategy and, above that, blackmail. Know that what he tried to do to me has not been forgotten. Quite the contrary, really. It is well etched into the forefront of my mind."

He huffed abruptly, then cocked his head, taking in what I had said.

"Is he a threat to you here?" he asked, arms crossed tightly over his chest.

"No more than he has ever been."

"I don't like that answer."

"You do not have to like it, but it is the truth all the same," I rebutted, leaving out the fact that my plan was to use Deimos' disturbing antics against him, or at least try to, to get the information I sought. I did not think that would help to ease Casey's mind. "Does Oz know of his return?"

"No clue. That's why I've been trying to find him. Though, if he did know, I'm pretty sure he would be all over your ass. Why do you ask?"

"Because I think the reunion of those two will be far more disconcerting than that of Deimos and me."

He scoffed.

"If you are convinced that nothing will happen between you two, I'll let it go. For now. But I'm still going to track down Oz, shady motherfucker that he is."

"Plan on inciting a riot?"

"Something like that," he replied with a dark smile. "I'd pay good money to see that showdown. There isn't any love lost between those two."

With that, he turned and continued in the direction we were originally headed, though he seemed utterly unconcerned that I did not follow. Casey was not prone to coddling me, and it was a trait in him that I found admirable. Even now, with so much uncertainty regarding what I was and who I was vulnerable to, he viewed me the same way—as a member of the Petronus Ceteri. As an equal.

"Then, if I should find Oz first and lead him to Deimos, I will be sure to call you when the battle breaks out," I called down the hall after him before making my way back to my father's room. I could hear the rumble of his maniacal laughter reverberating down the corridors behind me.

For it would be a battle indeed.

One that I wished to avoid at all costs.

If Oz and Deimos were to stand off against one another, the outcome would be bleak. Only one would walk away from it, and I could only assume that one would be Deimos. I was not inclined to believe that even Oz could overtake him, and the reality was I needed them both alive, though for different reasons.

With that in mind, I instead strode past Hades' room, continuing on toward the Great Hall, then the Warriors' Wing beyond that. Deimos would certainly find me eventually, so I saw no point in hiding from him. Seeking him out would take him off guard.

An advantage I would sorely need.

5

It was also an advantage I would not get.

Even in my attempt to seek him out, Deimos found me first. I felt him long before he announced his presence from around a shadowy corner, as the familiar shiver he evoked ran down my spine. As always, I did not outwardly falter, nor did I deign to turn around and acknowledge him when he stepped out of the darkness he had shrouded himself in. He would demand my audience eventually. Forcing him to work for it seemed a favorable tactic.

"You are hard to get alone these days, Khara. You travel with quite an entourage," he mocked, letting me know that he viewed none of them as a threat. "Your pet Dark One is especially fearsome."

"Is there something you would like to discuss, Deimos?" I asked, finally turning to face him. I ensured that everything about my countenance epitomized impassivity.

"Many things," he purred through a wicked smile, coming to hover ominously above me.

"Perhaps we could get on with it, then," I volleyed, standing steadfast against both him and my desire to escape him. "My entourage will likely be looking for me. They will find me any minute. If privacy is what you seek, you will not have it for long."

"You have complicated my plans for us, *vasílissa mou*. At first, I found the change of events most disagreeable."

"And now?" I asked, shuddering internally at his pet name for me. "My queen" would, for most, be a term of endearment. To Deimos, it was a reminder that he sought to own me, a fate I wished to avoid— now more than ever before.

"Now I find it more entertaining than ever."

"You do so love the hunt, Deimos."

"Like nothing else," he drawled, moving closer to me. His size was formidable—even more so than that of Oz—and with it, he sought to enclose me in his cage of fear. It was one of his greatest powers. He could cow his prey easily; the terror he inspired proved disabling to those ensnared by it.

I would not be that prey.

"Then I am confused," I said, straightening my body against the wall of fear that threatened my resolve. "If you are married to the chase, then why change me to that which you could claim so easily? Where is the sport in that?"

His maniacal grin wavered.

"Because I grow tired of chasing you. I do not wish to hunt you any longer."

"You wish to own me?" I stated, clarifying his intentions, though I already knew what they were.

"Not wish, Khara. I *will* own you." The intensity of his gaze ate through my defenses momentarily, and my expression fell. There was a sense of conviction in his words that was immediately unnerving. I had long known that I was the object of his desires, the one he wanted for himself and himself alone. I had maneuvered around this desire of his for centuries. Sometimes successfully. More frequently not. It was the game we had always played.

But after my transformation—my awakening—I had hoped for some kind of shift. A balance of power between us. That night in the alley, before Sean banished Deimos back to the Underworld, I had thought I felt differently in his presence. Perhaps I had been high on the moment, having just defeated the Stealer sent to darken my soul. Doing all I could now to not cower before him, I realized little had changed. The anger I felt rising within me as a result was nearly enough to override the fear.

Nearly.

"I have staved you off this long, Deimos, and I will continue on that path unhindered," I bluffed.

"No," he said abruptly.

"No?"

"No."

It was his only response.

"Why are you suddenly so convinced of this?"

"Because I do not lose, Khara. Ever."

"And yet you have, Deimos. From the time I arrived here so very long ago, you have continuously lost," I argued, trying with a concerted effort to keep the tremors I felt coursing through me out of my voice. "You may be able to own my body, but you will never own my affections or my mind. Nothing about that has changed. Nothing ever will."

"On the contrary. *Everything* has now changed."

"I fail to see how."

He scoffed at my words.

"That is because you do not see how he looks at you." His words were a puzzle he willed me to solve. "I will not lose."

In an instant, the immense weight of his body crushed mine against the jagged rock wall behind me. I could feel the sharp edges bite into my skin even through my clothes. I would be bleeding soon. It proved a pleasant distraction.

He looked down at me, the hall so dark that I could barely see his midnight eyes boring into mine. Boring into my soul. The fear I had narrowly managed to stifle quickly turned to terror. Whatever torment I had known from Deimos in the past was child's play. He had been holding back his power. There, cornered by his weighty stare and bulk, I knew that his claim was true: He would own me eventually.

And eventually started now.

6

"Well, well, well, what have we here?" Oz drawled, his voice carrying down the hallway that separated him from us, cutting the tension between Deimos and me, if only slightly. Though I could not see him, I knew the expression he wore: a smug grin with a fierce gaze. "You will not lose? What game is it that you're playing, exactly? Perhaps I can throw my lot in to make things more interesting."

"Your lot is not welcome," Deimos growled. His gaze never faltered; he stared fixedly at me, refusing to turn and face Oz. His unwillingness to do so illustrated just how little he feared him. To Deimos, Oz was little more than an annoyance, a distraction in his quest to possess me.

"My lot rarely is," Oz retorted, a noticeable bite to his tone. When he came into my view, standing only paces away from Deimos, I saw the bitterness in his expression. "Thankfully, that never stops me from throwing it in anyway." His eyes fell on mine, and my urge to scream abated. "Hades is looking for you, Khara."

"Are you his errand boy now?" Deimos mocked as he pressed against me with even more force, blocking Oz momentarily from my view. The pain in my back instantly increased. "How fitting."

"I'm just trying to keep you and me on an even playing field, Deimos. You've been his lackey—or bitch, as I like to say—for a long time, but I think he's taking a real shine to me. Better watch yourself. Your replacement could be imminent."

That premonition claimed Deimos' full and terrifying attention. His head swiveled slowly to face Oz, who was just shy of flanking him on his left.

"Careful, fallen one."

"It's Dark One now, if you please," he replied, feigning pleasantness. "I've been upgraded—or hadn't you heard?"

"I heard, but it doesn't matter. You'll be downgraded to dead in a minute if you do not shut your fucking mouth and go back from whence you came. There is nothing here for you."

"Oh, I think you and I both know better than that, now, don't we?" Oz tsked. Whatever effect Deimos had on others, it was clear that he did not hold that power over Oz. The Dark One proved utterly immune to it, and the patronizing expression on his face served to irritate Deimos further.

A perk of his dark nature, no doubt.

Deimos released me before turning to advance on Oz, closing the distance between them slowly and methodically. Everything about his approach was designed to intimidate. Oz, however, remained unfazed. No longer entrapped by Deimos' body, I peeled myself off the wall that I had been so forcefully pressed against, which caused the sharp pain in my back to morph into a dull, throbbing ache. I could feel the rivulets of blood seep down my back while I watched the dark angel and my father's soldier face off. I had never known anyone to stand so defiantly against Deimos—other than myself. If they had, they surely did not live long enough to speak of it.

"You think I cannot end you?" Deimos asked, his voice more curious than heated, as if he was in awe of what he perceived to be Oz's ignorance. If it was ignorance, his education in the matter would likely be delivered in the form of his death.

"I think," Oz began, leaning toward Deimos rather than cowering in fear from him, "that just because you can navigate the in-between does not mean you can relegate me to it."

Deimos laughed heartily for a moment, but he then stopped abruptly, his sharp eyes piercing Oz's.

"I think I can do far, far worse than that, and you know it."

Oz merely shrugged in response.

"Maybe. Or maybe your arrogance serves only to conceal your shortcomings. What I am one hundred percent certain of is that we're done here—for now. The rest I'm willing to take my chances on," Oz replied. He winked at me before offering me his hand by extending it just beyond the wall of Deimos' mass. "Shall we, new girl?"

"If my father requests my presence, then I shall go to him." I did not take the hand Oz offered, but instead I walked around Deimos, giving him a substantial berth. "I do not wish to keep him waiting."

"Remember what I have told you, Khara," Deimos called after me while Oz and I took our leave. His words were a warning. "You too, Ozereus."

"Remember them? Impossible," Oz replied dismissively. "I've already forgotten." His words were a taunt. He intended to start a war with the terror-inspiring one. A war against a yet-undefeated entity. Whether it was out of hubris or boredom, it mattered not. Oz had thrown down the gauntlet against the one that no one knew how to conquer.

No longer was I the batshit crazy one.

Falling in step behind me, Oz ushered me away from Deimos, down the winding tunnel, and toward the Great Hall, ultimately accompanying me to my father. There was an uncomfortable silence between us for part of the journey there. With him walking behind me, I could not read his expression to get a sense of what he was thinking. Perhaps he was not thinking at all. Judging by his actions toward Deimos, there was ample evidence to support that hypothesis.

"Want to tell me what your little rendezvous with Deimos was all about?" His voice was cool and controlled, just as it had been when we first met.

"What it is always about," I replied, feigning as much indifference as he had. But I felt anything but indifferent. I was truly rattled by my encounter with Deimos that day. I realized that the menace I had long thought him to be was just a scratch on the surface of his true power. The implications were grim at best. At worst, they were deadly.

Deadly, indeed.

"Enlighten me." He bit the words out as though they pained him.

"Me. He wants me. You already know this. I have said as much before."

"Yes. You have. But what I find interesting about that, new girl, is how you do nothing to stop his endeavors to achieve that end."

I stopped in the middle of the hall, which nearly caused Oz to slam into me. When I turned to face him, a heat boiling inside me that was as foreign as my newfound wings, I was met with a fiery stare. We were both raging on the inside.

"Please, Ozereus, tell me. What would you have me do? Kill him?" I asked, knowing that it was an impossibility. At least it was for me. "If you have suggestions on how best to thwart his advances, I am open to hearing them, but I know that you do not. No one could possibly know how to do something that cannot be done. Deimos is a storm you weather, not an opponent you slay. You would be wise to keep that in mind the next time you challenge him so derisively, Oz."

He cocked his head, curiosity playing upon his expression.

"You sound as though you're concerned for my safety, new girl."

"I am simply informing you about the enemy you have most certainly just made."

"Will you do the same for him, I wonder?" he pondered aloud, raising his eyebrows in contemplation. "Will you tell him all my secrets for him to use to his advantage?" I could almost feel him ruminating over all the possibilities.

"I know none of your secrets," I countered.

"Playing both sides would be wise."

"I do not wish to play at all."

His gaze dropped to my chest for a moment and then back to my eyes.

"Pity that."

I stepped toward him briskly, forcing his eyes to meet mine.

"Is that why you sought me out? To 'play,' as you so eloquently put it?"

"I came because your father wanted to speak with you, just as I said before."

"And precisely when did you start taking orders from my father?"

"I didn't," he scoffed, disgust marring his features. "I wouldn't say he sent me at all. I may have overheard a conversation he had been having with his beloved. I wanted to get to you before he did."

"So you were spying?"

"Not spying, just listening attentively," he corrected, tapping the lobe of his ear. "You can't blame me for having keen senses, can you? It was all very innocent, I assure you. Like I said, I simply *overheard* their conversation."

"Innocent?" I replied incredulously. "Just as you innocently happened upon Deimos and me?"

"No." His tone was suddenly harsh, losing any hint of its earlier, darkly playful nature. "That was most certainly intentional."

I leaned toward him, my face only inches away from his.

"And now whose voice betrays them? I think it is you who is concerned for my well-being, Oz, not the other way around."

His jaw flexed tightly, creating harsh angles on his face. Angles I suddenly felt compelled to run my fingers along.

"He cannot have what has already been claimed."

"He can," I said flatly, pressing closer to him still. "Because, as he sees it, he laid claim first."

A darkness shadowed Oz's face, making him look as though he was born of the purest evil. Uncharacteristically, I flinched.

"We shall see about that, new girl," he breathed harshly. "We shall see."

As he seethed with anger, his fiery rage pulsating from within him, I collected myself, recovering from my lapse in control. That pure hatred that he exuded was not for me, nor was it born of our encounter with Deimos. That degree of anger took time to develop, making me question precisely when and where it emanated from.

"Tell me something, Oz," I said, looking at him intently. "You recklessly bait Deimos—a fool act, indeed. I want to know why."

"Because I can," he replied, his lips suddenly closer to mine. The narrow margin between us begged to be closed.

"No," I argued. "There is something more there. I can see it. For all your projected indifference, it is plain to me that this is personal. What happened between you two on the rooftop that night?"

"Why do you assume something happened at all?" he countered, pushing me away just enough to eye me haughtily.

"I know he was there."

"Maybe he was. Maybe he wasn't," he replied with a Gallic shrug.

I grabbed his arm; my grip was tight, but not threatening. He slowly turned his gaze down to my hand that held him and then lazily returned it to meet my eyes. Though the gesture was casual, his eyes were sharp and cautioning.

"Either you are after something from him or he is after something from you," I continued, ignoring his silent warning. "I want to know why."

"That's none of your concern, new girl."

"A wise man would be wary when dealing with Deimos."

He cocked his head condescendingly while he peeled my hand from his forearm with ease.

"And you, of all people, should know that I am anything but wise."

"I know that you are evasive, argumentative, and arrogant, but I have never known you to be unwise. You are calculating. That takes a measure of intelligence that many lack, but you—you do not. So I will ask you again, what happened on the rooftop the night of the attack?"

"You grow bold after your change," he purred, assessing me as he had in Detroit on more than one occasion. I had said something worth consideration in his mind. "Perhaps you should heed your own advice, though, and exercise wisdom and caution when dealing with *me*. Or have you forgotten? I'm under new management now. The rules of old no longer apply."

"There were no rules where you were concerned," I reminded him, remembering our time on the eagle-adorned rooftop of the Penobscot Building in Detroit. He had spoken of freedom that night, tempting me with it. Oz had never known rules. Not since he had fallen long ago.

A cocky smile spread wide on his face.

"Fair point, new girl."

"So you refuse to tell me still?"

His eyes narrowed.

"There is nothing to tell." He clipped his words through a clenched jaw, clearly irritated by my insistence. "I was overtaken by the Stealers. End of story."

"Or so you say . . ."

"Would you care to offer your account of what occurred up there, since you seem so convinced it is not as I say it was?"

"I do not know for certain, as I had been shoved rather abruptly from said roof," I replied curtly before hesitating for a moment. "I just have this feeling. I cannot explain it, but it will not abate. I feel that something else happened up there. Something that you are clearly unwilling to reveal. I find it curious that Deimos did not kill you, which means either he did not perceive you as a threat at the time or it somehow behooved him to let the Stealers overtake you. Either way, I did not see what happened. And yet, somehow, I know there is more to this than you claim. My curiosity persists."

"Well, you know what they say about curiosity." For a moment there was a familiar twinkle in his eye—one of mischief—but it faded as quickly as it had come, replaced by a seemingly endless darkness. "I have to say that I find it mildly amusing that you are now so dependent on these feelings of yours. This from the girl who formerly felt nothing? I cannot help but be skeptical of this new dependence," he said, unable to hide the incredulity from his tone.

"I will not endeavor to explain it to you any further."

He scoffed, pulling away from me to assess my expression intently.

"Taking a stand . . . how interesting. Fine. I concede. Deimos was there."

"What did he say?"

"Maybe you should ask him that."

"I am asking you."

"You know I won't tell you."

"Yes."

His brow furrowed.

"You're asking me knowing that I won't tell you?"

"Yes."

"Why?"

"Because I wanted you to prove me wrong."

"Ah, yes. The eternal flaw of women, both human and not: hope." He once again leaned toward me, his eyes blazing with rage. "That emotion is lost on me, new girl. How unfortunate that you seem so full of all these new feelings now but lack the discernment to know how and where to apply them," he cautioned, his voice low and gravelly. "I am all you think I am and worse. Every assumption you've ever had about me is right. If you're searching for even an ounce of redemption in me, your effort is in vain. There is nothing left to save, new girl." He took my chin in his hand, his lips hovering just above mine, whispering his warning. "There never was."

I steeled myself against his words.

"So you say."

His expression darkened.

"So I know."

With that, he turned abruptly, releasing my face only after squeezing it to punctuate his remark. He wanted to cement that fact into my consciousness—drill it into my mind. I could not help but wonder why. His insistence on highlighting his irredeemable qualities only piqued my interest. It all seemed contrived—an attempt to derail me. What puzzled me still was why.

Perhaps I just wanted to see his response as an act. An affectation. In reality, however, it remained very possible that his words were indeed true, that his soul was lost to the darkness. That it had finally found its rightful home.

The home I had single-handedly relegated it to. While I stood still, frozen by my thoughts, he pushed past me, continuing in the direction of the Great Hall. He left a trail of fury in his wake. His abrupt departure left me alone and slightly addled. His inexplicable near-obsession with me after turning Dark had, at first, seemed explicitly sexual in nature. I could not deny that my body craved him, too. But what I had previously been so adept at denying was the possibility that his interest in me was anything but physical. Watching the change in him when we discussed Deimos, though, made me question that assumption, and it contradicted his claim that there was no longer anything of worth left in him—that there never had been. There was indeed something under that arrogant façade of his, something ignited by the presence of Deimos and the threat that he posed to me. Whatever changed in Oz when he had first donned his new wings may have still remained a mystery, but it would not remain so forever.

It was a mystery I swore I would solve.

7

While I stood there, lost in thought, Hades approached, calling my name as though surprised to find me loitering in the hall.

"I was coming to look for you," he explained as he approached. "I have something I wish to discuss with you. Alone."

"We are alone now," I noted as I looked around at the empty corridor.

His expression was dubious.

"No, we aren't, but we will be momentarily," he replied, gently taking my arm to usher me into the nearest room. Throwing the door open carelessly, he revealed the private chamber of one of his servants, who happened to be sexually involved at the time.

"Out!" Hades barked, and the three participants scrambled from the bed, grabbing what clothing they could as they scampered out of the room.

Hades slammed the door behind them, turning a conspiratorial smile my way.

"I don't think they were expecting any further visitors." I nodded in reply. "Khara," my father started, his voice suddenly laden with a heaviness that was uncharacteristic, "I have learned something recently. Something I do not want to share with you because I fear it will only fuel your desire to find answers to things you should not, but I know you. You are smart and strong and will not abandon this quest you have decided upon embarking on. So, with that in mind,

I will tell you what I have just learned, though it is against my better judgment."

"What is it?" I asked, the question escaping me a little too eagerly. The fact that it did served only to give Hades further pause; he frowned slightly before continuing.

"It's about your mother. Celia."

"Tell me. Please."

"She is not dead."

His words slammed against me, halting my breath for a moment.

"You are certain of this how?" I asked, wondering how he had come to learn this when only hours earlier he had attested to all the reasons he thought her to be deceased.

"I asked Persephone. She knows things that very few others do. After you and I spoke, I went to her and asked if she knew where your mother was—if she was alive. She looked at me strangely and then said that Celia was indeed alive. She replied in such a casual tone, as though it was common knowledge and she was surprised that I knew nothing of it."

"Why would you not have found out more about my mother before now? All this time . . . I could have known so much more about her."

"No," he corrected tersely, "you could not have, because what I knew I could not share with you. And what Persephone knew, she was unable to share with me."

I was taken aback by his reply, but, in truth, I had always known that my father was bound by the covenant he entered with Demeter. Even if he had known everything there was to know about Celia, he could not have told me. But why Persephone could not have shared what she knew with him made little sense, unless . . .

"The agreement prevented those bound by it from discussing anything related to it—anyone related to it—with anyone else." My words were not a question, rather a realization.

"Precisely."

"Does she know anything else? Anything that could be of use to me?" I asked hurriedly.

"I do not know, my princess. As soon as I found out Celia was indeed still alive, I came to find you."

"I must go to her now," I said, turning to leave. Hades caught my arm before I could take a step.

"Khara. Please. I would be remiss if I did not reiterate my concerns about your learning more about your mother. I fear you will only incur disappointment and pain as a result."

"Why are you convinced of this outcome, Father?"

"Because she abandoned you as an infant, Khara. Abandoned both you and your twin to very different but somewhat cruel fates," he explained, his expression softening. His dark eyes warmed as he reached out to cup my cheek affectionately in his hand. "Anyone who could not see your value, even as an infant, cannot be of sound mind, my princess. Coming face to face with the one who discarded you will only bring you heartache, and that is something I cannot bear to witness."

"I seek answers from her, Father. Not her love."

"I wish I believed that was true," he said sadly, speaking as though he saw something hidden in my words and actions that I was blind to.

"She cannot hurt me," I argued softly.

"She already has, my princess. She already has."

His words lingered, hanging heavily between the two of us. From him, they evoked further sorrow. From me, they elicited more questions.

"She is a Dark One, is she not?" I asked bluntly.

He was silent.

"You are not telling me something, Father. Withholding the truth from me is pointless. If Persephone has told you something else, I suggest you tell me yourself, for I will get her to tell me eventually. And when I do, there will be no undoing this moment between you and me. I will not forget it."

Instead of incurring his wrath with my blatant challenge and disrespect, I received his embrace. Resting his chin atop my head, he held me tightly, as though the truth he affirmed would tear me apart. As though he saw me as uncharacteristically fragile when it came to this particular subject.

"To my knowledge, yes. She is," he started, loosening his grip on me slightly. "But she was not always. Your shady companion would be the one to ask about that. He, more than anyone, will be able to tell you about her. More than Persephone or I ever could."

"Unfortunately for me, he is not that forthcoming in all matters, especially those where my mother is concerned."

"Indeed," he drawled; his tone lacked any hint of surprise. He pulled away from me, releasing me from his hold to address me more directly. "Tell me something, my princess. I know you said that Oz lived at your brothers' house in Detroit, but how, precisely, did that come to pass? They seem an unlikely troupe."

"I do not know the particulars. All I know is that they seemed to have a long-standing but precarious arrangement. Over time, he seemed to have become an unavoidable fixture in their lives. While I was there, he became one in mine as well."

"How convenient for him," Hades mumbled as his expression fell sour.

"And inconvenient for me. Oz has an undeniable knack for complicating matters."

"Of that I am certain," he replied, his eyes narrowing. "I'm curious about something else, Khara. Your wings—you have not told me much about how they came to be. I would be lying if I said I was not surprised to see them when you returned home."

"My mother was an angel. Why should it be so unfathomable that I, too, would be one?"

"This is true," he replied, hedging slightly.

"Then explain your surprise, Father, for I do not understand why you should possess it."

He sighed heavily.

"Because I knew that Aniketos—or Sean, as he is now known—was not," he admitted, his tone and shoulders sagging under the weight of his words. "I had assumed that you and he would have the same traits."

"So you had assumed that I would be like my twin? Invincible and ruthless?"

"I did not know what to think, but I had no way of knowing for sure."

"But my markings? Did they not give you pause?"

"Khara," he replied with irritation in his tone. "I hardly ran around staring at you while you disrobed. And those that cared for you in that way made no mention of your markings. They likely would have taken them to be scars. And you never said a word about them. Would you hold me accountable for something I could not have known?"

"No. I would not."

"Surely you knew that you had them. What did you think them to be?"

To be honest, I had never thought much about them at all. I assumed they were scars. Demeter, early on in my time with her, was not opposed to taking out her anger on me. The first day that Persephone was taken to the Underworld, Demeter beat me so severely that I could not move for an entire day. She brutally whipped me with a thin branch that eventually shredded the robe I had been wearing. I was only a child then. It was after that time that I remembered seeing the markings. I never told Hades of either their emergence or the beating that I had believed led to them. There was no point. It was in the past and would do nothing to change the future.

Or so I had thought.

I looked at my father; his beseeching expression caused a tightening in my chest. I did not wish to tell him the answer to his question. It would only cause him pain. But he was shrewd and intelligent. He would see through my lie, if I were to respond with one.

"Scars," I said curtly, hoping the concision of my response would forestall further questions into the matter.

"Did the Dark One find these scars?" he asked, a suppressed rage lingering just below the surface of his question. A question I would need to answer carefully so as not to unleash his fury.

"They were exposed to him and my brothers. Oz recognized them immediately. He then said that I was an impossibility—that an adult Unborn could not exist."

"Did he help you reveal your wings?"

"In a fashion."

"The evasive nature of your response does not inspire my confidence."

"It is a rather long and convoluted story."

"I will accept the abridged version, providing you do not omit anything pertinent in the name of brevity."

"The short of it is that Oz was backed into a corner, so to speak, when he realized that there were Soul Stealers after me. We had no other options to ensure my purity, so, after they attacked us at my brothers' home, Oz pulled me to relative safety and birthed my wings."

"Interesting," he replied, tenting his fingers in front of his mouth. "And what precisely did he do after that?"

I hesitated for only a second.

"He threw me off the roof of our home."

Hades' eyes widened before he roared with laughter. It was far from the reaction I expected. Knowing that Oz had nearly killed me should have enraged him. For some odd reason, he looked relieved by my response.

"You cannot trust the fallen, Khara. Of this I have long warned."

"That you have, Father."

"And yet you stayed under the same roof as him. The roof that he ultimately threw you off in the end."

"I had few other savory options," I countered, knowing that had been the truth only until my twin had offered me refuge with him and our other brothers on the East Coast. At the time, I had declined, not fully understanding why I had done so. There was a connection I had felt to my brothers who had taken me in. Now, reflecting upon that time, I wondered if I had not felt a connection to Oz as well. "He was not as despicable as you may have assumed, Father. Though he was the indirect cause of the battle we all found ourselves embroiled in, he was not entirely evil."

"No?" he asked, unable to hide the incredulity in his tone.

"No. Not entirely."

"How would you have described him, then?"

"Disgruntled. Arrogant. Loathsome at times. But not evil. He was not as he is now when I first arrived in Detroit," I explained. "And I am afraid I may be to blame for the ultimate change in his character."

"You are not to blame for his actions, Khara," Hades said, reprimanding me.

"I am not to blame for his antics, no. But I am to blame for the darkness that overtook him and created the being he is now."

"You caused his darkness?" The disbelief in his expression was plain.

"So it appears."

"That is preposterous. How could you have done such a thing?"

"The exact method remains unclear. The details of what happened to Oz after he threw me from the roof remain cloudy in my mind. What I do know is that when I returned to the Victorian and found him lying on the couch, dying from the emptiness, I did something to him—gave something to him—that he accepted. Whatever it was, it made him what he now is. A Dark One."

"Impossible . . ." he breathed.

"I am afraid not. My brothers were there. They witnessed the entire thing. They, alongside me, watched Oz spring to life and sprout his obsidian wings before escaping through the back window and flying off into the night."

"I do not understand this."

"Nor do I, Father. My brothers seem to have some theories, but I left before any of them could be tested. I abandoned my home in Detroit to come here. To see you."

"And you used him—that *thing* you created—as a means to return to the Underworld?" he uttered, disbelief marring his noble features.

"Yes."

"Why, Khara? What would possess you to risk so much to return home? He cannot be trusted. I have seen how he stalks you like a hawk circling its prey. He could have taken you—" Hades cut himself off before disclosing something he did not mean to. "You could not have been certain that he would bring you here, Khara. You had to have known that I would send my army to find you. All those I could spare were dispatched. Deimos alone should have been enough—"

"Oz was my best option," I answered firmly. Now was not the time to explain what had occurred with Deimos. Perhaps there never would be such a time. I questioned whether or not my father was capable of understanding the depths of Deimos' insanity—his depravity—given that he had not noticed it already. Was there a chance that my father could see Deimos' plan to make me Dark and claim me as his own as a way of ensuring my safety by relegating me to the Underworld permanently, thereby insulating me from any threats from above, both known and unknown? He could view it as a strategic maneuver rather than the machinations of Deimos' maniacal mind. Regardless, to gain confirmation that my father would rather have my soul tainted than face an unknown future was a truth I preferred to remain ignorant of.

But Hades seemed to have a strategy of his own, and it revolved around obtaining his own answers.

"Something is amiss with you two—you and Deimos," he noted, his eyes narrowing. "First your brother speaks of Deimos as though he were the enemy, and now you cut me off at the first mention of his name. What is going on that I don't know about?"

"As I said before, my brothers and Deimos have a history of sorts."

"Yes, you did say that, but what I want to know is why you suddenly seem so reluctant to discuss him."

"I am not reluctant, Father, nor is my distaste for Deimos sudden. He is not my favorite. He never has been. His methods for accomplishing what he must are often objectionable and unscrupulous, and though you find Oz to be unsavory and untrustworthy, one could argue that Deimos is no different. But it just so happens that he is under your command," I stated calmly. "For the sake of efficiency, I capitalized on the opportunity presented to me at the time. Deimos was not there. Oz was. It is as simple as that."

The finality in my tone seemed to surprise Hades. The quirk of his brow when he pulled away from me just enough to better assess my countenance was proof of that. He had not expected that response.

"Fine," he said, still sounding somewhat dissatisfied. "What is done is done. However, that does not mean that I will allow this tarnished angel to linger in my kingdom uninvited to do as he wishes with *my* daughter." He hovered before me, his large frame looming ominously. "As for Deimos, know that he is a necessary evil in my world. I do not find all of his antics palatable, but he gets me the results I need. I cannot argue with that." He was right. I could not either. My father's realm was one that required a tyrannical rule. Employing one who thrived in such conditions was a crucial part of maintaining order in the Underworld. The fact that he was diabolical and fixated on me was subsidiary to my father's needs to have one such as Deimos serving under him. "But if he has done something to you directly—"

"He has not," I interrupted emphatically. My words were not entirely a lie. Deimos himself had done nothing to me in my time above. It was his legion of Stealers that had attacked both my brothers and me, not him. Bringing up Deimos' thwarted plan would serve only to disturb and distract my father. He needed order, not dissonance and doubt. I would deal with Deimos, just as I always had in the past—without the aid of my father.

"All right, then. Now, about your Dark One," he started, heading toward the door to exit the room he had claimed for us. "I think it's time we rid ourselves of him, don't you, my princess?"

"You have no power over him," I said plainly. It was not meant as a slight. It was a gentle reminder of the truth he had so militantly ingrained in me—that the Dark could not be controlled. It was also a reflexive answer that had escaped me before I put any thought into it.

"I have plenty of power," Hades growled, standing in the doorway.

"But you hold none over him."

"Perhaps. Perhaps not. But there are ways to deal with the likes of him, Khara."

With that, he stormed off down the hall; I followed closely behind him.

"What are you going to do?"

He looked back at me over his shoulder.

"Whatever needs to be done."

8

Hades had appeared far too determined for my liking, and his words left much room for interpretation. If his initial plan had been to distract Oz, it seemed as though his intentions had escalated to something far more sinister. The distress I felt at the thought was unnerving. The only solace I found was the knowledge that Hades himself could not kill a Dark One. Had he possessed that ability, I never would have been abducted from my home.

For the second time that day, I found myself standing in the middle of the hallway, alone with my thoughts. But it was not time to think. It was time to act. I needed to find Oz—though I was still unsure what I would tell him once I did.

But I also had a pressing desire to find Persephone to see if she did in fact hold more information than Hades had revealed to me. Or more than she had even revealed to him. She was a resource I needed to consult either way, and I found myself uncertain who exactly I should locate first.

The labyrinth that was the Underworld could be challenging to navigate, even for those familiar with it. It seemed to have a way of changing over time—evolving. So as I made my way toward the epicenter of it, the Great Hall, I was not surprised to round a corner only to find a rather perplexed Kierson wandering aimlessly.

"Hey!" he called out. His relief was nearly palpable in his tone.

"Kierson," I replied with a slight smile.

"I thought I was on my way to the kitchen, but now I have no clue where I'm going." He looked around, surveying the various tunnels that branched outward from where we stood. "And I'm so hungry . . ."

"The kitchen is this way. I will take you to it."

"Where are you going?"

"To find Oz. Or Persephone. I am not yet sure which."

"How do you know where either of them is? This place is a bitch to find your way around in."

I stopped for a moment to ponder his question.

"I am hoping to serendipitously encounter one or the other. Perhaps both, though not simultaneously."

"Oh," he replied, scrunching his features up in confusion. "Whatever. As long as you can take me somewhere to eat, I'm happy. We need some time to talk, anyway."

"About?"

"Leaving." His demeanor took on a seriousness that had been absent only seconds before. "I know Casey already talked to you about it, but I'm going to throw my two cents in, too. This place is a real blast and all, but we need to get back. You don't seem to be getting the answers you came for very quickly. Can't we just say fuck it and go?"

"You are not enjoying your time with Aery?" I asked, unable to keep my eyebrow from rising quizzically.

Kierson blushed, a reaction I had never before witnessed.

"Don't get me wrong, she's . . ."

"Fun?"

"Yes. Fun. But I know that Drew is probably going postal by now, and with Deimos back . . ."

"He is no more a threat to me here than he is in the world above. Most likely, the opposite is true."

He looked over at me as we continued to walk. I could feel the weight of his stare on the profile of my face.

"You're really not going to give up on this, are you?"

"Can I afford to, Kierson? We know nothing of what I am. What I can do. If there is a chance that we can find answers to my questions here, is it not sensible that we get them before returning to Detroit?"

"Yeah . . . that makes sense," he grudgingly agreed. "But you have no guarantees that you're going to find the answers that you're looking for here. It seems like a risk."

"Perhaps. But today I learned that, though my father may not have much to offer me in the way of information about my mother, Persephone is a far more promising source. One that I need to consult with soon."

He sucked in a breath through clenched teeth.

"About that," he started, sounding concerned about my plan. "Sean is not a big fan of hers. I haven't heard good things."

"This changes nothing."

"Fine. But be careful, okay? Sean isn't one to overreact about things, and he's been known to flip the fuck out about her."

"They have history. Histories are not always pleasant."

"Right, but in this case, I think that might be an understatement."

"I will take your warning under advisement, brother."

"Good," he said with a nod. "Now do me one more favor. Take Oz with you when you go to talk to her."

"I think he will prove only to be a distraction. Persephone stares at him as though he is food and she is starving. I wish to interrogate her, not watch her drool."

"Speaking of starving," Kierson muttered as we made our way down another corridor.

"So, brother, what do you think of my home thus far? Is it all you had thought it would be?"

Kierson and I passed some of Father's men, all of whom nodded brusquely in acknowledgment of me.

"Hell?"

"I find that name so crass," I replied, running my hand along the rocky wall. "But, yes. This is your so-called hell. Is it not what you expected?"

I looked up at him while we continued on; his face displayed his consideration of my question.

"No. Not really."

"Interesting. In what manner does it fall short, precisely?"

"I guess I thought it would be, you know, hotter. More fiery and flamey." The befuddled expression he wore reminded me just how entertaining he could be at times.

"Flamey?" I asked, quirking my brow as Oz often did.

"I couldn't think of a better word."

"So it would seem."

He shot me a sideward glance. My face sought to contain the smile that begged to be displayed.

"Traitor," he mumbled.

"Is there not some human idiom about loving the ones we tease the most?"

"Yes."

"Well then."

"Fine, but I did think there would be more roaring fires and flames and . . ."

"Tortured souls?"

"Well, yeah. You did kinda sell that vision."

"There are copious tortured souls here, Kierson. It is just that not all of them are permitted to roam the common areas." My explanation left him with a dubious expression, so I continued on in hopes of clarifying the issue. "There is a caste system in the Underworld, Kierson. Not all dead are relegated to the same existence here."

"Meaning?"

"Meaning that there are specified areas for certain souls. Others are granted more privileges, as it were. They are condemned, but less so."

"Varying degrees of damned?"

"Exactly."

"Didn't see that coming."

"I saw no reason to mention it during my time with you in Detroit. It is not a widely known fact outside this realm. I felt a sense of duty to Hades not to shed light on information he endeavors to keep largely secret."

"Loyalty," he said softly. "I guess that's one of those traits we share." He took my hand in his, a gesture that still made me moderately uncomfortable, but he found solace in touch, so I allowed him that. For whatever reason, I made concessions for my brother that I never would have for others apart from Hades. My heart seemed inexplicably softer when it came to Kierson.

"It would seem," I replied, smiling faintly at him.

The light at the end of the stony corridor grew brighter as we approached the kitchen. I had hoped to encounter Persephone on our way there. She and I had much to discuss, and I wished to get our conversation underway. Instead of my father's wife, Kierson and I came upon a room full of the dead. Dead that I had seen before, but did not know. Only Hades possessed the capacity to know all whom he housed in his domain.

Those present were souls of the highest caste—those who occupied the Elysian Fields. The ones who were subject to virtually no torture or torment, unlike the rest. But they were still in the Underworld. That in and of itself spoke volumes.

I entered the vast room, scanning it quickly for any sign of Oz or Persephone. Seeing that neither was there, I departed, hoping to find either in one of the hallways that branched out from the kitchen area.

Before I made much progress, Kierson grabbed my arm, forcing me to halt. When I turned to ask him why he had stopped me, I was met with a look of sadness that pierced my heart like nothing ever had. I did not like seeing the pain of loss in his eyes.

"Kierson," a male voice called from behind me. "It has been a long time."

I looked over my shoulder at the one who spoke. He was tall and formidable in appearance, and handsome. Had it not been for the chalky paleness of his skin, one would never have known he was dead. But he was.

"Cassius," Kierson exhaled, his voice barely audible. He then scanned the many faces that stared at us, absorbing every one of them. He appeared to know them all, that was clear. Why and how were less so, but I had my suspicions. And they were quickly confirmed.

"It's good to see you, brother. Though I wish it were under different circumstances," Cassius continued, walking toward us. "Have you come to be with us?"

"He is a guest here," I said, seeing that Kierson was, for once, at a loss for words. "He has come for me."

Cassius stopped a pace or two behind me, and I turned to face him, a silent Kierson by my side. His arm slowly drifted up past me, reaching toward his fallen brother. Our fallen brother.

"Can I . . . ?"

"Touch me?" Cassius replied with a grin. "Of course you can, but keep it above the waist, if you would, please."

Without further ado, Kierson snatched him up in an embrace that told me all I needed to know. Cassius had been dear to him at one time. His loss had wounded Kierson deeply.

When they separated, Kierson's gaze drifted to me for a moment, and a look of realization settled in.

"Do you know Khara?" he asked Cassius.

"Yes. We all know of the princess of the Underworld."

"Touch her," Kierson said, coaxing Cassius toward me.

"I do not wish to offend Hades," he replied cautiously, a look of concern on his ghostly face. He had a sense of honor. It made sense that he was placed in the caste he was.

"It's okay," Kierson pressed. "Just touch her arm. I need to see something."

Cassius' eyes met mine, a look of reservation plaguing them. To abate it, I lifted my hand slowly and placed it on his arm. Nothing happened.

"What is the meaning of this?" Cassius asked, his confusion plain.

"You cannot feel it?" Kierson asked sadly.

"Feel what?"

"The connection. She is one of us. She is PC."

"Impossible," he whispered, bringing his hands up to clutch my shoulders. He closed his eyes, willing himself to feel what he would have felt so easily in life. Then his arms fell heavily to his sides, a look of dejection marring his expression.

"What he says is true," I concurred. "I am what he says I am."

"But there are no females born of him."

"Khara is the exception," Kierson told him, a note of pride in his voice. "She is the exception to many, many things."

"She must be, to still be alive," Cassius said tightly, undoubtedly knowing the rumors that the others long believed to be true as well. "Who is her mother?"

"Celia."

Cassius' eyes widened dramatically at the mention of that name.

"So she's—"

"Yes."

"Does Sean—"

"Yes."

"Holy shit, Kierson."

"I know, right? It's a total mindfuck."

By the time the two had finished sorting out the implications of my being born of Celia, the rest of the crowd had tightened around us, engulfing us with their curious stares. When Kierson noticed this, his body became rigid and he pulled me closer to him. He was protecting me from some threat I did not sense.

"He cannot find out about her," Kierson said, his voice stronger and more authoritative than usual.

Cassius looked at the brothers surrounding us; his eyes bored into theirs. He then nodded to the group once, held his right hand over his heart, and looked back to Kierson.

"On our honor."

Kierson mimicked the hand gesture and inclined his head.

"Good."

I realized that his sudden change in mood came solely from the fear that he had just exposed both me and my secret to over one hundred of our brothers. His childlike excitement had gotten the better of his judgment, as it so often did. But there was little for him to fear. There was no one for the fallen PC to share that information with who had ties to the world above and the ability to freely go there. With the exception of Deimos and Aery, the inhabitants of the Underworld were as cut off as the dead were, with little to no ability to expose me and my secret, even if they had desired to.

"You have little to fear, brother," I said softly to him.

"Ugh," he replied with a roll of his eyes. "You and the no-fear thing again. You're like a broken record, Khara."

"Your argument does not negate my point," I countered. "Besides, I am hardly without the ability to defend myself now."

"True," he acknowledged grudgingly. "There is that—not that you have a fucking clue how to do whatever it is you can to protect yourself yet." He smiled brightly, his relaxed nature easily sliding back into place. "And I'd suggest keeping your newly acquired powers—whatever they are exactly—to yourself down here for a few reasons, not the least of which is me not wanting to be on the receiving end of them."

"You wouldn't be," I replied flatly. "Not intentionally, of course."

The twinkle in his eyes returned.

"Of course not."

A cold hand on my shoulder snapped my attention to the dead warrior behind me. He looked young. Far too young to have served a brotherhood wrought with violence. To the human eye, he would have appeared only a teenager.

"I'm Thomas," he said shyly.

"Khara," I said in return.

What then followed could best be described as a mass introduction to my brothers that had fallen. Some recently. Some centuries ago. But all had one thing in common: They were all sent to the Underworld. It gave me little hope that any of my brothers would ascend. That thought plagued me. They deserved better than that—even Casey. My home was acceptable to live in if one's soul was not bound to it. To be eternally damned, however, was a different matter entirely.

It seemed like hours had passed by the time our brothers dispersed, heading back to their eternal home. Though it was not rare to see souls from the Elysian Fields roam about when permitted to, it was strange to see so many of them out at once. In my experience, it was unprecedented. While I considered that, Kierson collapsed into a chair across from me at one of the countless wooden tables in the eating area. He no longer looked as though he wished to eat.

"So this is it? This is how my fallen brothers spend the rest of their existence?" he muttered under his breath, holding his head in his hands as though he lacked the strength in his neck to support it. "It does not seem right."

"Now that I know you and know what you and your brothers do, I must agree. I think that you should be better rewarded for doing the job you have been charged with." My words did little to console him; the creases of worry remained etched deeply around his eyes. "At least you do not have to fear for them, Kierson," I said softly, taking his hand in mine as he had done with me so many times. It was not for my benefit, but his. Contact seemed the best way to soothe my sensitive brother. "They are not tormented as you might expect. I think I may have done a poor job of illustrating just how complicated the Underworld and its many layers can be."

"So, they're okay? They're treated well?"

"Those that we saw here today, yes. Though I imagine there are others who met far less enviable fates."

"How does it all work, then? How do you know where you'll go? Where I'll go?"

"You," I said commandingly, "will go nowhere because you are far too strong to be taken down. As for the brothers I have not yet met above, they will likely go where the other noble warriors we met today went: to the Elysian Fields. It is a relatively pleasant place compared to all others here. I can take you there if you'd like to go. Perhaps there are even more fallen brothers there whom you might know. Others that you would like to see."

"I would like that," he replied, lifting his head up to smile weakly at me. "But if they don't go there . . . ?" Worry furrowed his brow; his countenance betrayed his unease with the subject.

"Then they are relegated to realms for the far less savory of souls." I did my best to deliver my words delicately, but there was no gentle way to tell someone that their brothers in blood and arms may be bound to an existence of great torture and pain.

"Can I go there?"

I shook my head no.

"It is not a place for you, Kierson. I know that you are a fearsome warrior in your own right, but I also know that your emotions run deep. Seeing someone you know there would wound you in a place that could not heal. I will not subject you to such a fate." His expression fell. "Perhaps there are particular individuals you suspect to have gone there. I can check for you if you like. I can travel to virtually all of those realms freely and without personal consequence. I bear no ties to those that suffer there. For you, I would do this."

"Thank you," he replied, reaching across the table to lightly squeeze my hand. Then he leaned across the table awkwardly, pulling me toward him to kiss my cheek. He pressed his forehead against mine after he did. "I would feel better knowing where my brothers are. Having been here . . . seen all of this. The uncertainty is starting to wear me down."

"I knew it would," I said somberly. "I wish you had not come. This is a place far better suited for Pierson or Casey. I fear Drew would not have accepted my home well, either."

"You should have seen how torn up he was about not being able to come here, Khara. He was so distraught about your disappearance."

"I will do my best to make it up to him when I see him again," I assured Kierson. I thought about my time above and realized how heavy my heart had become in the absence of my brothers. "I miss him. I miss you all."

"Then come home," Kierson whispered in a soft plea. "Check on my brothers, get Casey, and let's go. There's nothing for you here. This place is death, Khara."

"There is everything for me here, Kierson," I countered, pulling away from him. "There are secrets here that I must learn—and that I can learn. All save the ones that Demeter holds dear; I doubt that she will ever be forthcoming with me, whether she is able to do so or not. So I must stay until I learn them."

"If you think Demeter has answers, then why can't we go to her? Start there?" he continued, his concern once again etching lines in his boyish face. "I will *make* her talk."

"The Underworld is both the path of least resistance and a land of plentiful resources. There are many here who potentially know things about my past. More than I had originally thought. I will do all I can to learn what they have long kept secret. Then I will leave."

"Did you ask Hades about this?"

"It was difficult, but yes."

"Then who is next?"

"Persephone."

"Right! You said that," he replied, shaking his head a bit as if to jump-start his memory. His lack of food was affecting his cognitive functions. "Great! Then let's go find her, make her tell you what you want to know, and leave."

"Your plan could work, but you seem to be overlooking one small but crucial detail, Kierson. We cannot leave on our own."

"Fine. We'll get that crazy nymph chick to take us out."

"Aery is a fickle thing. She may or may not do this. Not unless Hades orders it."

"Then we'll get Oz to—" He did not finish his sentence, the reality of what he was about to suggest sinking in too quickly to allow the words to escape him. Even Kierson, in all his optimism, could not keep the incredulity from his tone. He knew that beseeching Oz for anything was an ominous task at best. Dark One or otherwise, Oz was hardly the accommodating sort. "Okay. I see your point. But isn't there someone else that could?"

"Yes, though you will enjoy that option even less."

"Ugh," he groaned. "I forgot about Deimos."

"A dangerous oversight indeed, brother."

"Yeah. I kinda gathered that back in Detroit."

Frustration overtook his countenance, and he abruptly stood to pace the room, thinking of a way to rescue me from the home I did not yet want to leave.

"When the time comes, we will find a way," I told him, hoping to ease his worry. "If it would please you, I could see if Aery would take you back now. She likes you. I think for you she will make an exception . . . though it may cost you."

"I'm not leaving you here!" he shouted, wheeling around to glare at me.

"Then let us go find Persephone. Perhaps we can learn from her what I came to the Underworld to ascertain. If not, surely she will know from whom I can obtain the information I seek."

"And then we can go home?"

"Possibly."

"I'll take that as a yes," he said with a wan smile.

I rose to join him, and we headed for the corridor to the Great Hall. Kierson fell into step beside me, flanking me protectively. I wondered if it would be wise to tell him that I was not the one that needed protection in the Underworld, but then I thought better of it. That knowledge would have changed nothing for him.

"You said it would cost me if Aery took me back," he recalled while we strode down one of the narrow and winding channels that cut through the rock of the Underworld. "What did you mean by that?"

"I meant you would have to pay her whatever she wanted in return for escorting you out."

"Any idea what that would be?" he probed.

"Yes."

"Care to share?"

I felt the increasingly familiar tug at the corners of my mouth when I thought of what the nymph would seek as compensation for her efforts.

"Just know that it is something you would be more than happy to give her, Kierson." He looked down to find me smiling wryly as we turned the corner, nearing my father's quarters. "Something you are more than happy to give many women . . ."

"Ooooooh," he drawled, before laughing to himself. "Well, why didn't you say so? Hell, I'll pay for all of our rides out of here, no pun intended."

"You are a thoughtful one, brother."

"What can I say?" he replied with a shrug. "I'm a giver."

"And Aery is a taker. Perhaps you two are a match made in heaven, as they say."

"Maybe. We'll have to see about that."

As I continued on, I soon realized that Kierson was no longer with me. When I turned to see where he had gone, I found him standing motionless in the center of the hallway, a blank expression on his face.

"Kierson?" I called, turning back to approach him warily. Something was very wrong with him, though I could not tell exactly what. He said nothing, his eyes remaining fixed on something in the distance that did not exist. At least not in our realm.

"Kierson, please. What is happening?"

"Drew." It was his only response.

"What about him? What do you see?"

He paused for a moment.

"Blood." His voice was barely a whisper.

Then his piercing death cry rang through the corridor; echoes of it bounced endlessly off the stony surroundings. It was only seconds before we were engulfed by Father and his men.

"What is the meaning of this outburst?" Hades demanded, accosting Kierson.

"Father, please," I said softly, placing my hand on his arm. His dark eyes fell on mine, confusion and anger tightly packed into his glare. "Kierson, is Drew all right?"

His head dropped in dejection, avoiding my gaze as well as my question. When I stepped closer to him, he took me roughly into his arms, burying his face in my shoulder.

"No."

"Is he—"

"Yes," he bit out, his admission muffled. "He was ambushed. Pierson arrived too late."

"But," I started to argue, not willing to accept the truth in Kierson's words, "Pierson sees things *before* they happen. Perhaps there is still time."

"No. Not this time."

"How do you know?"

"Because that scream was not my own. The banshee cry signals the death of someone important." His words ran through me like ice down my spine, and I shivered involuntarily as he spoke. My brother had been lost, and all because those that had so often been there to aid him were down in the Underworld trying to bring me back. In my selfish quest for answers, I had failed Drew. I had failed them all.

Panic. That is what I felt when my mind finally accepted Kierson's words.

"Father," I called beseechingly. "Is this true?"

He closed his eyes for a moment as though he was reaching through his mind to the fields that spanned far and wide below the Earth's surface in search of my fallen brother. When his eyes shot open again, they instantly fell on mine. Sadness abounded within them.

"My princess . . ."

His words were both an apology and an affirmation.

"Where is he?" I demanded.

"Khara," he began, his tone patronizing. I would have none of it.

"I will search every realm until I find him myself if you do not disclose his location."

With a heavy sigh, Hades conceded.

"He will be in the Elysian Fields, as he should be. He was one of the PC's most noble warriors. I will see that he is treated as such."

Without a word, I started off in that direction, running faster than I had known my legs to be capable of. In my frenzied state, I did not notice any pain when my wings shot forth. But shoot forth they did. Narrow though the hall was, they spread wide, rubbing against the stone walls that surrounded me. They should have been a burden, but, inexplicably, they were not.

Kierson's shouts faded behind me while I sprinted for the fields that now housed my brother. In truth, it housed many of them. But he was the only one I needed to see. For whatever reason, I had to see him with my own eyes to fully accept his passing.

I also had to see if there was a way to get him out.

9

When I arrived, it took me a moment to retract my wings into a manageable position behind me. It was a pause I should not have taken. Just as I went to step through the thin veil that separated me from the Elysian Fields, a voice near me caused me to falter.

"He will not know you," Oz said frankly. His breath was hot on my ear, and it caused me to shudder. "You must remember that when you see him."

"I do not require your escort in this."

"I am aware of that," he said snidely. "But have it you shall. Like it or not."

"Infuriating," I muttered under my breath, pushing through the membranous border. His response was muted by it.

Once on the other side, I realized the magnitude of the task I had embarked upon. Hundreds of thousands—if not millions—of men and women occupied this particular realm of the Underworld. If Oz was correct and Drew would not recognize me, I stood little chance of finding him.

"It's as if you don't know the advantage of having those things," Oz groused, gesturing to the mottled-gray wings folded behind my back. In a grand show, he snapped his own out wide, creating a gust of wind that blew my hair back wildly. His obsidian wings were an awesome sight indeed. "Care to join me? In the interest of saving time, of course."

"In the interest of saving time," I agreed, focusing to unfurl my wings and take flight. It still required effort to connect with that side of my nature—that portion of my DNA. "How will we find him, even with an aerial advantage?"

He shot me a backward glance.

"Let's hope we get lucky."

With that, he leapt forth into the eternal dawn of the Elysian sky, and I followed his lead, soaring just above the valley of souls. We covered miles upon miles without catching sight of my fallen brother. Hours passed. My body tired. And still, we could not find Drew.

"There are too many," I called to Oz as I pulled up to flank him on his right. "Our search is in vain."

He did not respond immediately; he instead stared fixedly at something in the distance. When he did turn his attention to me, he was unable to contain his self-satisfaction.

"Oh, ye of little faith," he replied, then swooped down with lightning speed toward a mass of bodies below. They were all gathered around one individual.

"Drew," I whispered to myself before diving through the air after him. He looked exactly as he had when I had last seen him. It was hard to reconcile that with the knowledge that he no longer was alive.

I landed somewhat inelegantly in my haste, staggering a few steps to right my balance. When I looked up, I was staring into the face of my brother, but he may as well have been a stranger. He knew not who I was. His lack of recognition was written all over his face.

"Drew . . ."

"He will not know you," Oz reminded me. It was a harsh truth indeed. I nodded in understanding.

"Who are you?" Drew asked calmly, seemingly unaware of his state and whereabouts.

"I am Khara. I am your sister."

"Sister . . ."

He rolled the word around on his tongue strangely, as if he had some memory of saying it before.

"Will he eventually remember?" I asked Oz, thinking of Cassius and the others that I had encountered with Kierson. Their recognition of him had been immediate, but what if it had taken them years, decades, centuries to acquire those memories? My sadness at the possibility weighed heavily in my voice.

"Yes. But I do not know how long it will take." His expression remained unchanged. "You have seen what you came to see. We must leave now."

"I want to know what happened to him," I countered in protest. I was not ready to abandon Drew yet.

"I don't know," Drew replied, confusion in his tone. "Where am I?"

"You are in the Elysian Fields of the Underworld, Drew. You were killed."

He looked off in the distance, searching for something he was not likely to find.

"Yes . . . I was. I remember the blood."

"Pierson saw it all happen. He shared his vision with Kierson. Do you remember them? The twins?"

Fierce concentration furrowed his brow while he tried to recall his siblings.

"No. I don't."

"Khara," Oz said firmly. "His mind must heal. Bombarding him with further questions will only slow the process—if not derail it entirely. We must leave him be. You got what you came here for. You know that he is all right."

"He is not all right," I snapped, wheeling on the Dark One with a venomous glare. "He is dead."

"And you cannot change that," he growled, leaning toward me.

His advance was met by my hand on his chest, which forced him to take a step back. In that instant, Drew moved forward to stand between us, bewilderment still running wild in his countenance.

Little in life surprised me, but there, in that moment, I felt my eyes widen at the sight of Drew's interference. What his mind seemed unable to recall, the fiber of his being easily could. He was defending me, just as he would have above. He knew me—he just was not yet aware that he did.

"Time to go, new girl," Oz ordered, looking past Drew to me. "I'll allow his affront this time. Next time, I will be far less forgiving."

"You threaten my blood, you threaten me, Dark One. Shall we see how forgiving I am?" I growled. Oz and I stared at each other for a moment, both mentally preparing to battle.

"You should go," Drew said softly to me over his shoulder.

"If that is what you wish. I will return tomorrow, and the day after that. I will return here until you greet me with the inexplicable joy you did when we first met, Drew," I declared, grabbing his arm and turning him to face me. "And then, brother of mine, I will find a way to get you out of here."

"Until then," he said; a ghost of the smile I had grown to expect from him pulled at the corners of his mouth.

"Until then," I replied with a reverent bow.

I shot a glance in Oz's direction before taking to the air, not awaiting his company. I knew that he would be at my side soon. As the wind rushed around me and the silence was replaced by the rhythmic beating of my wings, I contemplated all the ways I could return Drew to Detroit. None seemed plausible.

"What you seek to accomplish will not so easily be done," Oz called to me, his voice cutting through the noise that surrounded us. "There is no undoing death, Khara."

"And yet I will try."

"Your energy would best be focused on something you can accomplish."

"And exactly what would that be?"

He paused for a brief moment.

"Revenge. Retribution for your sibling's life."

"That will not bring him back."

"No," he replied coarsely, flying over the top of me, his body hovering just above mine. "But you have no idea just how good it will feel to watch the life of the guilty party slip away knowing that they're destined for a place far worse than Drew's."

A part of me ignited at his words. If I could not release Drew from my home to return to his, then I would make sure that the one who sent him to the Underworld would suffer for their crime. They would beg for death.

I would see to that myself.

10

What had originally been a mission to return home and acquire the knowledge of my past quickly transformed into one of saving Drew at any and all costs. There was only one individual that could potentially do that, and that was my father. Storming through the maze of the Underworld, I searched for him until finally I came upon him.

"Father," I said cautiously, trying to rein in my anger at the situation. The task was far more taxing than I would have ever imagined.

I was uncertain how best to broach the subject of Drew. In all the time I had spent with Hades, I had never known him to have released a soul. Not from the Underworld itself. I did not even know it to be possible, but my unwillingness to accept Drew's death clouded my thoughts. Hope settled in like a fog. "My brother . . ."

"I am sorry for him and you both, Khara, but I know what you will ask of me, and I am afraid that the answer is no. I cannot release him."

"Cannot or will not?" I asked, an edge to my tone that I had not ever taken with Hades. None ever did. Not if they wished to remain amongst the few living souls in his kingdom.

He turned his sharp gaze to me, putting down the book he had been poring over.

"What are you implying?"

"Nothing. It was a direct question. I simply want to be clear whether this is a matter of your inability to send him back or your unwillingness to do so."

"And why, if I could help my princess, would I not?" he countered. "Have I not always done right by you? Has one week away from me in the world above changed that somehow? Distorted your memory of how well I have always treated you?"

"Of course not—"

"Then why, Khara? Why accuse me, however indirectly, of something like that?"

"I just—" I started, collecting my thoughts while my desperation scattered them about in my mind. "I just cannot bear the thought of him being relegated to this place. Father, if you had known him, you would see that his heart is truly pure. Pure enough to deserve the heavens. The Underworld is my home—your home—but it is not Drew's, no matter how peaceful the Elysian Fields may be. He deserves more than that."

"You barely know him."

"I have seen his worth."

"You have little to compare it to, my princess. I'm afraid that perhaps your evaluation of him may be unfairly biased. He is a warrior. He has killed."

"As is his calling to do so when need be. But I have seen the guilt that plagues him. The remorse he feels for every death he has brought, deserved or otherwise. If it is possible to be pure of heart and do the job he has been charged with, he is, and the world above needs him. The Underworld does not."

He eyed me tightly, pondering my words.

"You truly believe that he is above this place."

"Not above it," I corrected gently. "He is just—he is special. He is unlike any other I have ever met. Noble. Loyal. Just. There is no gray area with Drew. Things are right or wrong, and he would never deviate from the path of righteousness, not even to serve a purpose. Not even to save me."

"I do not know that telling me that he would let harm befall you because of his moral code is an argument on his behalf," he argued, coming to stand before me.

"And yet it is. You know as well as I that there is not a soul in this land pure enough of heart to have such a statement made about them."

"And you are sure of your statement?" he pressed, staring at me intensely.

"I would swear my life on it." Again, he mulled my words over as though they were more than just a testament to Drew's character. He was weighing something. Something incredibly important. "What is it that vexes you, Father?" I asked, placing my hand on his arm. "I can see it in your eyes. There is something you both wish to tell me and wish to keep secret. I implore you, please, tell me what it is. If there is a way—"

"You know not what you ask of me," he muttered, turning away from me to walk to his wall of books. He always found solace in them. Wisdom. Strength. With a great sigh, he unburdened himself, sharing with me something that he had told no other. "I lied to you when you returned here, Khara. There is a way to release a soul, but it has never been done. Ever. And I cannot be certain that your brother would survive it, even if I met with him and agreed with your assessment of his character. Further, if your assessment proved wrong, the ramifications would be both unenviable and permanent. Not even I can undo them." He turned to face me, his sad eyes pleading with mine. "Would you risk his soul if failure meant an eternity in the Oudeis?"

His words gave me great pause. The Fields of Oudeis were reserved for the most depraved souls that both man and gods had ever spawned. Its name meant eternal nothingness—an allusion to the realm's unique torture for all who inhabited it. The Oudeis was nothing like the Elysian Fields, where relative peace pervaded. Drew had likely sent beings to the depths of the Oudeis. That fact alone was reason enough why he did not belong there. He and those he slew could not have been more opposed in nature.

"If there was a way to know that it would work—"

"There is no such way," Hades interrupted, breaking me from my thoughts.

"You have never done this before?"

"Never. Though the ability was granted to me, there has never been one worthy of such elevation before."

"Let us suppose for a moment that you do this and it succeeds. What then? What becomes of Drew? Will he be as I knew him? How he was before he died?"

"I cannot say," he replied honestly, "though I know there is always a price when magic such as this is cast."

"To maintain balance," I whispered to myself, a reminder of the message Hades had long imparted to me.

"Yes, my princess. Yet another unknown to be concerned about." He came to my side, wrapping his arm around my shoulders. "I know you care for your brother a great deal. That fact is clearly displayed on your face, but if you love him, it may be best for you to leave him where he resides. Wagering souls is a dangerous game, Khara. Both here and above. It rarely, if ever, ends well."

I could not help but think of Deimos in that moment. He had done precisely that—wagered my soul—and lost. The only difference was that he had not employed magic in an attempt to corrupt mine, merely dispatched the Soul Stealers to do the dirty work on his behalf. Neither he nor I had paid a price for the failure of his endeavor. Oz, however, had. A fact that I needed to keep tucked away in my mind. If magic had a price, I wondered what it would cost to cleanse the Dark One's soul.

"Then I will ask Drew what he would choose," I said firmly, removing myself from my father's embrace. "If he is the warrior I know him to be, he will not flinch. He would welcome the chance to return home and resume the job he was charged with."

I was nearly out the door before Hades called after me.

"Only ask if he has fully recovered from his loss of memory, Khara. And be painfully honest with him. You ask him to wager much in this. He must understand the inherent risk."

"I am nothing but honest with my family," I reminded him.

"Yes . . ." he uttered under his breath as I entered the corridor. "I fear that will be both your and his undoing."

His words halted me, if only for a moment.

He knew that I would present the facts as I knew them to Drew, but he also knew from what I had told him that my brother would accept, regardless of the risk. If our efforts failed and Drew was lost to the Oudeis, that would be his undoing. But what would be mine? That I would not forgive myself? That Drew would not forgive me, not that I could easily go to him to obtain his forgiveness? The Fields of Oudeis were not meant for outsiders aside from my father. Drew would be lost to its barren torment for eternity. And I would be left with that knowledge weighing on my conscience.

That was the undoing Hades feared I would face.

In that moment, I saw the situation for what it really was. I was not nobly trying to free my brother as I had thought. I was trying to do for him what I seemed unable to do for Oz, and it was clouding my judgment. Further, by bringing the decision to Drew, I felt absolved of whatever outcome might befall him, thinking that I will have allowed him to choose his own destiny. But, in truth, presenting him with the choice was a mere formality, an illusion of volition, for I knew what he would decide, just as I had told Hades. And my foreknowledge of that would condemn me in my mind should Hades fail to send Drew back.

Weighty were the thoughts in my mind.

Crushing was the vise on my heart.

Leaden were my feet as I walked toward the Elysian Fields, my resolve strengthening with every step.

I was prepared to risk it all—wager everything for a chance to free Drew. But by tempting him with the opportunity to reclaim his former life, I knew I could potentially lose him forever to an eternity of suffering.

Heavy was the crown of judgment I wore.

Heavy was the crown, indeed.

11

The banks of the River Styx had long been my sanctuary. The calm water lapping at the shore was meditative. For the first time since I had returned home, I found myself taking the time to clear my cluttered mind. So much had happened since my return that I could not process it all. I needed time to think.

And I needed to free Drew.

The breadth of the river was considerable. I sat and looked onto its deceptively serene surface, staring off into the red glow of a fiery horizon that burned eternally. It was by far the most placid scene to be found in the Underworld. Or at least it was until Oz came to stand before me, his wings blacking out the orange light that had surrounded me.

"The calm amid the chaos," he muttered curiously, as though he had just realized something that should have been obvious to him.

"It is," I agreed, trying to look past his legs and back to the river behind him.

"As are you," he countered. I stretched my neck skyward to find him looking down at me, his expression unreadable. It was too shadowed by his own darkness to be discerned. "This place provides the perfect metaphor for you, Khara: the calm amid the storm."

"I fail to see how I personify that."

"One rarely sees oneself clearly."

"Then I am pleased to have you to succeed at that task on my behalf," I replied sardonically.

"Are you not drawn to this place?" he asked, unable to hide his irritation at my mocking.

"I am."

"Interesting, is it not?"

"It is quiet here. Normally."

"Touché, new girl."

"Why have you come here?" I asked, hoping to find the reason for his presence so I could then find a way to make him leave. My previous desire to warn him about my father's intentions seemed to pale suddenly in comparison to my brother's situation. Oz was more than confident in his ability to survive. Maybe it was time for me to let him test it.

Or maybe that was my grief speaking on behalf of my rational mind.

"I wish to be alone," I said flatly.

"Perhaps I came for the same reason you did."

I scoffed at his reply.

"If you had wished to be alone, then you should not have come to the Underworld."

"If I had not come, you would not be here."

"I do not require your persistent chaperoning. You may leave at any time—escape the growing chaos."

"I may do whatever the fuck I want, new girl," he snarled in response. "A fact I am well aware of."

"I require no reminder of that. I, too, am well aware of your freedom, which you so flagrantly flaunt."

"So enlightened," he mocked, sitting down beside me.

"Tell me why you are really here. I do not believe your presence does not involve me in some way."

"My, my, my, aren't we vain?" he said sardonically, picking up a stone that lay by my foot and throwing it into the water. The river sizzled and spat at the disruption. It may have appeared placid, but it was anything but. The Styx and Oz had much in common. "But you are correct. I came for you."

"Running another errand for my father?" I inquired condescendingly.

"I run errands for no one."

"Yes, yes," I sighed, dismissing his response with a wave of my hand. "You do as you please; that needs no further reiteration."

"Good. See that it doesn't. My patience has limits, Khara. Even with you." He stared at me long and hard, his nearly black eyes boring through mine as if to sear that fact into my mind. He would not be made a mockery of; that much was clear to me. When he finally looked away from me, he took another pebble and threw it into the water, breaking our silence. "I came here because I wanted to talk to you. Alone. It proves difficult to create such an encounter in this place."

"Why do you wish to speak to me alone?"

"I have something to ask you."

"Then ask it, and we can be done."

He laughed aloud, the acerbic quality of the sound cutting through the stagnant air surrounding us.

"You and I will never be done, but I will get what I came for and leave if it helps support that fantasy for you."

"Ask."

He paused for a moment.

"Do you really wish to free Drew?"

I turned to face him slowly, my eyes narrowed while they assessed his expression.

"Yes," I said curtly. "I told him I would and I will see it done, though I cannot fathom why this is of such great concern to you. Great enough that you would seek me out privately to interrogate me on the matter." I let my gaze fall back on the water before me, dismissing him with my indifference.

"Releasing him would be a mistake."

"Saving you was a mistake, Ozereus," I replied sharply. "Saving Drew would be righting a great injustice."

"Is that what you think you did? What you think you are doing?" he asked, grabbing my chin to turn my face toward him. "Saving us?" He released me with a snap of his wrist. "I have never, nor will I ever, need your saving. Is that clear?" I only stared at him in response. "As for your brother, he has met his fate. Intervening on his behalf undermines his sacrifice as a warrior, though I am quite certain you do not see it that way. He has fallen, as many of the PC have. He is surrounded by those souls. He is home now. Leave him be."

"Why is this of such great concern to you? You care not for my brothers or how their souls rest."

"I know this guilt that follows you around like a black cloud will poison your every pure intention," he said sharply. "Having known you before your transformation, I find it incredibly hard to understand. You were far more entertaining when you were cold and detached—unaffected by anything."

"I was not devoid of all emotion when we met," I countered. "There was a barely perceptible shift in me when I met my brothers, as if my being had finally found a place that it belonged to. I would not have fought to stay there if that had not been the case."

He quirked his brow at me.

"And now you are the Khara-equivalent of a hormonal teenage girl. Fascinating."

"Are you finished? You got your answer."

"I got my answer but have not made my point." His eyes bored into mine, and he leaned in closer, speaking softly as though we were surrounded by others whom he did not wish to overhear us. "If you will not leave him here for his own good, then do so for yours."

"My well-being is not a factor in this," I argued, holding his stare.

"You know not what powers you possess or how they work. You are an oddity—something this world and the world above have never seen. Do not think for one moment that you could not be used to inflict pain and suffering on those you care most for because of your own exceptionality."

"Why do you say this?" I asked, cynicism in my tone. "You care about nothing but yourself, and, in some bizarre way, perhaps me."

He smiled widely.

"True. And I do love it when things go sideways, but I thought I would share this bit of information if for no other reason than to remind you at a later time that I did warn you. I do so hate to have petty things held against me."

"I absolve you of any and all responsibility, Oz. Do you now feel better? Perhaps you feel well enough about things to leave this place altogether?"

His smile grew impossibly wider still.

"I am not leaving the Underworld without you. That is a delusion you will need to let go of sooner rather than later."

"How about leaving me in peace now, then?"

"Soon. I have another question to ask first." He looked utterly unapologetic for changing the topic of our conversation. "Have you gotten the answers you came here for yet?"

Of all the things he could have asked me, I did not expect that to be it. I stared at his darkened profile in silence, trying to discern why he would ask such a thing. It mattered not to him.

"No," I replied simply, letting my gaze fall back to the vast body of water before us.

"And if you do not get them?"

"Then I will search for them elsewhere."

"And if you do not find them?"

"Then I will seek the source of the controversy—my mother."

He hesitated only slightly.

"And if she is elusive?"

"Then I will find Ares and ask him."

I heard Oz shift beside me, undoubtedly staring at me as though my reply was the most asinine thing he had ever heard. Perhaps it was. Sourcing answers from the one who, by all accounts, would order my death on sight was not the sanest plan ever proposed.

"I wish Casey were here right now," he murmured.

"Why is that?"

"Because I do love it when he calls you batshit crazy, and that is precisely what that idea is. Bat. Shit. Crazy."

I shrugged ambivalently—a habit I allegedly shared with my twin.

"My mind is unsettled. The feeling is foreign to me, and I do not enjoy it. I cannot rest as easily as I used to when I was content to simply know that she had given me up. When I knew not of my family, my true father, and what I am—what I was to become." I felt the heat of anger rising within me, and I fought to contain it. The swell of emotions surrounding the mystery of my abandonment threatened my calm—the indifferent façade that I had so long held in place.

Something in me had changed with the birthing of my wings. When I became whatever it was I had been destined to become. It was yet another circumstance I needed to adapt to. Unfortunately for me, I was doing a poor job of it. "I need to know the truth, even if it results in my death. That is an outcome I would accept. But the torment of never hearing the reasons behind her actions is an unacceptable fate. I will not allow it."

"And you think that Ares is the place to find truth?" he asked incredulously.

"I do not. But if all else fails and he is my last resort, I will use him, come what may. I would rather die trying than not try at all."

I looked over my left shoulder to find him still staring at me, his jaw flexing wildly—his wings twitching behind him. They were begging to unfurl.

"You will not die," he said, barely restraining the anger that clearly coursed through him as well. "But as your father has told you before, there are fates worse than death."

His reply was enigmatic and heated, precisely what I had grown to expect from Oz. Fallen or Dark, some aspects of him seemed to change very little.

"Such as?" I asked, baiting him. It may have been a dangerous decision, but I was frustrated and irritated, which made me feel like pressing him. I wanted to see just how much it would take to make him snap.

He narrowed his eyes at me, his glare ferocious.

"Like angering a Dark One." He punctuated his statement by standing and snapping his wings wide.

"Is that what I have done?" I asked, uncurling from my seated position to stand against him.

"Not yet . . ."

I leaned in closer to him.

"Then I shall try harder next time."

With some effort, I forced my wings through the flesh and clothing that entrapped them, and extended them to their limits. They may not have been as grand as Oz's, but they were a sight to behold. A muscle to flex.

It was only seconds before he closed the distance between us, his bare chest in my face pumping wildly.

"I don't have to be your enemy, Khara, but that does not mean I won't be. Do not push me."

"I will push if it pleases me," I said, straining my neck to bring our faces closer together. "In fact, I may do whatever the fuck I want. This is my home. Not yours." I hovered there before him; the proximity of our bodies became something I was increasingly aware of as the seconds dragged on.

He leaned down to my ear, his lips grazing it lightly.

"This is not your home, new girl," he whispered. "Be careful whose doorstep you lay your loyalty upon."

I felt the soft brush of his feathers on my bare shoulder when he stormed off past me, leaving me alone on the shore—exactly how I wanted to be. But now there was no peace for me there. He had tainted my haven.

I could not shake the impact of his final thoughts. If his words were true and the Underworld was not my home, where was it that he thought I belonged? It was clear I was not one of the Light Ones, as I had assumed I would become. Surely he did not believe my place was with them.

And why did he allude to my loyalty being misplaced? If his allegations were against my father, Oz was wrong, plain and simple. Hades had always done his best for me. There was not a traitorous bone in his body where I was concerned. I would not believe that about him. Ever.

Frustrated, I threw a stone into the water, and it splashed wildly. A drop of the river's water fell on my skin, burning a hole into it within seconds, again reminding me that what belied the Styx's calm exterior was not to be underestimated—a lesson best applied to my dark-winged chaperone, perhaps.

12

It took far less time than before to locate Drew when I returned to the Elysian Fields to talk to him. Though it had not been an unpleasant place before his arrival, it seemed brighter now with him in it. Happier. More full of life, ironic though the thought seemed. Drew had an infectious inner strength and joy that could not be contained.

I hoped those qualities would serve him well when Hades tried to send him back to the world above.

The last time we had seen one another, Drew had not remembered me. Oz assured me that should change with time, though my confidence in his words wavered minutely when I approached my brother. I was in his periphery, choosing my angle of approach intentionally. Something dissonant inside me stirred with every step I took. I wondered if I would not be able to handle his unknowing stare and if I had therefore chosen to avoid it.

However, without warning, he turned to face me, his eyes narrowing for a moment.

"You . . ." he said curiously. "I know you."

"Yes. You do," I replied as I came to stand before him. "I have been here to see you before."

"No . . ." His voice was soft and distant; his brow furrowed while he fought hard to recall the memory he sought. "I know you. From somewhere else. I . . . I just can't remember."

"It will come," I reassured him, realizing that I could not possibly present him with the choice I had intended to when he could not even remember who I was. It would have been cruel and unfair, two things he did not deserve. Especially when he was already somewhere he should not have been.

Without another word, I turned to leave him, walking away slowly. I could feel heavy eyes watching me. Just before I would have been too far away to hear him, he called after me.

"Khara!" My feet stopped instantly. "Your name is Khara."

I looked back to see him running toward me, confusion still marring his expression, though it was apparent his mind was clearing.

I could not withhold the ghost of a smile that his remembrance had brought forth.

"Yes. It is," I replied, turning my body to face him. "I told you that when we last saw one another."

"That's not it," he said, shaking his head in frustration while he strained to remember something else. "I found you . . . in . . . in Detroit." His mind was working vigorously, trying to keep up with the demand he placed on it. The effort was evident in the harsh set of his features. "I tried to kill you—"

"You almost did," I corrected. "But you stopped."

"I stopped," he whispered to himself. "Why did I stop?"

Judging by the expression on his face, he was asking himself and not me, so I allowed him to work through his memories unsupported. When his gaze snapped up to mine, disbelief in his eyes, I knew he had fully recollected that night in the alleyway.

Not saying a word, he threw his arms around me, tightening his grip as though I would otherwise slip away. Perhaps I already had—in a sense.

"How could I forget you?" he asked shakily. "How could I forget the sister I had only just found?"

"That is not your fault, Drew. Bear it no mind."

He pushed me away from him gently, capturing my face in his hands.

"Why are you here?" His words were commanding, just as they had been at the Victorian when he was able to compel those around him to answer. Unfortunately, that ability was lost to him in death. With any luck, it would return when Hades righted the injustice of Drew's death.

If he could.

"Fear not, brother. I am here of my own volition. I am not dead."

"Fear not," he muttered under his breath. "You always said that, didn't you?" His question was rhetorical; I only smiled in response.

"It is why Casey insists upon calling me batshit crazy."

"Yes . . ." he said, enlightenment dawning in his eyes. It was all coming back to him slowly. "Where is he—wait! He is here, too, isn't he? And Kierson? And Pierson . . . did he—" He stopped short, unwilling to state aloud the fear that now ran through his mind.

"He is well, as far as I know. He is still in Detroit." Drew exhaled heavily. "Do you remember anything about what occurred before you awoke here?" I asked.

"No. Not yet. I am still missing parts of that day. The day after you left." He turned hurt, angry eyes to mine. "Why did you leave without consulting me first? It was a selfish and irresponsible thing to do, going to the Underworld with *him*. Alone."

"The opportunity presented itself, and I was loath to let it pass. There are things I need to obtain here. Answers that I could not possibly have gotten above."

"You cannot trust him, Khara," he said curtly, his expression souring. Though he had lacked any memory of his former life when he entered the Elysian Fields, it now seemed almost fully restored. Except for the day following my departure. "I know what he did . . . how he nearly damned your soul."

"He did."

"He betrayed us."

"He did."

"Then how, Khara, can you align yourself with someone you know will only do the same to you again? It's only a question of time."

"He seems to have a vested interest in my well-being," I told him, keeping my answer vague. I did not wish to upset him by sharing the depths of Oz's bizarre obsession. An obsession that even I did not yet understand.

I only knew that a small, carnal part of me enjoyed it.

"Oz is vested in himself. Do not let him fool you."

"He does not, Drew. I see him for what he is, but you must trust my judgment. If he has plans to betray me, then they are unlikely to transpire during my time down here. For now, all is well."

"Until it isn't," he replied caustically.

His statement was true enough. Nothing was certain until I knew precisely what Oz had planned for me. Claiming that I was his could have been little more than a ruse—a way to capitalize on whatever ties bound us.

"Drew," I said warmly, directing the conversation back to my original purpose. Now that he seemed to remember his former life, I thought it best to put forth my offer. "I came here to tell you something. I have a possibility that I wanted to raise with you."

"What is it?"

"If there were a way to return you to Detroit and have you resume your life there, working for the PC, would you take it even if its failure would result in eternal damnation?"

He eyed me tightly.

"Is that not where I am now? With the damned?"

"The Elysian Fields are reserved for the noblest souls residing in the Underworld. You will find that it is filled with many warriors, both PC and otherwise," I replied, keeping my tone even, my expression soft. "There are other realms here that one would never willingly enter nor wish to be condemned to. Where the worst of the world have been relegated to in death. That is where you would be sent, should this plan fall short of success. Hades seems to think that failure is precisely what will happen if we attempt this, but I am less convinced. So I am bringing this to you for your consideration. If there is even the most remote chance that I could see you freed of this place, then I would very much like to see that plan through. But the decision is yours to make, and you should weigh it heavily. The Fields of Oudeis would be your soul's undoing, of that I am certain."

"Who would be responsible for sending me back? You or Hades?" he asked plainly.

"Hades."

"And you trust him?"

"Implicitly."

"Has he done this before?"

"No. Regretfully, he has not. It is an ability he has always had—to send worthy souls back to their former lives—but he has never seen fit to invoke the magic before. He hasn't deemed any other soul pure enough."

"Why me?" he asked, a solemn tone overtaking his voice.

"Because I vouched for you. I do not believe you belong here, for I have never known a warrior nobler than you. Not even Kierson possesses such an inherently strong moral compass as you do."

He thought for a moment, then laughed aloud.

"Not when it comes to monogamy, that's for sure."

"Indeed," I agreed with a hint of a smile that faded far too quickly. "Please think about all I have told you. You need not answer yet. I will come back to receive your reply."

"I'll do—"

"No!" I interrupted, staving off his reply with my outstretched palm. "I know what you wish to tell me now. I told Hades it was what you would do, but I implore you to fully consider the weight of this decision. My father is convinced we will fail, and I fear that the blame would be on me that your soul was forever lost to the nothingness of the Oudeis. That is an unacceptable fate to me on myriad levels."

"Okay," he replied softly, taking my hand in his. "I will give this decision the consideration you feel it deserves. When you return, I will give you an answer."

"Then I shall see you soon, brother. Farewell."

I slipped my hand from his and turned toward the thin veil that divided Elysian from the labyrinth of corridors that wound their way through the Underworld.

"Do not forget my warning, Khara. Beware of Oz's lies."

"I am aware, Drew," I replied, looking back over my shoulder at him. "Fear not."

My reply brought a tugging smile to both of our mouths before his figure was swallowed by the crowd of souls that had surrounded us. The very souls I was determined to extricate him from. I needed some measure of reassurance that Hades would not fail in this endeavor—that Drew did indeed have a chance. To do that, I sought the one closest to him. Though of questionable morals, she was reputed to be an expert in dark magic, especially instances when such magic dealt with death—a quality that would make her the perfect ally in this endeavor. With that in mind, it was not long before I found myself standing in front of the fuel for much of the Underworld's gossip.

Hades' wife.

13

"So you wish to set him free?" Persephone drawled, looking at me keenly. There was a shimmer in her eyes; the fire that wrapped around the perimeter of the room danced in their darkness. "Just so that I am clear, are you asking me to help in some way regarding your endeavor, or did you come here solely to share your doomed plan with me? Because my help typically comes at a price. . . ."

"I have come because I wish to learn that Hades is indeed capable of succeeding. He believes he is not."

"And he would be correct," she replied, snapping her gaze to the door before turning it back to face me. "That bit of information I give freely because we are all family. If you care for this warrior brother of yours, I suggest you leave him where he resides. It is a far more enviable location than the potential alternative."

"Why are you so certain that Hades will fail?" I pressed. Something about her resignation to that outcome did not sit well with me; a dissonance coursed through me at the thought.

"That," she said curtly, "is information I am not certain I can yet trust you with, though I am sure that if you know your adoptive father at all, you would see that not all is as it should be." She sauntered toward me, assessing me as she did. "Family of a sort we may be, Khara, but I do not *know* you. I only know what Hades has told me over the years. He speaks of you highly, of course, but one cannot be certain until one is able to judge for oneself. Do you not agree?"

"Something is awry with him?" I continued, ignoring her question.

"Persistent, aren't we?" She let her head loll to the side as she stared; an expression of curiosity intruded upon what otherwise would have been a vacant expression. "You love him, don't you?"

"Hades?" I clarified. She nodded. "Yes. As much as I could love anyone."

Her dark eyes narrowed.

"You speak the truth. Good. See that that behavior continues, and we shall find ourselves allies. If not . . ."

"Will you tell me what I wish to know or not?"

"In time," she purred, a sly smile creeping across her face. "I will in time. For now, however, I suggest you focus on another matter."

"And that would be?"

"Your Dark One."

"What is there to focus on? He brought me here. He will return me when I have acquired what I came here for."

"Is that what you think?" she asked, a mocking lilt in her voice. "How very interesting." She closed the remaining distance between us slowly and deliberately. "I shall offer yet another bit of information to you because I know it would break Hades' heart if anything unsavory were to ever happen to you." Taking my arm, she leaned in close to my ear, her cheek brushing mine. "The Dark help no one—work for no one. Not really. If you think that he has brought you here for your purposes and not his own, you are a fool." Her lips fell gently on my cheek, kissing it lightly before she pulled away from me, a warm smile on her face. "I will consider your request for information, Khara. But, in the meantime, be careful. You may be familiar with the perils of the Underworld, but those pale in comparison to the wrath of the Dark. Know your enemy, sister. Know him well."

I watched her elegantly stride out of the room, leaving me alone with my thoughts, my concerns, my frustrations. I had sought her counsel, desirous of answers, but all she left in her wake were more questions and more quandaries than I had been aware of. I was not ignorant of the reality that Oz's intentions were not entirely noble. Only a fool would have believed otherwise, but her warnings were severe, making me wonder if, once again, I had underestimated both Oz and his motives.

Complicating things further was her confirmation of Hades' inability to do what I wished of him. And she did so without hesitation. She required no time to consider my question; she instead fired back an answer that she knew to be true: He would fail. But since I did not have her trust, she would not tell me why. I found it inherently ironic that I needed to obtain her trust when I was not convinced that she had mine. The rumors I had long heard proved hard to dismiss.

All I was left with after my encounter with Persephone was a greater sense of uncertainty. I found it unacceptable. Too much hung in the balance for Hades to fail. So, in an effort to learn as much as I could about how exactly one could bring someone back from the dead, I turned to one of my father's advisors and Persephone's confidante. She was an expertly skilled necromancer in the world above. If anyone might know how to release Drew, it was she.

I would need to pay Casey's mother a visit.

14

Hecate preferred to dwell away from the rest of the inhabitants of the Underworld, choosing to reside nearer to the fields of souls. I think she found peace there. The dead brought her a sense of comfort. The only times I saw her were when Hades demanded her presence. Otherwise, she was a veritable ghost.

When I reached her room, at the far end of the tunnel that led to the wall of veils, I questioned the prudence of my course of action. Coming to her meant exposing Hades' weakness. Though Hecate was a loyal servant of both his and Persephone's, I knew I could never be too safe with whom I shared information in the Underworld—no one could be. I was not certain I could trust her, but I was certain that Drew could not remain in the Elysian Fields. Confiding in Hecate was a calculated risk on my part. One that I was willing to take. Whether that was for Drew's well-being or my own sanity, I could not say for sure.

Either way, I would do it.

Just as I reached up to knock on her door, it opened. Hecate stepped out; an amused look lit up her face as she stood before me.

"I knew you were here," she offered in explanation. "There is something very different about you now." She cocked her head as she looked me over, her dull gray eyes analyzing me. I was a puzzle she wished to solve. "I could never feel your presence before . . ."

"I have come to ask you something."

"Of course you have," she said, sweeping her arm toward her room to invite me in. "Nobody but Persephone or Hades ever comes to me without a reason."

I accepted her unspoken offer and stepped into her tiny room. It was an oppressive space, the ceiling far too low to be comfortable. I could barely stand upright. A dying fire faintly lit the room, showing only a bed in the corner and a wall of books on the opposite wall with an adjacent shelf full of glass bottles. Some contained liquids of various shades—most of them blood red. Other shelves contained what appeared to be desiccated body parts.

"So," she started, demanding my attention. I pulled my thoughts away from the vials to focus on her. Her long gray-white hair hung straight down her back like a cape, wrapping around her willowy frame. "How can I be of assistance to the daughter of the Underworld?" There was something about the way she called me by my title. A barely perceptible prickling sensation traveled over my body when she addressed me that way.

"I have been to Persephone regarding this matter. She is convinced that what I wish to do cannot be done. You, however, are the necromancer, not her. I need your opinion."

"On what matter precisely do you wish to consult me?"

"I would like to deliver my brother from the Elysian Fields. My father possesses the ability to do this, though he has never done so. Both he and Persephone have reservations about how successful his endeavor to do so would be. I want to know what you think, Mistress of the Dead."

"In order to offer my opinion on his ability to do so effectively, I would need to know more about the magic necessary to do this," she said thoughtfully. "That is presupposing that Hades can indeed send someone back, as he says—rebirth a soul."

"You question the veracity of his claim?" I asked, narrowing my eyes at her intently. My body coiled in response to her words, my muscles tightening in preparation of a fight. It was an instinctive reaction. Hecate was flirting heavily with insubordination, something my father, should he hear of it, would not tolerate. In light of the odd occurrences that had transpired since my arrival, maintaining authority was even more paramount than ever.

"Of course not," she replied hastily, what little color her pale face possessed disappearing in an instant. "I only suggested as such in the unlikely event that he had been misled about his ability. The gods were never above such trickery. If he has not done it before, then there is no way for him to be certain he can perform such an act, not beyond a shadow of doubt."

"Which is why I am here. I need to know if he would be more successful in releasing Drew if he were to have the most powerful necromancer in history at his side. Surely your magic combined with his would be enough."

Her brow furrowed while she contemplated my words; then her eyes darted to her wall of supplies, and she walked hurriedly toward it.

"I would need time to make preparations and talk to your father."

"No," I said tersely. "I will speak to Hades about your involvement. It will be received far better from me than you. I will send word once I have discussed the matter with him."

"Fine. In the meantime, I will gather all that I could possibly need." She looked over her shoulder at me, her face harsh, her expression cruel. "If it can be done, it will be so. If not, your father has been misled, and there will be consequences for that. You know all magic has a price, Khara. And that of death magic is infinitely greater."

"I am aware of the risks, as is Drew."

"Good," she replied, her features drawing tighter. "Now, go see your father."

Turning back to her shelf of gore, she dismissed me. As I took my leave, something occurred to me that warranted mentioning.

"You do know that your son has returned to the Underworld, do you not?" I asked, my mind wandering back to the night Casey and I interrogated the gargoyles in Detroit. Our discussion that had followed regarding the Underworld and, ultimately, his mother left me wondering. The raw anger and resentment he felt toward her was still fresh in my mind.

"I do."

Silence.

"Will you see him?"

She paused in mid-motion as she reached to return a book to its position on the shelf.

"Whatever for?"

"Because he is your son," I replied plainly, as though that were reason enough.

She cackled in response.

"He is a product of my body and nothing more." The callous nature of her words made sense of so much and validated Casey's assessment of her. She was not worthy of meeting her son. My cheeks burned with a sudden rage that I fought ardently to control.

"He came to my aid when I required it while above. He is a great warrior and a prized member of the Petronus Ceteri." My threatening tone commanded her attention, forcing her to turn and face me. *And he is also my brother,* I thought to myself, having retained just enough composure not to share that information with her. "As far as I am concerned, he is my family. You may not value that which is yours, but I do. You would be wise to remember that, and wiser still to never disparage him again in my presence. Have I made myself clear?"

"Yes," she uttered with disdain.

"What did you say?" I asked, taking a step toward her. When I did, that strange prickling sensation—that feeling of power—ran over my skin tenfold.

"Yes, *princess*," she spat, her eyes a mix of surprise and rage.

"Good."

I stared at her for a moment longer, then removed myself from her presence. Once I did, my body started to calm and settle into its normal state. While I made my way back to the populated section of the Underworld, I could not help but wonder what had come over me. I had never been prone to intimidation or violence, though surrounded by it for an eternity. But hearing Hecate renounce Casey sparked a fire inside me that burned fiercely. He was not something to be discarded and forgotten. I would beat that point into her if need be.

Right after she helped me free Drew.

15

I strode through the cavernous Underworld, trying to quiet my mind. I needed rest if I was going to be of any use to Drew. Facing my father, demanding that he do as I have asked, would likely be a battle. It would demand the best of my negotiation tactics. Diplomacy was always key when dealing with such sensitive subject matter, but with Hades it would prove especially essential. Telling him that I had acquired outside help in the event that he was unable to do as requested on his own was going to prove challenging to spin.

The passage of time is an odd thing below. Without the cardinal rhythms one experiences above—no cues of sun or moon—sleep comes when exhaustion prompts it. And that was precisely the point at which I found myself. Mentally and physically fatigued, I reached my room, wanting nothing more than to lie down and recharge. But as fate would have it, another hurdle was set before me in the form of a lithe nymph hovering by my door, worrying the ends of her long, platinum blonde hair between her fingertips.

"Khara!" she called out in a hushed voice.

"What is it, Aery?" I asked, unable to conceal my frustration with her presence.

She gestured to my room with her head, eyes darting around the hallway. She was nervous. Aery was never nervous.

With a nod, I opened the door and entered; the sprite followed me closely.

"Something happened, Khara," she started, biting her lip while she hesitated to continue.

"To my brothers?" I asked, stepping closer to her.

"No. They're fine. I left them in the Elysian Fields with the fallen PC. They'll be good there for a while."

"Then what is so important that you feel the need to skulk outside my room and speak with me privately?"

"I heard something . . ."

A quirk of my brow willed her to continue. Immediately. Instead, she began rotating her upper body left and right, increasing the frequency of the movement while her silence dragged on. It was then that I realized: It was not nervousness that afflicted her. She was afraid. Afraid of something that she was about to inform me of. In the century or more that I had known her, I had never seen her fearful.

"What did you hear?" I asked, my words crisp and clear.

"That's the problem," she explained, desperation in her voice. "I don't remember. You know how feeble my mind can be sometimes. I remember hiding . . . voices . . . shadows. The rest is just gone. I'm sorry, Khara."

"Why have you bothered to come to me with this? It serves no purpose."

"That's the thing I can't escape," she explained, shaking her hands before her as if she hoped the answers would come flying out of her fingertips. Her agitation was plain, and it was also infectious, fueling my own. "It's this feeling, you know? Like I needed to come here. I needed to tell you."

"And bring me what? Mystery? Conjecture? Lately I have enough of those things infesting my days, thank you. I am in no need of more."

Suddenly her hands quieted, slowly dropping to her sides. Her expression went slack. Dull, vacant eyes turned to me. Aery was there physically, but not mentally; her mind had gone adrift in the special place that it sometimes went when her memories grew dark. Too dark.

"Evil . . ." she said numbly. "It comes."

"For whom?" I asked carefully, not wanting to dislodge her mind from its train of thought. "For whom does it come?"

The empty expression fell from her face, one of worry overtaking it.

"You," she whispered. "It must be you."

"Are you certain?"

She looked thoughtful for a moment.

"It has to be. Why else would I be here?"

"Did you remember anything else just now? Anything else of importance?"

"No. I'm sorry, Khara."

"Very well," I exhaled, my exhaustion deepening. "Go back to Kierson and Casey. Keep them entertained however you need to."

"What about you?" I saw true concern in the set of her features.

"What about me?" I countered. "If evil comes for me, then it comes. Just be sure that you keep my brothers far from it. I know not what they can do here in the Underworld—how effective their traits will be. If something wicked comes for me, then best it find me alone. Without them. I will not jeopardize another of my brothers; is that understood?" She nodded frantically. "Go now, and say nothing of this to anyone. Not a word. Not even to my father."

Her eyes narrowed tightly. The fierceness within them was surprising.

"I'll keep them busy."

"Good. And not a word."

Without anything more, she turned to leave, giving me only the slightest glance over her shoulder when she pulled the door closed behind her. I immediately made my way to my bed, collapsing upon it in a heap. Though my mind was plagued by various unsettling matters, I could not stay awake long; the pleasant tug of slumber pulled at my consciousness. One by one, the crises that ran through my brain were

plucked and thrown aside for a later time. As a fog of nothingness settled inside my head and lulled me to sleep, one last vision shot through
my mind. It flashed like lightning through a black and stormy sky.

But it wasn't a stormy sky—it was a pair of vast, black wings that
spread wide above me, and what appeared to be lightning was instead
a piercing pair of blindingly white eyes that etched an image into the
back of my mind, one that lingered long after sleep overcame me. *"Oz,"*
I mumbled, turning onto my side and sheltering my face with my arm.

All at once, the lightning stopped.

Darkness engulfed me.

16

I awoke with a clear head; no fatigue remained. My confidence in what I was about to do grew with every second. I was going to get Hades to free Drew. The thought brought a reserved smile to my face.

Then the smile fell.

As I pushed myself up to sit on the edge of my bed, the comforter still beneath me, I saw an unmistakable indentation in the vacant spot beside me. The covers had been disturbed by the weight of another. The storm and the lightning.

Oz.

He had been in my room—in my bed.

With that befuddling realization, I scanned the rest of my room for any sign of him. There was none to be found. If he had indeed been there while I slept—and I saw no viable alternative to that theory—then why had he left without so much as a word? Oz lived to taunt me, fallen or Dark. I could so easily visualize him lying beside me, his smug grin intact while I awoke to some snide remark about me drooling in my sleep or something equally crass. The fact that he had not capitalized on such an opportunity only gave me further pause.

But there was no time for ruminating. I needed to find my father, inform him of what I had done, and start the process of sending Drew back. I made my way to the standing mirror that was propped against the far wall of my room. My hair was disheveled, my clothes a wrinkled mess, but I had no inclination to change. So, I instead smoothed my hair back as best I could in an effort to make myself more presentable, and I turned to head through my bedroom doorway and into the corridor that would eventually take me to Hades' chambers. I hoped he would be there.

"Khara," he said with a measure of surprise when he stepped out of his room, nearly running into me in the process. "I was just coming to find you."

"As I was you. I need to speak with you. It's about Drew."

"Yes, I know. Hecate told me," he said, somewhat tersely. There was an underlying irritation in his tone, though I could not discern if it was aimed at me or his necromancer.

"She has spoken out of turn, then," I replied, thinking that she had gone against my wishes and approached my father.

"She told me that you went to her. . . ." He studied my expression as he spoke, looking for something in it that he was unlikely to find. "That you told her of my concerns about Drew."

"I did. I thought that if anyone could be of service in the matter—"

"Enough," he said, holding his palm toward me to cut off my explanation. "It is clear to me that you will not let this go, or you would not have done something as bold as going behind my back about it."

I did my best to look contrite, though I did not feel it.

"I am sorry for sidestepping your concerns—"

"I will do it," he said, cutting off my apology.

"You will?"

"Yes," he affirmed, though his expression darkened, as if in forewarning of the outcome he saw as inevitable. "I have spoken with him myself. You were right; he did not hesitate for even a beat when I made the offer."

"When?"

"Momentarily. That is why I was coming for you. Hecate has already pulled Drew from the Elysian Fields. She is waiting with him in the temple. We must go now."

Time moved both quickly and slowly. My hurried pace and racing heart contrasted greatly with what seemed to be the endless journey to Father's temple. It was his private room for those who needed more punishment than the various realms of the Underworld could provide. It was secure and secluded, and the most inconspicuous place to attempt what we were about to.

When we strode down the final hall, my father's heavy footfalls out of cadence with my own while I struggled to keep up, he looked down at me. There was a morbid uncertainty in his gaze. I met it with one of confidence. His magic would work.

It had to.

We arrived to find the others already there. Hecate said nothing upon our entrance; she instead lurked in the shadows cast by the torchlight. Drew, however, turned to smile at me when I arrived. Though he did not speak, that one simple gesture said everything. He was once again himself. Once again how I remembered him—finding joy in the most inexplicable situations. This time, it was the chance to return home that had his spirits high.

"I will give you one last chance to abandon this," Hades said aloud, addressing Drew. He shook his head in negation. "Then so be it."

With a sigh, Hades closed his eyes tightly and started murmuring under his breath, the melodic Greek words spilling from him like a lullaby. But it was anything but. Those words would, if the Fates allowed, raise the dead. While the cadence of his words and the volume of his voice increased, I stood stoically in silence, waiting for my brother to change. To return to the warrior he had been. Drew, however, stood in the middle of the room, looking mildly concerned;

his eyes constantly darted to the dark corner where Hecate stood. He knew who she was and what she had done to Casey. It was clear that he had little trust in her, which only further cemented my resolve not to utilize her in the ceremony unless absolutely needed. If Drew were to be forever relegated to the Oudeis, I wanted it to be at my father's hands, not hers.

I could feel the magic coursing through the room, dancing over the surface of my skin gracefully while it pulsated toward Drew. The intensity grew along with my father's voice until suddenly Hades threw his arms up and yelled, "Rise!" The very second the word left his mouth, everything went wrong.

Drew's head snapped back to look up at the ceiling; his entire body was rigid but vibrating. The pain was evidenced by the tight grimace on his face. I took a step toward him, but Hecate's voice held me in place.

"Do not touch the dead when death magic is in play, Khara, unless you should wish to trade places with him." I would be lying if I did not admit that her warning momentarily fueled me to go to him. I would have been willing to trade places with my brother. The only reason I did not was the inherent knowledge that, when he realized that I had sacrificed myself for him, he would never forgive himself. His guilt would prove more torturous than the Underworld ever could be. Sean would never forgive him either, the implications of which were beyond grim for Drew. So I stayed, standing steadfast against my raging desire to aid my brother.

I watched as sweat ran down Hades' face, a look of impossible concentration etched deeply into it while he struggled to right the wrong that the Universe had dealt Drew. I had no idea if he was accomplishing what he had set out to do, but I was certain that he could not have done more. He stumbled back a step, arms raised, as though he was trying to magically lift Drew up and out of the Underworld.

But Drew did not move.

Instead, he remained where he was, his body nearly convulsing in pain by this point. His mouth ripped open; a soundless cry threatened to escape him, but nothing did. He looked as though he was being torn apart from the inside, and I wanted nothing more than for it to be over. I could watch him suffer no more.

"Father," I whispered, afraid to break his concentration, but even more afraid to witness the destruction of my brother.

But Hades was in another place, his mind fixated on the task at hand. He did not hear my plea.

Just then, Drew's hands shot to his head, clamping down on it so hard that I feared he would crush his own skull. Collapsing to his knees, he dislodged the scream that had undoubtedly been trying to escape for what had seemed an eternity. The sound was nearly deafening, and the power it carried forced the rest of us against the walls of the room.

Wind whipped wildly at our faces.

Fiery flames erupted around our bodies.

The stench of burning flesh clung to our nostrils.

And then, suddenly, in a white-hot flash of lightning, Drew disappeared. One moment he was there. The next he was no longer. All that was left was a smoldering scorch mark on the floor where he had just stood.

The three of us who remained in the room were released from our invisible shackles. His scream had evaporated with him. Now able to move, I ran to the ashen black mark on the stone floor while Hades and Hecate stayed where they were. Father's face was a mask of horror. Hecate's was unreadable.

"Father?" I asked, imploring him to tell me that all was well. That his endeavor had succeeded. I was met, however, with silence. "Father!" My tone was brash, trying to elicit some sort of response from him. Again, I was met with his silence.

"He has failed," Hecate replied, drawing my attention to her. "For what it is worth, there is nothing I could have done to help. The magic needed to come from your father alone. I felt that during the ceremony."

"So, you are saying that he is in the Oudeis?" Her lips pressed tightly together, unwilling to confirm what I already knew the failed outcome to be. "Then it is I who has failed," I whispered, wandering toward the vast room's door. "I have failed them all . . ."

It was only then that my father found his voice, calling after me while I mindlessly walked out of the room and down the hall, uncertain where I was headed. All I knew was that I could not remain where I was. Soon enough, I would have to tell Kierson and Casey that the plan had not worked, an outcome I was loath to admit. They had all done so much to help me in my short time with them above. I had wanted to do the same for them—but I had my selfish motivations as well. Spending time on Earth without my loyal, noble brother seemed unfathomable. Detroit needed him. The PC needed him.

I needed him.

And as that thought punched a hole in my heart, seizing my chest so tightly that it was hard to find my breath, I continued off into the darkness, hoping that it would swallow me whole.

I should have traded places with Drew when I had the chance. Sacrificing myself for him would have been the noble thing to do. It is what Drew would have done for me, and that reality only served to highlight my shortcomings as a member of the PC. They did not need a female whose powers were uncertain. They needed warriors. I had told my brothers once that I was anything but. They had argued the point with me then.

Now, I had no doubt that they would concede it.

17

By the time I had found Casey and Kierson, the self-loathing I felt was intolerable. It made me long for the days when what little emotion I possessed was utterly unreachable. It was a far simpler time.

Sitting silently at one of the massive feasting tables, the two of them started when I came in the room, both turning their attention to me. It did not take long for them to read the failure that was so plainly evident in my countenance. I had made no attempt to hide it.

"So he's—"

"Forever lost," I stated, interrupting Kierson. "Hades was not able to do what Drew and I had both hoped he could, though I do not blame him. I blame myself. Hades was transparent when he told me of his reservations. I chose to ignore them, as did Drew. And now . . ."

"He's fucked for eternity," Casey added, his voice a growl.

"Yes. He is."

Casey shot up out of his seat, instinctively pulling his daggers from the sheaths that were strapped across his back and chest. He wanted something to kill; he knew he would find solace in the act. Unfortunately, the only thing he could kill for retribution was me. For a moment, his black eyes met mine from across the room. With his blades raised, I wondered if he was assessing the ramifications of killing the princess of the Underworld—his own sister. But he did not attack. His eyes blinked hard, then his weapons lowered, a twinge of sorrow in his expression. As sorrowful as one so soulless could ever appear, at least.

Then, without warning, the feasting table went flying across the room, smashed into the far wall, and broke into two formidable pieces. The screeching cry that accompanied it was a familiar one. Kierson stood behind Casey and me, breathing hard as his wild, unfocused eyes stared off at the carnage he created.

"Kierson," I said softly, as though coaxing a wounded animal. "This is my fault, and for that I am sorrier than you can imagine." I did not wish to admit what I then knew I had to, but my brothers deserved the truth, and I would provide them with it, consequences be damned. When he finally came back to his senses, his head slowly turned toward me, his body quieting itself somewhat. "I could have spared him by changing places with him. I chose not to. His damnation hangs over my head."

His eyes narrowed keenly at me.

"You could have changed places with him?" he asked. For once, in all the time I had known him, his voice was devoid of emotion.

"Yes."

"And you considered doing this?"

"Yes. But in the end I refrained."

He paused for a moment, then charged toward me, stopping so close to me that our bodies were nearly touching.

"It's a goddamned good thing that you didn't," he seethed. "And I don't give a shit if you think this is all your fault or not. You didn't kill Drew. You didn't force him to try this sketchy ceremony bullshit either. Death is a part of our lives, Khara. You may think I'm too soft to accept that fact, but I've been dealing with it for longer than you could possibly imagine. So you can give up on this guilt that you are clinging to so desperately. Drew would have never forgiven you for trading places with him . . . and neither would I."

"Me either," Casey echoed. I turned to face him, shocked by his admittance. He shrugged ambivalently. "What can I say? Chaos follows you around like a shadow. And I'm always up for a little chaos."

"Well, this has all been very touching to witness," a familiar voice drawled from a shadowy corner of the room. "But now that we have established that Drew is eternally fucked and Khara is not to blame, can we move on to more pressing issues?" Oz stepped into the firelight of the room, his dark appendages retracted neatly behind him.

"Such as?" Casey snapped. Those two were apparently not yet on better terms.

"Getting you two idiots out of here and Khara getting the answers she came for."

"I'm not leaving without her," Kierson growled protectively.

"Listen, just because Drew is gone, that doesn't mean there's an opening in the 'most loyal brother' department," Oz retorted, much to Kierson's irritation. "You can rest assured that Khara won't be far behind."

"And I'm not leaving until I get what I came for. We have had this discussion before," I told him, watching something flicker through his deep brown eyes when I defied him.

"You're not safe here," he rumbled in response.

"Is that not why I have you?" I mocked. "Are you not here to ensure my safety, for whatever reason you find it necessary to do so?"

Flames flickered in his pupils. They were mesmerizing.

"I think it's time that you and I have a sidebar, new girl," he said, taking me by the arm to lead me out of the room.

"I think not," I countered, twisting out of his grasp. "I have an agenda here." I addressed the three of them, knowing that, like it or not, they all needed to be reminded of something. "And my agenda has not been satisfied. You may not see Drew's relegation to the Oudeis as a failure, Kierson, but I do, and I refuse to fail also in my attempt to discern precisely what I am and why I have been kept a secret all these centuries. Until that is done, I will need to be protected by those who care about me, which will only result in more death and sadness. I cannot stand by idly and allow such foolishness. If knowledge of my mother can remedy this, then that is precisely what I am going to get," I declared, turning my focus to Oz and Oz alone. "You may not be willing to provide me with it, but there are those who will. For a price."

A battle of wills drew out between us when our eyes met. I did not wish to further explain, and Oz seemed reluctant to have me spell out, in no uncertain terms, what "for a price" meant. I could not help but wonder if he was weighing his options while he stared at me harshly, his eyes cutting through me. He opened his mouth as if to speak, but a spritely voice interrupted his attempt.

"What are you guys doing?" Aery asked, feigning ignorance of the tension in the room. Much to the contrary, I had no doubt that it was that very tension that had drawn her to us. When none of us responded, she clasped her hands behind her back and rocked back and forth on her feet, awaiting an explanation. The hostility being projected at her did nothing to deter her.

"Nothing," I said, breaking the silence that threatened to continue ad infinitum. "We are finished in here. Do you need something, Aery?"

"Oh, no. I just wanted to come and see how you were doing," she said sympathetically, her oversized eyes wide. "I heard about Drew. For what it's worth, I'm sorry."

I could feel my teeth protesting under the pressure of my clenched jaw.

"Thank you."

"He seemed really sweet," she continued, making her way farther into the room.

"I need to go," I said abruptly, pushing past her on my way to the door. She caught my arm before I could advance very far.

"There's something else, Khara," she said, her eyes darting warily to the others. Leaning in close to me, her body pressed close to my side, she rolled up onto the tips of her toes to whisper in my ear. "An army of darkness comes."

Pulling away from her, I looked down to find a steady but concerned expression on her face. She had remembered more of the message.

With barely even a nod of acknowledgment, I turned back toward the door and walked away.

"Did you hear me?" she asked, confusion in her tone.

"Yes. Thank you for letting me know."

"What should we do?"

"You should entertain my brothers and keep them out of trouble," I replied without looking back at her.

Her riotous laughter let me know that she rather enjoyed my plan. Oz's immediate presence at my side in the hallway, however, told me that he was less amused with my quick dismissal of them.

"You're up to something," he snarled under his breath. "I can see it in your eyes."

"You see grief. Nothing more."

"No," he replied, grabbing my arms and pinning me to the stony wall. "I see anger and recklessness, two things that I'm far more versed in than you. You think you can fool me, but you cannot. This is not the time for foolhardy actions, new girl."

"Your advice has been taken under advisement," I drawled impassively.

"My advice is an order, and it will be heeded." There was something different about his behavior in that moment. Something far less sinister. Sincerity, perhaps? Though I could not be certain that he possessed that quality at all or even had access to it. He was cold and calculating, even more so after his change.

But the resemblance to the way he acted on the roof the night that the Stealers attacked—the night that everything changed—was impossible to ignore.

"Why are you so concerned? You are never far. Surely you can keep me from endangering myself, can you not?"

The harsh lines etched in his face when he flexed his jaw stole my attention momentarily.

"I need to leave for a bit," he admitted grudgingly. "I need to know that you can keep your shit together in my absence. Stay close to your father. He's the only insurance you have down here."

"Are you attempting to tell me something you think I do not already know?"

"I'm trying to reinforce something you seem to have forgotten, new girl," he growled. "You don't seem to have any idea who your enemies are down here. As far as I'm concerned, you have no allies. Your father is the closest thing to one."

"And yet I have survived for centuries without your aid."

"Things have changed. You are not what you were then. Remember that while I'm gone. Question everything and everyone—including your father." His eyes were dark and pleading as he stared at me in the dimly lit hall. "You want revenge for Drew? I will make sure you get it, but until then I need you to keep your head down and your shit together. Understood?"

"Yes," I lied. The ease with which I did so surprised even me. His advice, though thoughtful, fell on deaf ears.

"Good." He stepped back from me enough to rake his eyes over my body as though he was trying to memorize it. As though he thought he might never see it again. "If I'm not back in twenty-four hours, I want you to get Aery to take you and the boys back to Detroit and wait for me there."

"And if you do not show there?"

"Then I want you to call Sean and tell him that he has a big fucking problem on his hands."

"Shall I tell him what the big fucking problem is?"

He laughed in response.

"No. If I don't return, he'll already know what's coming." While I stood silently, ruminating on the possibilities, Oz's signature smirk overtook what had been a mask of apprehension. "Remember what I've told you," he said as he started to walk away from me, toward the Great Hall and presumably the Acheron and the gate to the world above. "And for the record, new girl, I like seeing that fire in your eyes. I'd just rather see it there when you're under me . . ."

18

His sinister laughter echoed in the hall long after he disappeared from it.

The second it stopped, I was able to tear my mind away from the temporary distraction Oz's words had provided and head toward the River Styx. I needed to regroup. I needed to plan. I needed to accomplish what I had returned to the Underworld to do, and perhaps find a way to cheat death without the aid of Hades. I held some measure of sway over lost souls; that was apparent from my interaction with the Stealer in Detroit and upon my return to the Underworld. If there were a way to understand that power—harness it—then perhaps I would not need Hades to aid me at all.

But I would need help from someone.

And that someone found me not long after I sat down on the rocky shore of the Styx.

"Why have you come?" I asked Persephone, trying my best to determine what her true intention was. At that precise moment, I wished to be alone—to stew in my overwhelming emotions and plot my revenge. I was not ready to discuss matters with her yet. And if she had come to gloat about the outcome of Drew's rebirthing ceremony, then she would soon find herself on the wrong side of my anger.

"You and I have something in common," she replied, slowly pacing along the riverbank while she ignored my question. Casually, she picked a rock off the shore and started turning it over in her hand.

"Do we?" I did little to keep the incredulity from my tone, which was only fueled by my irritation with my failure. "From all I have heard of you, sister, one thing in common is one more than I would have assumed."

Her hand faltered at my insult, causing a fraction of a second's pause between flips of the stone.

"Yes," she affirmed tersely. "We do. Our love and admiration of Hades." When her eyes drifted from the river before her to meet my gaze, she was met with my empty stare. I would give nothing away. "I can see that the gossip surrounding him and me did not dissipate during my absence from the Underworld."

"No. It did not."

"Of course," she nodded, dropping the rock back to the ground. "Then let me be frank with you. Contrary to what you may have been led to believe, I love your adoptive father—or at least I have grown to love him. The circumstances surrounding us have always been controversial. Such circumstances do not lend themselves to a traditional love affair. In fact, quite the opposite. However, time and proximity have led me to not only accept my place at his side, but desire it."

"Your point?" I asked. I wanted to know the real reason she had come to me, not listen to her defend her relationship with my father.

"My point is that regardless of how unconventional our pairing may be to outsiders or their reservations about it, I would never want to see harm befall my spouse. The man you consider your father."

"Your words imply that harm awaits him."

"Just as I had intended, because it does. I alluded to something the other day—something I needed to share with you but was not certain I could. Now, I feel as though I must, regardless of my feelings." She paused for a moment, giving herself a chance to choose her words wisely. "Your father is in danger."

"Is he?" I asked flatly.

"He is." Her tone mimicked my own.

"How is it that you have come to know of this impending danger?"

She sighed heavily, elegantly folding herself into a crouched position at my side in preparation for the discussion we were about to have.

"Khara, how much do you know about the falling of the gods?" she asked. Her question seemed disjointed from the conversation at hand, though I did not doubt it had a point.

"Enough to know that few are left after the emergence of the Christian God."

"This is true; we lost many, but it is not their loss in and of itself that is pertinent. It is how they were lost, and, more importantly, how some managed to persist." Her keen stare was piercing, demanding that I keep pace with her subtext. Once she seemed confident I was paying adequate attention to her words, she continued. "When the takeover began, an ultimatum was put forth: conform or perish. It was that simple. The gods, full of pride, found those terms unacceptable. Many challenged the Christian God. From all that I have learned over time, those that did were met with a swift death. And not the kind that earns you a place in the Underworld." My eyebrow quirked slightly at her words. She smiled wickedly in response. "I am certain your father has long cautioned you that there are fates worse than death." I nodded. "Then you know of what I speak?" I shook my head slowly in negation. "Ah, well, that is a topic for another day, I think. Just know that you would not want to travel down the path they took."

"How many of them met this fate?" I asked curiously.

"Most," she replied tightly. "I believe there is a saying in the Christian Bible that speaks of pride going before the fall." She shrugged Gallicly. "The gods that perished seemed to embody that cautionary tale."

"If many fell, then who remains?" I asked, wondering which of them had chosen the path of survival.

"Of the true Greek gods? Ares, Poseidon . . . Demeter, of course . . ."

"That is all?" I asked, unable to conceal my disbelief.

"And Hades, though his fate was orchestrated differently from the others. It was rather poetic, really, given that many on Mount Olympus looked upon him as unworthy of his position amongst them. He was the only one granted reprieve from His mandate."

"How were the gods to 'conform'?"

"That was the most interesting part of all, I must admit. The Christian God is not without His sense of cruel irony, I must say. To punish those that remained, He stripped them of their previous gifts and relegated them to a life in which they could only enjoy the opposite of all they had previously loved. For example, Ares, instead of leading armies into battle, is now charged with peacekeeping between the species that inhabit the world above as well as preventing humans from learning of those pesky supernaturals that inhabit their mundane planet. He did not take this offer well at first, but he is self-preserving, if nothing else. I was told that when he watched the others deny God and subsequently fall as a result, he was all too quick to accept his new position with every ounce of grace that he could muster."

"Poseidon?"

"Bound to the shores, never to set foot in a body of water again."

"And Demeter? What of her abilities?"

"God seemed to be far kinder to her than the others, most likely because her penchant for mischief and abuse of power was far less prominent. She still wields some authority over the elements, though it is a pitiful amount. She is a mere shadow of her former glory—barely a step above human, though still immortal. It pains her to be so out of touch with nature. She laments her new station. I think, if given the chance again, she would choose the fate that befell the other gods."

I pondered her words for a brief moment, wondering if perhaps Demeter's always-sullen behavior had less to do with me specifically and more to do with her detachment from the earth she loved. With that thought came a light tightening of my heart. Guilt settled there for a brief moment before dissipating entirely. It was a misplaced emotion. Memories of Demeter's loathing of me, regardless of the reason behind it, were enough to rid my body of any regrets I had where she was involved. My resentment of her was well earned as far as I was concerned, her behavior's possible justification notwithstanding.

"So only the four remain?"

"Well," she hedged, her eyes darkening in the flickering firelight around us. "There is some conjecture surrounding one or two of the others, my father included."

"Zeus did not perish?"

"I do not know for certain. He was the last to meet his fate, allegedly. The others had all chosen by then—there were no witnesses. But I do know that I have not seen him since that day. He is nowhere that I can find him. Above or below." Her shadowy eyes narrowed. "And there is virtually nothing that I cannot find and even less that I do not know."

There was heat in her words as well as a certain hint of warning. Persephone, despite her rumored shortcomings, was powerful in her own right. A fact that I would seek to use to my advantage.

"Perhaps that is his punishment? He has been cut off from all he loved?" I offered, thinking it a plausible and sensible explanation for the one who fathered so many and ruled so many more.

"A perceptive observation, sister," she purred. "Especially for one who did not have the privilege of knowing him as I did. It is also an observation that I had long ago made, but my faith in its veracity grows weary." Her eyes softened for a fraction of a second, exposing a sad and exhausted depth. Then they hardened again. "But I digress. My point in telling you all of this was to highlight the fact that Hades was not subjected to the same treatment as the others. For whatever reason, which you may feel free to speculate about later on, the Christian God did not strip Hades of his previous reign. This statement may seem rather obvious to you, but it is the underlying subtext that is most fascinating. He allowed Hades to rule the

Underworld—an unsavory place—but from that point on, all who came here would be supernatural or former deities, though minor ones. Humans would no longer be cast into the bowels of this place."

"And because Hades agreed to this, he experienced no change in power?"

"Correct. For the most part." She paused, worrying her bottom lip between her fingers while she processed her own thoughts carefully. She was weighing her words. "Hades has lost some things—things that I dare not divulge here because the shadows of this place have ears. Such things should never be said aloud. Ever. But the losses of which I speak hinder him in ways that could potentially leave him . . ."

"Vulnerable?" I asked, my voice low and cautious. The darting of her eyes around the room was response enough. She looked mildly paranoid. "Impossible."

Her crazed eyes landed on mine, giving me pause and undoing my resolve, however slightly.

"Is it? Would you wager his life on that?" she hissed, lunging toward me. With her face hovering just before mine, she fought to regain her composure. Taking a reserved step back from me, she smoothed down the various layers of fabric adorning her, then continued. "There is more to this story, Khara. More than I have time to tell you. More than I *can* tell you, for I do not fully understand what is happening myself. And, as I said before, there is precious little that I am not privy to knowing. But what I do know and can tell you is that much has happened since you last saw your father." A heaviness eclipsed her words and expression, her earlier exhaustion breaking through yet again. This time it stayed in the forefront. "The pact—the one that has bound you and me to the schedule we have held for centuries—has been broken, though by whose actions I have yet to determine." Her expression hardened yet again. "Regardless of who is guilty, Hades' powers are . . . eluding him in ways they have never before." She grabbed my forearm tightly, whispering harshly to me.

"My telling you this makes us allies, Khara. It means that I am willing to set aside my better judgment and trust you without truly knowing you. There are precious few in my world that I have trusted so."

My mind immediately brought forth images of Drew convulsing in pain and the expression on my father's face. From the onset of my plan, he had tried to warn me away from trying to save Drew. Had he done so not because he was inexperienced and uncertain, but because he in fact knew that his powers were waning? As that realization settled into my expression, Persephone pressed her lips tightly together in a sympathetic gesture, her features softening slightly.

"The chaos that you arrived to witness, Khara, should have been evidence enough, but Hades' failure to force Drew's rebirth clearly illustrates that his power is diminishing."

"You let Drew perish," I said accusingly, pulling my arm from her grasp.

"No," she argued quickly. "I did what I could to warn you, but you would not hear it. Instead, you went to Hecate in an attempt to undermine Hades and me. No, I stand by my decision to wait and share this—this *delicate* information about Hades—with you until now. You needed to see for yourself. I do not think you would have believed me any other way." I rose in anger, forcing her to lean away from me. Her initial shock turned quickly to controlled anger, and she stood to face me. "I did not come here to fight with you, but if you force my hand, I will defend myself, sister. That is not something you want."

"What I want is my brother back," I growled, my voice deadly serious.

"Which is partly why I have come to you. I think I have a way to solve both of our problems, should you be willing to set aside your grief-driven anger long enough to listen."

I closed my eyes, inhaling deeply. Though it took longer than it should have, I managed to regain an emotional state more reminiscent of the one I had lived in for centuries.

"Go on."

"I know the chaos that you witnessed when you returned to the Underworld, Khara. I also know it was stifled by you. You, sister, hold the power to contain that which threatens to overrun both the Underworld and, in turn, your father."

I eyed her quietly, digesting what she had said. She seemed to take my silence as evidence of my continued distrust.

"Khara," she started, softening her tone slightly. "I can see in your eyes that you think little of me, and, given all you have undoubtedly heard, it is easy to comprehend why. What I need you to do is reconcile your feelings with my intentions to protect the man you view as your father. I fear for what is happening. I feel a shift in all that surrounds me. If order is not maintained, he may fall victim to those he was charged to reign over."

An army of darkness . . .

"Impossible," I affirmed for the second time, dismissing Aery's warning, though it screamed in my mind.

"That word," she said, clicking her tongue against her teeth as she leaned closer to me again. "The impossible is only so until it occurs. Then it is an oversight of epic proportions. A legend. A cautionary tale. Would you hang your hat on what you believe to be impossible while risking the stability of the Underworld because your mind cannot conceive of any other possibility? Because your mind is too consumed with what you have already lost to perceive another, even greater, loss?"

I opened my mouth to respond, then promptly snapped it shut. Her words were harsh but true, and they were ones that I, above all others, should have understood. I had been an impossibility—an adult Unborn. All thought it could not happen until it did, and the ramifications of such ignorance nearly cost me my soul. My freedom. I knew in my heart that I would not risk Hades' well-being if I could somehow stop harm from befalling him. And if, in that endeavor, I could somehow bring Drew back, too, I would stop at nothing. If Persephone thought my assistance was integral, then she would have it.

"You are convinced that I am somehow the solution to this?" I asked, uncertain how or why she was so convinced, but that mattered not.

"Yes."

"Fine."

Her brow rose amusedly at my reply.

"That is all? Just 'fine'? You have no questions? Require no explanation?"

"I will do what needs to be done for my father's and Drew's benefit, if you believe I can help. I see no other options."

She then cocked her head, eyeing me with a mix of curiosity and bewilderment.

"May I be frank with you?" she inquired, her eyes quickly scanning the room as if she were reassuring herself that we were indeed alone. When she returned her gaze to mine, I nodded in response. "I have heard of what you did while away from here . . . in Detroit."

"From whom did you hear this?"

"In the spirit of transparency, I will tell you, though you mustn't say a word."

I nodded. "Deimos. I overheard him one night—just after he returned. He was manic, rambling about things I could not understand, but the longer I listened to his insanity, the more I started to piece together the gist of what had occurred between the two of you." She looked at me expectantly, her wide eyes searching for acknowledgment of what she had learned. I gave her nothing, which only spurred her on. "More specifically, what happened between you and a rogue Stealer. The *how* of it all remains unclear to me, but what I understood implicitly is that you annihilated it—and not with a weapon. He seems to think that you somehow drained the Stealer in the same way that the Stealer should have drained you."

"And this is why you view me as the solution to the management issue in the Underworld? I fail to see the connection."

"I have a theory," she said, stepping so close to me that her body pressed against my own, her lips at my ear. "If you were in fact able to take the souls that the Stealer contained into yourself, then I am left to wonder what else you can do with them—souls, that is."

"Your theory, though intriguing, sister, is one that has no means of being tested. Not without bringing attention to that which you seem so intent on keeping secret."

"Possibly . . ."

Her response was a seductive invitation—a crossroads. Her tone made it plain that she had thought about this for some time. She had a plan. I could either inquire what it was or walk away, potentially endangering my father in the process and eliminating any chance of learning what could be done for Drew. Rejecting whatever strategy she had in place would also burn the bridge between her and me, which would surely have kept her from telling me all she knew about my mother. Persephone's scandalous reputation may or may not have been warranted, but I knew she was powerful. I may have suffered at the hands of the Underworld in my past, but Persephone most certainly had not, which was a clear testament to her power. And if she thought that power was insufficient to aid Hades in his alleged time of need, that alone was cause for concern. Combined with all I stood to lose if I did not assist her, the decision was all but made for me.

"I am listening."

"Good," she whispered, pulling away from me. "Because we don't have much time." Again, her eyes quickly darted around the vast and open shoreline to ensure that we were not in the unwanted company of others. "I know you did something to those present in the Great Hall when you arrived; that much I have told you. What I have not told you is why I think you were able to. I believe that something about you calls to the evil surrounding you. In Detroit, you would have been in contact with a fair amount of it. Here, we are steeped in the darkest of the dark. Beings so wickedly depraved that there are realms where even I dare not go for fear of what wanders aimlessly there, waiting for the chance to exact revenge on those that keep them there."

"How could they? I know of what you speak, and I also know that there is magic that binds those particular souls to their place of punishment. There is no chance for revenge—no escape to be had."

"Unless that magic fails," she said, resting back in her chair. A smug smile tugged at her lips. It was an all-knowing expression that I was very familiar with. Oz wore it often.

As my mind pieced the puzzle together, I finally saw why she wore it. She already knew the answer.

"Hades . . . he is the power that binds them."

"Precisely."

"And you believe that if his power is waning—"

"So is the thickness of that which contains the most vile, nefarious, imprisoned souls that the Underworld has to boast. All of the veils are weakening, really."

I thought of all my fallen brothers, those that Kierson and I had encountered in the dining hall. That day, there had been so many of them out at once. Was that proof of Persephone's claim? Were they out because they had been permitted to be, or because that which contained them could no longer do so?

"Surely Hades must know this," I declared convincingly. "He must feel the drain."

"I believe he does on some level, though there is nothing he can do. But if he does indeed lose all control of this place, make no mistake about this, sister: The ramifications will be catastrophic for both the living and the damned."

"He would never let that happen," I argued, thinking of the militaristic yet noble man I had grown to care for—even love. He would do everything within his capability to ensure that never occurred.

But what if his capability to do so was lost?

"You must learn not to speak in such absolutes, Khara. Your brother, Sean, has that very same flaw. It is one that leads to unpleasant outcomes," she warned, her eyes narrowing tightly at her mention of Sean's name. "I believe what you meant to say was that Hades would never *willingly* let that happen. On that point, we can both agree. However, his intentions are not in question. His ability to do the job he was charged with is."

"I must speak to him," I said, my voice somewhat wistful and distant.

"No!" she cried, grabbing my arm when I moved to leave her. "I have already tried. He will hear nothing of it."

"But he must," I argued. "Especially in light of what happened to—"

"I agree, but he is a proud leader, Khara. You know this. To question his rule is to tear at his very fiber. His power is already unraveling. Would you unravel his being as well?"

I stared into her suddenly sad eyes and realized that I could not. But what price would be paid for my silence? That question plagued my mind.

"What will happen if I cannot do whatever it is you think I can do to aid Hades?"

"Then the walls between us and the damned will fall, and there will be true, unadulterated anarchy."

"And my father?"

"Will certainly be the first to fall victim to it," she said firmly. "There are too many locked away that blame him, not themselves, for their tortured existence in order for him to survive. Of this, I am certain."

"I would not stand idly by while Hades was under attack."

She smiled wickedly, squeezing my arm uncomfortably. Her eyes were murderous.

"Nor would I, but our efforts would be in vain. There will be no stopping the mob when they are in search of retribution. But that will not stop me from fighting, either."

"What do you propose?"

"We must go to the Fields of Oudeis. We must see if you are indeed capable of what I am desperately hoping you are."

"And that is?"

"Taking charge of all that call the Oudeis home. You will be a vessel for that evil until we find a way to restore the power that Hades has lost and return those souls to their rightful punishment."

"Even if what you suggest is possible, how will Hades regain the power he has lost? I have no way to impact that."

Her serpent's smile widened.

"Leave that part to me, Khara. I have far more tricks up my sleeve than any would give me credit for, and many in my debt that may be of use in this particular situation." She started off toward the main body of the Underworld, her graceful gait impossible to look away from. "I will keep you apprised of all I learn."

"And what of my brother?" I asked.

"I need to consult with Hecate in that matter, but I believe that, once the Oudeis has been drained into you, she should be able to remove his particular soul, but only when you return the others to the Oudeis," she explained. "As I said, I will keep you apprised."

The sway of her hips nearly mesmerized me, distracting me from the question that had burned itself into the back of my mind. The question I had originally set out to have answered. One of the main reasons I returned to the Underworld in the first place.

"I need something in return for doing this," I called after her. Persephone stopped short and turned to face me, a look of interest on her face.

"Is saving your brother not enough?"

"No. It is not." I could see that she was not used to having demands made of her, but I cared not. If she required my assistance to carry out her plan, then she would give me what I wanted. It was the only leverage I had. "Answers. About my mother."

Her eyes narrowed.

"Done," she said with a dismissive wave of her hand. She then resumed her retreat back to the depths of the Underworld.

"And the Dark One," I called after her, not forgetting that Oz, too, was a driving force behind my return to the Underworld. A driving force that compelled me to seek Persephone out specifically. "I have questions about him. About undoing what has been done."

My words halted her yet again.

"How very unexpected," she replied over her shoulder, her voice low and husky. "You surprise me, sister. It is strangely refreshing, and because of that I will entertain your request. Precious few things surprise me anymore."

"You admitted that there are things you know that others do not. I am certain that you are the only one who can aid me in these questions."

"And I am certain that if you know that much about me that you also know that I do not give without getting—that the information I provide comes at a price."

"You are receiving my aid in maintaining the Underworld and keeping Hades safe. Those are two separate outcomes for which I require two separate payments."

"Touché, sister," she purred. "Though your efforts are not the currency I typically deal in; for you—for family—I will make this exception, but only once. We have a deal, though I will not deliver until you do. There is no certainty yet that you will be able to hold up your end of the bargain, and I stand to lose much for what I can tell you about what you wish to know. If you succeed, I may be willing to divulge all I can, but I will not wager that until Hades is safe. Those are my terms."

"I accept."

"Of course you do. What choice do you have? You have had things stolen from you—your brother. Your mother. Oz. In a sense, I know what at least one of those losses is like. There was a time when I would have moved Heaven and Earth to find a way to right those wrongs. If I were you, that is precisely what I would do." Persephone turned to face me, her wicked smile impossibly wide. "Who knows . . . if I were you, I might even raise a little hell."

As I stared at her impassively, trying to appreciate her advice, she nodded at me and turned to leave.

"And what if we fail?"

"Then we will be raising hell for certain."

With a wink, she was gone.

I stood motionless, processing all that had just occurred while Oz's words reverberated in the back of my mind. He had warned me that now was not the time for recklessness—that I needed to be wary of where I laid my trust. But I did not care. I was blinded by the need to protect my father, free Drew, and get what I had come to the Underworld for. If Persephone's and my desires aligned to accomplish all of that, then it was a risk that I was more than willing to take. Oz's reservations toward all who dwelled in the Underworld were not mine. It did not help that I was still uncertain precisely what his intentions were. Should I accept the advice of a being whose agenda might be best served by my compliance if I did not yet know what that agenda was?

The answer to that question was both elusive and haunting.

19

The River Styx had always been my sanctuary, but I now sought an environment that mirrored my roiling emotions. The Acheron was the most fitting place. Its waters churned and crashed along the craggy rock walls that hemmed it in. If the Styx was an open oasis, the Acheron was a rushing divide, cutting its way between the dead and the living. With my feelings raging just below my controlled surface, I wondered if I wasn't destined to become somewhat the same thing. A violent force separating the two.

Standing on the cliff just above the water, I looked across to the other side, thinking it strange that a simple body of water was enough to withhold all that the Underworld imprisoned, but I knew it was. I had seen some of Father's disgruntled warriors attempt to cross it and escape. It was an ill-conceived plan. Their deaths were swift but grotesque, having been swallowed up in the acidic waves, bodies eroding in a matter of seconds. Strange that as I now gazed at the fast-moving river, I considered doing just as they had.

Reckless? Maybe. But perhaps not.

If my mother had been Dark, then why was it not possible for me to cross of my own accord? I could fly. Why not test my theory? I needed to know if I could personally extract Drew from the Underworld as quickly as possible if Persephone's plan worked. Perhaps I would need to bring him over while I still contained him. There were too many unknowns to chance—too many to relinquish to the control of others—and as that thought ran through my head, I felt myself lean forward, my body flirting with the cliff's edge. The familiar pain of my wings pressing through flesh seared in my back. I closed my eyes, hovering farther over the water. Just as my wings extended, I felt another familiar sensation travel along my spine. My heart raced the second his presence registered in my mind, and I stumbled back inelegantly from the water's edge.

"Tempting fate, are we?" Deimos asked, approaching from behind me. I turned to see him, his frighteningly rugged face fixed on mine. "Those are not the shade that I remembered them to be, nor are they the shade necessary for safe passage across the Acheron." He eyed me curiously. "But you know that, which makes me wonder precisely what it is that you are doing."

"Thinking."

"I would argue the opposite, given that your suicidal notion exhibits a clear lack of thought."

"I was not going to cross it."

He smiled menacingly.

"I know. That's my point. You were not." I felt my wings fold in behind me, shrinking under the weight of his stare. "You would have perished, and you see, Khara, I cannot have that."

"Is that why you are here? I now have two chaperones to ensure my safety?" I asked, controlling my expression as best I could.

His face, however, darkened at my question.

"You know why I am here," he growled. "The real question to be asked is why are you here? Why have you returned?" He slowly circled me like a lion. His casual pace and easy set of his shoulders did not fool me. There was nothing easy about Deimos.

Or the way he made me feel.

"I came in search of answers," I replied, doing my best to mimic his cool demeanor. "That cannot be surprising news for you to hear, knowing of all that has changed for me."

"Answers about what?"

"That is not your concern."

He stopped mid-stride. His face remained turned away from mine, and I saw his clasped hands tighten at my response. My challenge was not appreciated. Much to his credit, he kept his hands pressed together, instead of releasing one or the other in order to strike my face. I had expected that reaction when I answered. Something about him was different, and it made me want to test his boundaries.

"Detroit has changed you. Made you bold," he said calmly, though the tension in his expression betrayed him as he fought to maintain his composure. "Do not forget where you are or with whom you are dealing."

"I have questions about my mother. I came back to speak with Hades regarding them."

"I see. . . . And you think he has these answers you seek?" he asked, starting to circle me yet again.

"Some."

"Only some?" he asked with an unmistakable curiosity in his tone.

"If he has more than he has admitted to, then he is reluctant to share them with me. Whether that is because he does not wish to fuel my curiosity further or he does not dare share his knowledge, I cannot be certain," I explained. "You and I both know that there is little, if any, true privacy to be found in this place. It is hardly a secure setting to discuss sensitive subjects."

"That is an interesting assessment," he drawled from behind me—too close behind me. "Let us suppose that he knows nothing more about your dear mother. What then?"

"I have made arrangements."

"With whom?"

"Others," I answered defiantly, unwilling to disclose my deal with Persephone or its details. Knowing that my insubordination would only anger Deimos further, I steadied myself for the first blow.

But instead of a fist, I was hit with a roar of laughter so booming that I flinched.

"Fine, Khara. I will let you have this little victory if it pleases you."

I was glad that he was behind me, unable to see the astonishment that flashed through my eyes. In all the time that I had known him—been terrorized by him—he had never made such a concession.

He had never made any concessions at all.

"And why would you do such a thing?" I asked, pressing the boundaries of his evolving persona yet again.

Unresponsive at first, he slowly stalked around me to stand before me. His massive and intimidating form loomed above me, blocking out the flickering firelight behind him. My heart in my throat, I waited with bated breath for his next move.

"Do you remember having nightmares in your time spent above? The time you spent in Demeter's care?" he asked with curiosity, leaning in close to bury his nose in my hair. The chill that act sent down my spine could not have been more different than the one I felt when Oz did the same.

I had no idea why he had so abruptly changed the subject to inquire about the night terrors I used to endure. "Do you?" he pressed when my silence dragged on longer than he found agreeable. The simple response would have been yes, I did, though how he knew of my nightmares was a mystery to me. One that he would quickly solve.

He narrowed his eyes menacingly at me, and I finally nodded in response to his initial question.

"I'm afraid that I am to blame for those." There was nothing remorseful about his tone.

"You?" I asked, unable to conceal my incredulity. Then understanding settled in. "You were there . . ."

"Yes."

"Why?"

He hesitated for a moment, pulling his face away from my head to look down at me, his dark eyes unreadable.

"Your father sent me."

Yet another mystery.

"And he never saw fit to tell me this? That I was to be chaperoned during my time with Demeter?"

"I would not call it chaperoning per se. Consider it more like checking up on you," he said casually, winding a stray lock of my hair around his finger in a rhythmic motion. "As for not telling you, he never had the opportunity to. But he had his reasons."

I knew not how to process Deimos' bizarre and confounding revelation. I had always thought it strange that, though I seemed impervious to the fear that so many fell victim to, at night my mind was plagued by terror. Terror I could not explain.

Terror that I felt only in Deimos' presence.

Now that the nightmares had a name, the explanation for his presence still eluded me. I desperately wanted to press Deimos further to learn why Hades would do such a thing, but I was already surprised that he had disclosed as much as he had. I needed to make my moves carefully with him—employ strategy, not brute force. One could not strong-arm Deimos. Not unless one wished to lose said appendage.

With that in mind, I tried a different approach with him entirely.

"Why are you telling me this?" I asked, trying to project warmth with my voice when I felt none.

"Because," he replied, letting my hair fall softly against my cheek, "I have run out of options. I grow tired of your reluctance to join me and even more tired of chasing you. I cannot change what you are now; that opportunity has been squandered. So you leave me with little choice. I thought perhaps if I were to bend a little that you might do the same."

"Precisely how pliable do you expect me to be?"

"*Very.*"

"Then you will have to give me more than this," I said, leaning against his hard body while mine screamed at me to flee. "Why did my father send you to watch over me?" My blood pounded so loudly in my ears that I could hardly hear his reply.

"So many questions," he muttered under his breath, clasping his large hands around my arms. "I wonder if you really want the answers you seem so desperate for."

"Perhaps. Perhaps not. I will decide that once I obtain them," I countered, tensing under his grasp. His grip on me tightened.

"I have so much that you want . . ." he said softly, bending to rub his nose harshly along my face. "And you can have all of it."

"For a price," I whispered sweetly, though somehow the bitterness I felt still lingered in my tone.

He pushed me away from him, his stormy eyes dissecting my expression.

"There is always a price, Khara. Always. Do not be fooled by those who would tell you otherwise."

"And what is your price, Deimos?" I asked carefully. "My body? No, you have had that already—many times. My mind? I think not. What is it that you want from me?"

"What I have always wanted," he replied, his voice low and cautionary. "You. All of you. That has not changed; only my methods to meet that end have."

"And what, pray tell, will you do with me once you own me?"

His predatory smile pushed through his hardened expression.

"Whatever I want."

"You seem so confident that this new approach you have employed will be successful."

"I am."

"Why?"

"Simple," he told me while he leaned his face close to mine, his lips brushing against my cheek when he spoke. "I know far more than you could ever imagine. More than Hades ever will. And I also know that, once tempted by this information, you will stop at nothing to obtain the rest of it. It is only a matter of time before you give in. And when you do, I will capitalize on your weakness."

I flinched, though almost imperceptibly. There was veracity to his claim. I had returned to the Underworld to get answers, and, though that mission had been derailed by Drew's death, the fact remained that there was still so much I wanted to know—needed to know. About my mother. About what I was. About how and why I came to be in the hands of Demeter. Though the thought of willfully giving myself over to Deimos was repugnant, I knew that if no one else proved able to supply the information I so ardently sought, I would consider his terms.

An eternity with terror incarnate or one with amassing unknowns—neither seemed particularly palatable. If the time came, I would have to decide between the two. I would exhaust every option, though, before it came to that.

"But if I give in, you will have nothing to chase. To torment. I know how the hunt fuels your sickness, even if you have decided to play a more insidious game for the time being."

"Do not worry, Khara," he said, his voice so cold that I stifled a shiver. "*When* you give in, I will still find plenty to torment." I stood before him, forcing my legs to stay still. I had no doubt he would make good on his word. In fact, I had seldom been so certain of anything. "There are many ways to torture, *skoteini vasílissa*. I am confident that your mind will break long before your body ever would."

"We shall see about that," I said coldly, though my words lacked conviction.

His recognition of that was evidenced by the wicked smile that stretched across his dark face.

"That we will." He brushed past me, letting his hand trail across my chest as he did. The second his fingertips left my body, I felt the air

I had been denying myself rush into my lungs. "And Khara?" he called back to me. I did not turn to look at him. "I would not bother to ask Hades about my presence above. He will have nothing to tell you."

"I think he will have plenty to tell me."

"No," he corrected. "He will not."

His adamancy warranted my attention. I looked back at him to find a dark and foreboding expression dancing across his face. His words were a warning.

"He would not lie to me if directly confronted about this matter."

He scoffed in response.

"His denial would not be a lie," Deimos laughed. "It would be ignorance of the subject."

"He cannot be ignorant of an order he gave," I rebutted, confusion overtaking my countenance.

"Precisely," he purred. His dark, piercing eyes demanded that I decipher the subtext in his reply. Mulling it over in my mind, I finally came to a paralyzing realization. The smile he donned in recognition let me know that I was no longer schooling my reactions. I wore the revelation all over my face.

"Hades did not tell you to go." My words were barely a whisper.

He shook his head no, affirming my conclusion.

"Sweet dreams," he said softly, turning to disappear around a corner in the rock face beside us. "I did so enjoy watching you sleep."

20

Ares . . .

The name finally registered, but I did not speak it aloud. I could not. Saying it would give it power. Truth. And it was a truth full of unpleasant ramifications.

Before I could allow my mind to catalogue all of them, I once again found myself interrupted.

"*Skoteini vasílissa*, eh?" Oz's voice called from a shadowy crag. "His Dark Queen . . . I find so much irony in that name that I hardly know where to begin." He revealed himself, slowly stepping forward into the firelight that bounced hypnotically off the rock faces. The way that Oz could conceal himself amid the darkness was uncanny. I wondered if it was a gift of all Dark Ones or just a skill of his.

"After everything you have undoubtedly heard, that is the point you see most fit to address first?" I sneered. "Perhaps you were not listening carefully enough."

"Oh, I was listening, all right." He walked toward me, his usual swagger absent from his stride. There was heat in his words and anger in his expression. "But I think what I saw was far more intriguing."

"You could not possibly have been listening acutely, or you would have heard Deimos tell me that Ares not only knows of my existence but has had his son torment me for centuries while I was above."

"No, I heard that." His face had settled into a mask of calm indifference, but it was the fire that burned just beneath it that I was keenly aware of. If not chosen tactfully, my words would be fuel to that flame.

"How is it that you are not at all surprised by this revelation?" I asked incredulously. "It was what my brothers feared most while I was above—that Ares would be made aware of me."

"And how do you think he came to know about you, Khara?" He cocked his head with curious condescension.

"I do not know, but—"

"His son, one of his three favored children, is your father's second in command. Hades' number two. Surely you cannot be so naïve as to think that Deimos has had no contact with Ares in all these years?"

"Maybe he could not? Maybe he was part of the covenant for that reason?"

"Or maybe he's just as shady a bastard as he presents himself to be," he argued, looming over me. "But he's a problem for another time. They both are."

"Deimos is always a problem, but one I can handle. Ares, however, is not."

"Ares can't come down here because of his contractual obligations to the PC, nor should he want to. As long as you're here, you're safe," he countered before his features twisted into an ugly set. "And I saw how you handled Deimos." In a flash, Oz lifted me up painfully by my arms and rushed me backward across the room until I crashed against the wall. "You think you can play both sides, do you? That I'm as much a fool as Deimos?" he growled, pressing me painfully against the wall. Escape was no longer an option. Enduring the dark side of the Dark One was all I could do. I was about to see why Father had long warned of them. "I have pandered to your need for answers, but my patience for your tactics is growing thin. Do not, for one moment, think that my tolerance for your behavior is endless." He released an arm to run his index finger cruelly down my face, dragging it across my lip. He watched me with an intensity that was reminiscent of Deimos. He enjoyed what he was doing. Inflicting pain fed him.

Fear was his weapon as well.

He had been holding back his true nature from me. I had only glimpsed it when he first came to me that night in Detroit. After that, he was only a slightly more surly version of the fallen angel I had come to know. He showed nothing of the monster that would trap me in a cage of hostility in this corner of the Underworld. Though he did not evoke the same physiological response that Deimos inherently did, there was something far more sinister about him that left me disturbed.

I had underestimated him once again.

"My irritation with this place grows daily, Khara. Even where you are concerned. You would be wise not to cross me—especially not now. I am above the precious few laws that your beloved father enforces. Or attempts to."

"Then do as you will," I replied, my tone laced with indifference. Indifference I did not feel. "You are no different from Deimos in that regard."

"Deimos is an arrogant fool, and you are an ignorant one if you think that he and I are alike."

"You are far more similar than either of you can see. You both seek to own me, do you not?" I baited, hoping he would unwittingly disclose the reason for his obsession with me. It remained a mystery to me still. "Your methods are no different. Manipulation is the current weapon of choice for you both. Perhaps you are just as arrogant as he, and that hubris blinds you to your likenesses."

Judging by the look on his face, he was impressed with my tactic but saw right through it.

"So much you fail to understand," he replied, eyeing me as though I were a naïve child. "Let me state this in the plainest terms so that we do not find ourselves here again: Do not presume to play me, new girl. It will never work."

162

"Then I shall play Deimos instead," I retorted, still uncomfortably pinned against the stony corridor wall.

"Is that what you were doing?" he asked with a quirk of his brow.

"Yes."

"Interesting," he mocked. "It looked far more like you were trying to fuck him."

"As was my plan."

"Your plan was to look like you were trying to fuck him or to *actually* fuck him?"

"My plan was to do whatever necessary to get the answers I desire from him." He looked displeased with my response, so I elaborated in an attempt to assuage his growing anger. "To that end, I employed a strategy that was most likely to get me what I seek."

He cocked his head awkwardly while he considered my response.

"The only thing you will get employing that strategy is Deimos' dick crammed deep inside you."

"Not the only thing," I argued. "He tends to be rather obliging once his needs are sated."

His initial surprise quickly devolved to rage.

"You have fucked him solely to obtain information before?"

"Yes. Once. It is the only currency I possess that he is interested in accepting. Though he takes what he wants when he wants it, he seems to find it amusing when I come to him. His dark delight in my submission appears to make him rather forthcoming."

"And you would do it again?" He leaned against me so hard that my chest could barely expand enough to continue breathing. I assumed that was his intention. With his forehead pressed tightly against mine, his eyes blazed white, forcing me to shut mine. The light was blinding. "Would you like it?" he asked, his voice low and husky. But there was a note of warning there that could not be denied.

"I would endure it as I have before." At that, he scoffed.

"Of course you would," he muttered under his breath, an unmistakably demented edge to his tone. "A means to an end . . . and if there was another way to gain access to the information he holds?"

"I would gladly take it."

"Even if it involved fucking me?"

He ground his erection against my stomach.

"I recall trying that once before. You seemed disinclined to acquiesce then," I replied, mimicking his sultry but dangerous tone. "Had I known it may have benefited me greatly to do so, I would have been more diligent in getting what I had come to you for."

"Opportunities wasted," he tsked, pulling away from me only slightly. "Now you'll have to work even harder."

I leaned forward, closing the gap between our bodies again.

"I excel at hard work."

His eyes widened momentarily before resuming their maniacal glare.

"We shall see about that," he drawled, his voice tight.

Seeing that he was blinded by my sexual complicity, I endeavored to capitalize on the situation by asking an unexpected and untimely question.

"Tell me something, Oz, was my mother like this when she was Dark?"

"Ah, ah, ah," he chastised, wagging a finger in my face before capturing a stray wave of my hair. "No changing the subject." Those piercing eyes of his narrowed to a menacing glare while he tucked the dark strand behind my ear. "You have not yet paid the piper, Khara. Do not presume to dangle a carrot in front of me to get what you want—assuming I have it to give at all."

"You knew my mother, Oz," I countered while he placed his free hand against the wall by my head, caging me in. "You have something to give and yet will not. You are curiously evasive about her, which leaves me to question why."

"Maybe I just like toying with you." His response and its tone sounded far more normal.

"Maybe you have something to hide."

"We all have skeletons in our closet, new girl."

"I do not."

"Yes, well, you do seem to prove the exception in almost every way imaginable. I wouldn't expect anything less from you."

"And you continue to make yourself a hurdle I must overcome to get what I want."

"There is no overcoming me," he warned, still facing me. He pushed off the wall behind me with his hands, which had still been entrapping me, and walked away. "Your fate will not allow it."

"I will never be yours," I shouted after him, my well-practiced façade of control overrun by heated emotions. Conflicting emotions at that.

"That choice has already been made for you. Your insistence in denying that fact is both pointless and tiresome."

"Made for me by whom?" I pressed.

Before disappearing into the shadows of the tunnel leading away from the Acheron, he looked over his shoulder at me, a crazed look of self-satisfaction in his eyes. It served as his response. It was then that I realized that there may be no way to redeem Oz, even if Persephone did know of a way to try. He was not looking for redemption of any kind. He had finally found a form that allowed him what he desired most: complete control of his fate.

Apparently, he presumed that meant he had complete control of mine as well.

21

Though Deimos had informed me that Hades was not the one in charge of sending him after me in the world above, I still wished to confront my father about it. Deimos seemed to have his secrets. Perhaps my father did as well. With that in mind, I set off to find him. It seemed as though all I had done upon my return was storm through the maze of halls in the Underworld in search of others. Others with answers that I lacked. The monotony of it was beginning to gnaw at my resolve.

I was only yards away from Hades' office door when several of Father's warriors stepped out of the room, closed the door behind them, and headed in the opposite direction. The sight confirmed that my father was there.

I stepped up to the door and paused for a moment, not wanting to interrupt him if others were still present. Leaning my ear against the aged wood, I listened for voices. And voices I found.

"We need to proceed with caution," a male said, his words muffled by the thickness of the door. The shiver his altered voice sent down my spine told me who he was. "This matter should not be taken lightly, Hades."

"Do you think I am—that I have not been proceeding with caution this whole time?" my father countered, his volume rising with every syllable. "He cannot have her. That is final."

"Agreed."

"We need to be prepared for his arrival."

"The others have their orders. They are assembling now."

"He could ruin things for us. You realize that, don't you?"

"Of course," Deimos bit out. "But how do you intend to stop him?"

Even through the thickness of the door I could hear Hades exhale, frustration overtaking him. *Ruin things for us . . .* My mind turned the phrase over and over again until Hades' next question stopped my train of thought short.

"Can he be stopped? Truly stopped?"

"The Dark Ones can be put down, but it is no easy task."

I gasped. Never before in my life had the words of another shot through me to cause such a response. It was apparent that they were speaking of Oz. My father had already employed several tactics to attempt to dispatch him; all had proved unsuccessful. And now, just after Oz's most recent departure from the Underworld, it seemed as though they were conspiring to be rid of him. For good. The finality of that potential future had adrenaline coursing wildly throughout my body, and not in a pleasant way.

"But you can do it? You are certain?" my father asked, seeking confirmation from his second in command.

"He can be eradicated."

"That is all I need to know."

I felt panic rise within me when I heard Hades' unmistakable footfalls approach the door. Not knowing what else to do, I turned and fled with lightning speed, rounding a corner just in time to hear the echo of my father's door slamming behind him. Pressed flat against the wall behind me, I tried to control my racing breath. My control over my countenance was lost in that moment, but something else was gained in its stead: clarity. However much of a nuisance Oz may prove to be—however cryptic and brutal and smug—losing him was not an option. My body rejected that possibility, fighting it with every wild beat of my pounding heart. He would not fall because of me.

He already had once.

"Khara?" a high-pitched voice startled me when it called from beside me. I remembered that my outward demeanor needed to be reined in, and quickly.

"Aery. You surprised me."

"You are unwell," she said, her tone somewhere between a question and a statement.

"I was running. I am winded now." When I managed to compose myself enough to focus my gaze upon her, I found her to be as she had been when she came to me before. Agitated. Fidgety. Afraid. "What is it, Aery? Have you remembered something else?" She shook her head in negation. "Then what is it?"

She bit her lip between her teeth, tugging at it until it started to bleed.

"I just . . . I just felt like I needed to find you. Like I felt before."

"Are my brothers safe?" I asked, panic rising in me again.

"They're fine. The girls took them to get something to eat. They were in the Elysian Fields for a seeming eternity. They didn't want to leave, but Kierson's hunger eventually won out."

"It always does," I muttered to myself.

"They have asked about you. Several times. I cannot keep them away much longer," she admitted grimly.

"Perhaps you will not have to," I countered, thinking that her increasing unease with whatever evil was coming for me had nearly hit a fever pitch. I doubted I had much time left.

"Khara," she said beseechingly. "Can you go somewhere? Hide somewhere?"

"No."

"Then let me take you back to Detroit. I'll come back for the boys right after I drop you off there. I'll be as fast as can be. I promise."

"No. I will stay."

"Dammit, Khara—"

"Do as you promised, Aery. Keep Kierson and Casey far from whatever might hunt me." She stared at me while indignation marred her expression. "Besides this one request, I have never asked anything of you before. Will you do it or not?"

With lips pressed into a thin line, she nodded, though her frustration with my unwillingness to leave was plain.

"I'll go get them now."

"Excellent."

"And if they demand to see you? What then?"

I looked at her, quirking my brow mischievously.

"Do what it is you nymphs are notorious for. Twist the truth. Tell them I am to meet them wherever it is you take them. Tell them whatever they need to hear to concede. Surely you of all people can accomplish that."

Her anger gave way to an impish grin.

"Of course I can."

"Then do it now, while there is still time."

"Okay, but, Khara? Be careful. Please."

I returned her smile.

"Always."

Aery and I had not long parted when I heard chaos erupting from the Great Hall. The cries of those in it carried through the corridors toward me, bringing with them a sense of urgency that made my skin prickle and itch. Something was wrong—far more wrong than when I had arrived home. There was a sinister nature to the sounds that bombarded me while I stared down the hall. It reminded me of the attack on the Victorian.

Something had invaded the Underworld.

Though my mind wanted to discount that theory, my body did not give it the chance to. I charged down the hallway toward the ominous noises. Whatever the conversation I had overheard between Deimos and my father would lead to, it was no longer the most pressing crisis I faced.

When I neared the Great Hall, I was met with a wall of escapees crowding the narrow corridor. Whatever had come scared even those that dwelled amongst the damned. A foreboding sign indeed.

My body careened into the wave of bodies that were running for safety. I fought for every step, moving against the current of fear that hemmed me in. Once I was finally free, I sprinted the final yards toward the entranceway. The opening to havoc.

What I saw there was most unexpected.

From around the final corner, I peeked into the Great Hall to see a veritable army of Dark Ones, their black wings spanning the entire room. In all my time in the Underworld, I had never seen such a sight. In front of the mob stood two figures: my father and Deimos. Father's soldiers were nowhere to be seen.

Suddenly, the piercing cacophony that had erupted earlier stopped. A single dark angel stepped forward from his brethren, advancing slowly toward my father. And he was most familiar to me.

He was the one who had left me in Detroit to die.

"We are here for what is ours," he said, his voice a deep bass that nearly shook the rocky walls of the Great Hall. "We want the anomaly."

"Then you want a war," Hades replied, "for you cannot have her." It was then that Father's soldiers emerged from the various corridors that connected to the Great Hall, weapons drawn.

"You forget yourself, Soul Keeper," the Dark One sneered. "My asking is little more than a gesture of courtesy. We know what she can do and will take her by force if we must." His eyes then fell on Deimos, a curious look marring the familiar angel's expression. "And you and I are long overdue to have a chat."

Pressing as far forward against the wall as I dared, I strained to get closer to the entranceway—to get a clearer sense of what was happening. It was me they were discussing, of that I was certain. What I could not gather was why they had come for me at all.

"We have nothing to discuss, Kaine," Deimos replied, his tone a simple warning.

"So be it," the Dark One intoned, raising his arm as if to signal a charge.

And that was precisely what his signal triggered.

The wall of black wings advanced in an instant toward the various corridors with little to no regard for either Deimos or my father. They were merely obstacles in their way. One thing was plain: If caught, I would once again be abducted by the mysterious Dark One. It was a most displeasing fate.

Knowing they had not yet discovered me, I thought about running, but I steadied myself. They wanted me, nothing else. Surrendering myself would save my father from harm, if only temporarily. But no sooner than I had made that decision, a strong arm snaked around my waist from behind, pulling me away from the Great Hall. Oz dragged me down the tunnel toward my room.

"No fucking self-preservation whatsoever, new girl," Oz snarled while he ran, holding me captive in his grip as he stole me away from the approaching doom. "We don't have much time."

As we wound through the tunnels of the Underworld in an effort to evade the Dark Ones, I could hear the cries of my father. They sounded the same as the day I was ripped from his hold and taken to Detroit. I could also feel the terror inspired by Deimos' presence. He, too, was close behind me, though to protect me or help them, I did not know for sure.

"Hades cannot defeat them," I said as quietly as I could to still be heard by Oz while he ran with me, tucked under his arm. "We need to go back."

"They aren't going to go after him—not if he doesn't force them to."

"You cannot know that for sure."

"Yes," he bit out. "I can. They didn't come here to start a war."

"They came for me," I said plainly.

"Yes. But I have a plan."

Making a sharp right turn into an unfamiliar bedroom, he slammed the door, locking it behind him. He paused for a brief moment, raking his hand through his hair roughly before he lunged at me.

"Will you trust me?" he asked, holding my shoulder tightly in his hand. His fierce gaze zeroed in on me, demanding my attention.

"Tell me—"

"There's no time, Khara," he snapped, shaking me roughly. "Will you trust me?" he repeated. His eyes still bored through mine, as if to read my mind rather than await my response. I did not give him one. The dubious nature of my expression was answer enough. "Fine," he sighed with a shrug, drawing his arm back quickly. "The hard way it is."

I narrowly caught a glimpse of his fist as it sped toward me, cracking hard against my left temple.

Immediately, the world went blurry, then dark.

〰〰〰〰〰〰〰〰〰〰〰

I dreamt of the fall.

I felt my body plummeting toward the Earth as though I was reliving the night my wings emerged, not just remembering it. This time, however, it was in slow motion. I was keenly aware of everything happening around me. I was especially aware of Oz looking down at me as I fell to what could have so easily been my death. Surely he had known that I would survive the fall when he pushed me over.

My memory of that night, once replayed in my mind, afforded me access to all that I had not noticed when I was actually careening toward the ground. I clearly saw the faces of those that surrounded him while he gave them his back, ignoring them entirely. Watching what happened to me proved more important to him.

I could not help but wonder why.

Lines of distress etched into his brow, and his mouth moved when he called down to me. Just as I had that fateful night, I struggled to hear his words.

Lost in the place the mind wanders to when the subconscious reigns, I asked my questions over and over again, my fall seemingly infinite as I sought an answer.

"What are you saying?" I called up to him. "What are you trying to tell me?"

Just as my wings tore through my flesh, erupting in a downy-gray flash around me, everything stopped. The wind no longer rushed around me. The sounds of the world disappeared. I hung motionless in the air, suspended just above the ground, looking up at Oz. He was the only thing moving.

I watched while he leaned over the roof's edge; the shadowy stillness that surrounded him swallowed him whole. The scene foreshadowed much, to be sure.

In a moment of clarity, I strained to hear the words that had eluded me the night of the attack—the night that everything changed. "I'm sorry" carried down to me unobstructed, falling upon my ears like a whisper, though the phrase screamed through my mind.

It meant both everything and nothing.

Another mystery for me to solve.

I awoke on my back, shrouded in darkness and stifled by heat. It was not unpleasant, but it was disorienting. Once I could think past the ringing in my head, I remembered the scene I had escaped. The Dark Ones were coming for me.

Rolling onto my side, I attempted to free myself from the oppressive covering that weighed me down; a slight but growing sense of panic rose within me as I did. Black and soft and heavy, its silky texture glided through my hands temptingly as I slid them down to find the edge of the fabric. Eventually, I was able to burrow my way out from underneath it to find myself in a bedroom that was not my own; only a torch on the far wall lit the space.

When I moved to push the last of the unfamiliar bedding off me, I sliced the palm of my hand on something impossibly sharp. It passed through my skin so cleanly that I never felt any pain. Only when I saw the blood running down my arm did I know I was wounded. As soon as my eyes acclimated to the scant light of the room, I realized what had caused the gash.

I had not been covered in bedding at all.

Instead, a broad, obsidian wing had been draped across me, the owner of which still lay beside me silently looking on while I further inspected his ethereal appendage. Whereas the underside was the softest down one could ever have imagined possible—seamlessly silken in the most unexpected way—the top side proved even more surprising, comprised of layers of petal-like glass blades that only appeared to be feathers. They looked exactly like the soft plumage underneath, but were anything but. They were a cleverly designed weapon.

Not unlike their owner.

I ran my fingertip delicately along the edge of one; its shiny, oil-like reflectivity mesmerized me when I did. Just as I reached the tip of it, Oz stirred slightly, causing me to prick my finger. I watched the dark red liquid well up to the point of almost dripping. Before it could spill over, Oz took my finger in his mouth and sucked it away, his eyes penetrating mine as he did.

When he released my hand, he settled back into the bed, a look of satisfaction on his face.

"I think I might have hit you harder than necessary," he said with a smug smile. "I must have had some pent-up frustration to let out."

"Might you explain why you felt the need to punch me in the first place? If it was your attempt to get me to trust you in the future, your judgment may have been in error."

"Had you trusted me in the first place, we might not have had to travel down the path of most resistance, new girl. A fact that might serve you well to remember next time."

I eyed him tightly while a memory flashed through my mind: *I'm sorry,* he had shouted after me as I fell. I had trusted Oz then. Whether that had been to my betterment or detriment, I could not yet be sure. His apology only further confused the matter.

"I can assure you, there will not be a next time," I countered.

His smile widened.

"With you and me, there will always be a next time." Heat flared in my cheeks, reminding me of the pain that remained where Oz had hit me. Whether it was a flush of anger or something else, I could not be certain.

It was then that I became all too aware that I was naked. Oz, seeing me observe my state of undress, only smiled further.

"It was part of the plan, new girl," he explained, without a hint of contrition in his voice. "Like I said, you should have trusted me."

"Would you be so kind as to enlighten me about this plan you seem so utterly proud of?" I asked, gingerly sliding my legs out from under his razor-sharp wing. I saw no reason to hide my nudity from him, given that he had been the one to disrobe me in the first place. "I fail to see how striking me and stripping me naked spared me from abduction."

"Well, there was hardly time to explain, but I had a hunch," he said, sitting up to look at me more closely. I did not falter under his heavy gaze. "And since your father wasn't going to be able to stop them, I did what I had to do."

"Other than your own perverse obsession, why did you not want them to take me?"

"*Reasons.*"

"How did you know they were here?"

"I can sense my own kind. They are why I did not yet leave."

"Then I am not Dark, because I sensed nothing until the pandemonium in the Great Hall broke out."

He looked at me strangely.

"Was there ever any suspicion that you were?"

His question was confirmation enough.

"Are they gone?"

"For now."

"So, since I was inconveniently unconscious during the raid, would you care to tell me what happened, or shall I go and find my father? Perhaps ask him?"

"I would get dressed first if you're going to go looking for Hades. I don't think he would approve of your state of undress," he drawled, his eyes drifting lower and lower. "Especially not when he finds out that you were with me."

"He does not know I am safe?"

"You've only been out cold for about fifteen minutes, new girl. He's probably still searching the Underworld for you," he informed me, uncurling himself from the bed. The pants that he wore were unbuttoned and slung dangerously low on his hips. I could not help but notice when he walked past me and his leg brushed softly against mine along the way.

"Then I must go." I shot off the bed, hurrying toward what appeared to be a pile of my clothing in the far corner of the room.

"No!" he shouted, grabbing me by the arm and causing me to turn and face him. "No." His voice was softer that time, and he released his grasp. "Not yet."

"Where are we?" I asked, taking in the sparse room.

"The room I took over."

"And my father wouldn't think to come look for me here?"

"I'm sure he would if he thought that I was still in the Under-world. . . ."

"What do you mean?"

"I mean that he may have been led to believe that I left with the others. All part of my plan."

"Because you wish to appear aligned with them?" I asked. My eyes narrowed slightly, assessing his expression more closely. It gave little away.

"Because I did not want him to show up here," he replied, as though that fact were painfully obvious.

"How did you keep Kaine and the others from finding me?"

He laughed.

"I didn't. They were here not long ago."

"And they just left me with you."

"In a sense, yes."

"Care to expand on that?" I asked, knowing that he would not.

"All part of the plan, new girl."

"And this is why I should trust you?"

"Now you're getting it," he purred, a wicked smile darkening his expression.

"You still haven't explained the need to smash the side of my face in."

"No. I guess I haven't."

"All part of the plan?"

"Consider it an unfortunate Plan B," he explained most unapolo-getically. "You weren't ready to blindly trust me, and I didn't think that telling you to strip was going to inspire any more confidence in me, so I knocked you out so I could do what I needed to."

"Which was?"

He shrugged.

"Make it look like I was bringing you over to the favor of the Dark Ones." When I stared at him incredulously, he continued. "It was only a matter of time before they caught wind of your existence, Khara. You cannot still be so naïve that their desire to claim you comes as a surprise." In truth, it had. I had not had my wings long enough for me to contemplate all the potential ramifications of being whatever it was I had turned out to be. My expression betrayed me, and Oz laughed haughtily. "You need to learn who your enemies are, Khara, and you need to do it fast. The paranormal world does not accept anomalies well. They are either claimed as a prize or a weapon—or they are destroyed for fear that their powers will be used against the murderous party."

"And the Dark Ones wish to claim me for their side? Their use?" I asked for clarification.

He hesitated for a moment.

"They want you. For what, I cannot say."

"They trust you?" That question had been burning at the back of my mind since he had said that he had dismissed them from his chambers.

"They think I am loyal to my new family."

"But you are not?"

"I didn't say that."

Again, a serpent's smile spread wide across his face.

"Then you are?"

"I didn't say that either." He pulled my naked body tight to his, the pressure between us nearing an uncomfortable level. "I like to keep my options open."

"You plan to play both sides?" I said when the realization hit me. That hypocritical trait seemed to have weathered Oz's transition unscathed.

"I plan to win," he corrected, tilting his head so that his lips were at my ear. "You can thank me for that later." He released me abruptly, heading for the door. The flickering light in the room highlighted the muscles in his back favorably when he reached for the handle. Stopping just shy of it, he turned back to face me. "When you find Hades, and he sees the split above your eye and the growing bruise spanning the side of your face, you will tell him that Deimos hit you."

"Why would I do that? What do you hope that lie will accomplish, exactly?"

"I want to fuel Hades' distrust in him."

"Deimos is Hades' second in command. You will have to do more to create doubt than bruise my face."

"Hades knows something is amiss between you and Deimos."

"Perhaps, but Deimos has managed to minimize the extent of his curiosity."

He cocked his head at me strangely, like a raven locating its distant prey.

"Hades adores you. You are not ignorant of this fact. Do you think he would tolerate your face being used as a punching bag?"

"It has been used as one before. It did not result in the outcome you seek."

He growled, its echo tapering off slowly in the confines of the small room.

"It should have."

"Your plan will not work."

"Did Hades ever see evidence of the previous crimes against you?"

I thought long and hard, considering whether or not he had.

"I cannot be certain that he did."

"Then I will be certain on your behalf. I don't believe he would allow you to be abused under his care. I may not like your father or trust him as you do, but he has some degree of honor, especially where you are concerned."

"But how can you be so assured that he will react to the news in the manner you foresee?"

He moved toward me lithely, closing the distance in the blink of an eye.

"Because it would be my initial reaction to it."

"Hades is not you," I countered, standing stoically against his approaching form.

"No. He is not." He leaned forward, his lips at my ear. His voice was a breath against me. "For if he was, Deimos would be dead the moment Hades' realization of his treachery sunk in fully."

A sudden rush of wind blew my hair over my eyes. When I finally managed to remove the tangled mess from my face, I found myself alone in the room. Oz was gone, but his enigmatic words remained. He would have punished the one who had affronted me in the way he just had. It made no sense whatsoever.

But that was Oz—full of hypocrisy. There was little reason to be found in anything he did. And the reasons for that truth would forever remain a mystery to me.

⁓⁓⁓⁓⁓⁓⁓⁓⁓⁓⁓⁓⁓⁓

I stood outside my father's door, thinking about what Oz had said. He wanted to cast a shadow of doubt in Hades' mind. I just was not sure his plan would work. Casting doubt on Deimos was a dangerous plan, and I knew that Hades' power, weakening as it was, would not stand against an angry Deimos. Would I put my father in harm's way if I did as Oz had said to? Was that his plan? Did he wish to isolate me from those who cared for me, to meet some end I could not predict? When it came to fallen Oz, I had quickly learned his scruples were questionable at best. The Dark version of Oz, however, was an entirely different beast altogether.

When fallen, he had betrayed my brothers and inadvertently endangered me as well. He righted that wrong by birthing my wings and standing against those he had aided, but his initial actions still bred doubt in my brothers' appraisal of him. I had remained on the fence regarding the matter, but I was starting to lean toward their opinion.

Oz was not one to be trifled with nor underestimated.

I turned to leave, not wanting to approach Hades until I had spoken to Oz again and received the answers I desired, providing he was willing to share his plan with me in detail. To my dismay, the door opened before I was out of sight. A concerned-looking Hades stepped out, catching me as I walked away briskly.

"Khara! Where have you been? I have been beside myself with worry."

"I'm sorry, Father. I did not know."

"What happened? Did the Dark Ones not find you?" As I looked over my shoulder, my good eye facing him, the depths of the despair he had felt were still apparent in his eyes. In that moment, I made a decision which path I would go down. Which story I would tell.

"Oz found me."

I could not ignore the incredulity in his gaze.

"One and the same, Khara," he rumbled, stepping closer to me while I hovered outside the door to his office, shielding my battered face from him. "Khara. Come here, please." It was not a request, but an order. An order that had an unmistakable edge to the tone in which it was given. I hesitated for a moment before turning to face him. I had not personally confirmed the damage I had sustained from the blow I took, but given how my head was beginning to pound, I knew the evidence of it would prove easy for him to find.

The sucking sound he made through his teeth confirmed that.

"The Dark One did this," he seethed, lifting my chin toward the light to better assess my wound.

I hesitated again.

"No, Father. He did not."

"Who, then?" he asked, releasing my face from his grasp but not his gaze.

"I would rather not say," I said, hoping that I could afford myself the time I needed to speak to Oz.

"Tell me." Another order. Though I knew my father's powers were waning, I did not wish to treat him as such. I would answer him. But it would not be with the truth.

"Deimos," I sighed, fearing that I had unwillingly opened a Pandora's box. "But I do not wish for you to confront him, Father. I must learn better how to deal with him."

"Tell me what happened. Now."

Without hesitation, I pulled together the most believable lie I could.

"He came to steal me from Oz. He does not trust him. Perhaps he thought that Oz was working for those that had attacked. There was a struggle, and when I told him that I did not require his aid—"

"He did this intentionally?" he asked.

"It all happened very quickly, Father. I am sure that the circumstances surrounding the matter did not help. I cannot speak to whether or not he intended to harm me. This time . . ."

"Khara," Hades started, clearly reading meaning into my words. "Has this happened before?"

I did my very best to look sheepish and contrite.

"Yes, though I allowed it. I did not wish to trouble you with it at the time. But now I am stronger and have abilities. I will deal with him myself. Please," I asked softly. "Grant me that."

I could see the struggle in his eyes; his murderous intentions flashed through his otherwise impenetrable wall of pain. He viewed me as his princess, one that needed his protection. In fairness, I had always had it, in a fashion. But he, too, knew—now especially— what it meant to be challenged. He understood that if I did not stand and fight, rather than hiding under the security he provided, I would always be fodder. Even more than he wanted to protect me, he wanted to know that I could protect myself.

"I do not understand why he would do this," he said. The clarification he sought was not because he doubted me, but because he did not want to believe that Deimos, his most valued warrior, would have done such a thing to someone he cherished.

"Do what?" a voice called from down the hall. Right on cue, Oz strode toward us as though he had choreographed the scenario. Perhaps he had.

"You," Hades boomed. "This matter does not concern you. You are nothing but poison to her."

"This place is poison to her," Oz countered, coming to stand at my side. "And anything that happens here involving her involves me. So I will ask you again: Who did what?" He looked down at me, my bruised eye clearly displayed. He scowled as though he had not seen the marking before. An observer would not have had the slightest inkling that it had been he who had made it. "Ah, yes. This is what happens when you send your henchman to retrieve your daughter. Do you sanction this behavior? Is this how you take care of those in your charge, Soul Keeper?" he asked Hades while eyeing my face with great scrutiny.

"Deimos will be handled," Father snarled.

"He should not have to be, because it should not have happened."

"You forget yourself, Ozereus."

"No," Oz snapped, lunging closer to Hades. "You forget yourself. You are responsible for her. You chose to be her guardian. And you are losing control of those you employ. You would be wise to be more selective of those you keep in your closest confidence, Hades."

Without being dismissed, Oz took my arm and dragged me away from my father, leaving him alone in the hallway, surrounded by his guilt for endangering me and his anger at Oz's truth. His mission had been accomplished. Oz had most certainly fertilized whatever seed of doubt may have existed in Hades' mind regarding his second in command. The question remained as to what he could actually do to Deimos as a result of that revelation. As far as I had always known, Deimos was unstoppable. But perhaps he wasn't. Perhaps Oz knew something that I was not privy to. It would not have been the first time.

Once far away from Hades, Oz looked down at me, flashing me a proud grin.

"I'd say that worked brilliantly, wouldn't you?"

22

Before I could reply, the sounds of my approaching brothers caught my attention. They were shouting, presumably at Aery, who had done as she said she would and kept them away. But neither she nor they knew if I had survived the attack of the Dark Ones, and it was clear that if I had not, there would have been hell to pay.

"I am here," I yelled down the darkened hallway, hoping to assuage their fearful anger.

"Khara!" Kierson shouted, and within seconds he came into view. Casey was right on his heels. "You're okay! What the fuck happened?"

"I tried to keep them away," Aery called from behind them, apologizing.

"Yeah. We're going to have a little talk about that, too," Casey snarled, stopping in front of me while Kierson scooped me up in his arms and crushed me against him.

"The Dark Ones," I explained weakly; my breath was hindered by Kierson's overly tight embrace. "They attacked the Underworld."

"Holy shit!" Kierson blurted out, dropping me instantly.

"They came for you," Casey observed shrewdly.

"So it seems."

"It also seems that they were unsuccessful," he continued, reaching out to the bruise on my face. "Put up a good fight, did you?"

My eyes drifted to Oz. I was uncertain how much to entrust the boys with. As was usually the case, I did not understand Oz's plan, but when it came to the Dark Ones I had little choice but to defer to his judgment. I hoped that decision would not later prove unwise.

"She did," Oz affirmed, looking down at me with a hint of amusement. It was as if he enjoyed my deference.

"You were there?" Kierson asked, the guilt in his tone so thick that my chest tightened again.

Oz leaned forward.

"Why do you think I'm here, Kierson? The ambience? The five-star accommodations?"

"You knew they would come for her," Casey rumbled.

"No. But I wasn't willing to find out the hard way."

Silence fell over the group as the boys stared at Oz, disgust and appreciation warring in their expressions. They hated what he had become, but knew that I might not have evaded the Dark without him. And they were right. I would not have.

Kierson's features softened when he finally turned his attention back to me, gently taking my hand in his.

"Khara, I know you are hell-bent on finding answers here, but even you have to see that it's not safe. Your father couldn't keep you from the Dark Ones when they brought you to us, and he couldn't help you this time. He can't protect you. Here, you are essentially trapped with no means of escape that do not depend on the aid of others. That's a terrible defense strategy. Clearly you see this now."

"I know," I conceded, thinking that it was unlikely the Dark Ones would be deterred forever; regardless of whatever lie Oz had sold them, they would eventually see that he was unwilling or unable to deliver me to them. They would come back to collect what they saw as theirs and would undoubtedly instigate the war they threatened to bring about. I could not do that to Hades. Especially not with his powers failing.

Begrudgingly, I agreed.

"Good. Then let's get you out of here," Kierson said, pulling me behind him as he started off in the direction of the Great Hall.

"Wait!" I snapped, wriggling out of his grasp. "There is one final thing for me to do. Then we will leave. I promise."

His eyes narrowed at me, contemplating my demand.

"No."

"There is no option, Kierson. I must do this."

"Fine. Then we're all coming with you."

"No!" I cried. "You cannot."

"Bullshit," Casey spat, joining the argument.

"No bullshit," I countered. "Go to the banks of the Acheron. Wait for me there. I will not be long. I swear to you."

"Let us help you," Kierson implored, unable to keep the dejection from his countenance.

"If you could, I would. But you cannot."

"Can he?" Kierson's eyes snapped to Oz, who stood there looking amused.

"No. He cannot either."

Kierson seemed somewhat satisfied that Oz was denied as well. Oz, however, looked far less pleased.

"Do as she says," he growled. "Aery, you take them there and wait." He then turned his angry eyes to me. "I have something I need to do as well, new girl. Go do what you feel you need to. Say good-bye to Hades. Fuck Deimos. I don't care, but you'd better be standing by the Acheron waiting to leave when I get back."

"Where are you going?" Casey inquired.

"To see if my plan is working." Without any further preamble, he stormed past my brothers and me, Aery still hovering near the wall a fair distance away. Oz's speed increased with every step, urgency driving him onward. "See you soon," he called over his shoulder before disappearing entirely around a winding turn in the corridor.

I looked back up to Kierson, whose doubtful expression told me what I needed to know. He would do as I had asked, but the plan did not sit well with him.

"I will be fine, brother. Go and wait. I will not be long."

I forced a smile, then turned to Casey, who scowled at me in return.

"You're sure you'll be fine?" Aery asked. Her level of agitation was far lower than it had been earlier, but she was still unsure. She had every right to be. I was about to go find Persephone so that she, Hecate, and I could release the most venomous souls of the Underworld. If we were unsuccessful, I wanted my family where they could quickly and easily escape.

No more brothers would die if I failed.

23

The three of us stood at the veil that separated us from the most depraved beings that ever were, and, though I felt no fear, a sense of urgency fueled a measure of anxiety that I was not accustomed to. If we failed, Hades' demise seemed imminent, despite his unwillingness to acknowledge that truth. Persephone's brow creased with the weight of his fate. It marred her otherwise flawless face.

"We will have only one chance to succeed in this," she said, her voice low and serious. "Once the veil drops, I will not have the energy required to reinstate it, should we fail. Not even temporarily. Those that waste away in the Oudeis will be released." Her narrowed eyes fell heavily on me. "There is no room for error, Khara. I need you to understand the full weight of that."

"I do."

"Good," she replied, turning to Hecate, who stood at the gate, her shoulder nearly brushing the opalescent, swirling barrier. I wondered if she were to lean in just an inch closer if it would take her, sucking her into the vortex of nothingness that was the Oudeis. From what I knew, only Hades could both enter and exit that realm. All others would be lost to the endless emptiness. If Hecate's talents had not been needed for the task at hand, I would have been tempted to push her through. Her incarceration there would cause me no remorse, even if it was by my hand—not after her cruel dismissal of Casey.

Persephone's voice startled me from my dark ruminations when she spoke to her near-constant companion. "Are you sure you can reach them through the veil?"

"I can feel them," Hecate replied, her dull eyes focused through the opening to what lay beyond. Whatever it was that she could see, I could not see it. All I saw was an endless gray. "It is so thin." Her words were a mere whisper. "The order is collapsing . . ."

"Can you call to them?" Persephone pressed.

Hecate pressed her eyes shut.

"Yes."

"Can you control them once you do?"

Her eyes then shot open and a look of uncertainty fell upon her face.

"Of that, I cannot be certain," she admitted, turning her worried expression to Persephone. "Their combined power will be great. How great, I have no way of knowing. Once they amass at the veil, you must be ready. If I cannot compel them, I fear that their combined force may overtake the failing barrier regardless of your magic. We should proceed with that in mind."

"I am prepared either way," I told them. My confidence in the plan was of no consequence. We would succeed in this endeavor. There truly was no other option.

"So be it," Persephone said with a wave of her hand before she guided me several steps away from both Hecate and the waning veil that separated us from those we were about to release. "Do you remember how it felt when you absorbed the souls from the Stealer?"

I nodded.

"Good. Think of that. Let the feeling overtake your mind and body. You must be as devoid of emotion as ever, sister, for even the slightest hesitation on your part will be your undoing as well as your father's. Maybe all of ours."

With the heavy reality of the situation hanging over us, Hecate began to chant, her arms sweeping up wide above her. Her eyes rolled back in her head. She repeated a jumble of Greek over and over again until I felt the slightest shift in the air around us. My eyes shot to Persephone, and I found her looking back to me. She felt it, too. Our connection to the dead was awakened, however slightly.

As Hecate's voice rose, her words growing ever clearer, I looked to the veil, watching for those that she summoned. At first my stare was met with the same gray that had been there only minutes earlier. Then, subtly—slowly—an inky darkness wove through that gray, striping it hypnotically while it alone danced through the Oudeis, lulling me. Beckoning me.

I took a step forward, halted only by Persephone's arm across my chest.

"Hold steady," she warned while a shapeless, smoky soul intertwined with another, creating an entrancing pattern that I was unable to turn away from.

Straining against her hold, I looked on as the once-gray background turned to a mesmerizing black sea of the dead. They pressed against the pliable barrier, and it bulged against their desire to escape.

I could hear the strain in Hecate's voice while she chanted on. Forcing my gaze from the gate, I saw her, eyes still closed, rivulets of sweat streaming down her face. Her arms shook violently as though she was single-handedly holding back the forces the Oudeis contained. The forces I was about to take into me.

"I cannot hold them much longer," Hecate cried out, her voice straining.

Persephone turned her sharp and shrewd eyes to me.

"Do not disappoint me."

She then placed her hand on my forehead and mumbled incoherent words. Unlike Hecate's ramblings, which had aroused my connection to the dead, Persephone's words felt like they were tearing me in half, splitting me wide open.

"Now!" she screamed. The shrill cries of the damned disoriented me while they filled the space that surrounded us.

In the periphery of my vision, I saw Hecate drop her hands and collapse to the ground. Like a bubble bursting, the veil exploded; a rush of darkness swarmed my half-sister and me while we held steadfast against the surge. With Persephone's palm still pressed forcefully to my forehead, I looked over her shoulder while the wave of souls organized itself, swirling like a nearly opaque mass. As the black funnel cloud of death hovered above me, Persephone thrust my head back, forcing me to face what was about to inhabit me. The ever-concentrating mass of darkness stopped just short of me, pausing for a second. I could feel it—feel its pulsing evil. It was testing me. Taunting me.

It would see no fear in my eyes.

Then, suddenly, as though it was a single sentient being, the mass pulled back, tightening itself into a compact stream of midnight black before it screamed, shooting like a bolt of lightning at my face. I could not stop myself. I, too, screamed at its advance. That lightning struck down deep into my throat, gagging me while it burrowed deep into me. My back arched rigidly, my body pulled tight, my arms stretched outward painfully as though they would explode from my body under the immense pressure the evil caused as it overtook me.

I could not breathe.

I could not move.

My eyes bulged widely; my need to escape the sensations I felt consumed me. And then, finally, mercifully, it all stopped. The screams were silenced. The pressure abated. Dropping to my knees, I looked up at Persephone, who loomed over me with an assessing expression. Hecate, exhausted though she was, soon stood to join her. She cupped my chin in her hand, holding my face such that my eyes absorbed the scant light surrounding us.

"Gods be damned," she whispered, unable to suppress her incredulous tone.

"She has done it," Persephone continued. A mix of emotions swirled in her eyes, though I could not make them out; my mind and body were far too tired to focus with any measure of acuity. "Help me get her back to her room. We must return her there without being seen. Hades must not know of this." Her words carried a weight of warning in them. She knew he would not approve of what we had done. She did not know what the punishment for our actions would be if he were to learn of them. He may have loved her blindly, but, in his weakened state, I wondered if he would make an example of her, putting fear into those who served him. Mental instability in a leader was not a required trait, but it was effective when one wished to cow those beneath him.

"Will he not feel what we have done?" Hecate asked from beside me.

"No," Persephone replied tightly. "The souls are contained. The veil has returned. There is nothing to feel other than a momentary opening of the gate between the Oudeis and the greater Underworld. I possess the power to enter that realm, if I choose to. And that is exactly what I am going to tell him should he have suspicions. You, however, will remain mute on the subject." Her words were an order, laced with anger and authority. Persephone was protecting my father from Hecate's curiosity. She truly did love him. "Now help me with her!"

With great effort, they lifted my limp body, hooking my arms around their shoulders. I did my best to force my feet to move, but they were too leaden—dead weights attached to my uncoordinated legs.

"We will have to carry her," Persephone said, a strange urgency in her voice. My lids too heavy to open, I could not see what vexed her so.

"You will put her down," a male voice commanded, giving them pause.

I fought to see who approached, but my body failed me in every way imaginable. As they dropped me to the ground, my mind wandered away from the present, fogging with a haze of nothingness—remnants of the Oudeis. With its inhabitants trapped inside me, I could only wonder if my mind would somehow become a part of the isolation they'd been tortured by. Perhaps forever.

Magic always had ramifications.

And as my mind quieted—the dark imprisonment that beset it settling in—I wondered if the loss of my sanity would be one.

24

But imprisoned in my mind I was not.

When I awoke, I found myself in my room, lying on my bed while darkness surrounded me, comforting me as it always had. Pushing myself up slowly, I reached for my head, expecting a surge of pain and pressure that never came. I felt fine. Normal. That was most unexpected, given what we had just done. What I had just consumed.

"You are a fool," a voice called out from the far corner of my room, its owner lurking in the shadows just as he had when I first met him. "And you are playing with fire. You're lucky you survived that idiotic stunt."

"Yet I did, so there is little need to scold me," I countered, throwing my legs over the side of the bed to stand and face the disembodied voice.

"For now you have," he argued, slowly emerging from the blackness he shrouded himself in, wings hidden away. He looked human but not. No human could ever look like Oz. "Is that the pressing matter that you had to attend to before leaving the Underworld?"

"It is."

His expression darkened.

"I suppose absorbing the inhabitants of the most evil realm is still preferable to you fucking Deimos for answers."

"Why are you here?" I asked in my most put-upon tone.

"I brought you back here when the others could not," he replied, as though that fact was obvious. I remembered how incapacitated I had been immediately after absorbing the souls of the Oudeis into me. I was dead weight that both Persephone and Hecate could barely manage. I had no doubt that Oz did not struggle at all to return me here.

"How did you find us?"

Coming to stand right before me, he smiled wickedly, an all-knowing expression that said both everything and nothing. His hubris told me that he would not answer my question. I was not surprised.

"Tell me something, new girl; was it your idea to drop the veil between the greater Underworld and the Oudeis?"

"It was not."

"Ahhh," he drawled, arching his brow for effect. "How very interesting. I cannot imagine what would possess you to go along with such a self-destructive plan, then, especially if it was not one of your making."

"I did what needed to be done," I said curtly, turning away from his piercing stare. "My reasons are my own, not something for you to judge or make a mockery of."

"*Hades*," he said with distaste.

"You will say nothing of this to him," I spat, whirling back around to point a finger in his face. "You will not interfere, do you understand me, Dark One? This does not concern you."

His initial amusement with my challenge faded into an intimidating glare, and his eyes seemed to glow from within, casting harsh, angular shadows across the planes of his face. The effect was both menacing and mesmerizing.

"Once again, new girl, you fail to see things as they are," he whispered harshly. He moved closer to me, then continued. "All things concern me where you are involved, a fact that you should be thankful for, not spiteful of." When his face was only inches from mine, he snatched my chin in his hand, forcing my gaze to lock with his. The silence in that moment stretched on for an eternity. "I told you once that I would keep you around until it no longer amused me to do so. Do you remember this?"

I said nothing in response. He cocked his head at my insubordination.

"So defiant," he tsked. "What you fail to see is that your defiance does not constitute control, Khara. You have surrendered to the illusion that your wings' emergence has awakened a power within you—a strength you had not earlier possessed. This illusion will be the end of you if you allow yourself to be manipulated because of it. You are strong, but, as you know, you are not invincible. Strength without wisdom means nothing. It makes you a liability, something you will undoubtedly become in the wrong hands. Then you will be used and discarded, left to perish just as I threatened to do when we first met in Detroit. Do not believe yourself to be above this fate. Even the mighty fall, Khara. They fall fast and hard."

"You mistake my compliance for weakness—ignorance—but what you fail to see, Oz, is that I do not allow myself to be manipulated, because that requires emotional ties that can be exploited. Though something in me has awakened that allows me to feel, it does not rule me, nor does it blind me to reality, which would allow for such a lapse in judgment that can be preyed upon," I argued haughtily. "I assess the information presented to me and either accept or reject it based on merit. If you mean to imply that Persephone has somehow set a plan in motion that uses me as her so-called pawn, then you are overlooking one simple fact."

"Which is?"

"That, regardless of Persephone's motives, Hades is losing control of his kingdom, a fact which you have undoubtedly pieced together, knowing your penchant for skulking around and overhearing things that you should not." His unfaltering gaze gave him away, though it did not need to. I knew I was right. "The veils are thinning, Oz.

Persephone was right to fear what would happen if they could no longer retain those they were meant to. Whatever fields the souls would escape from, there would be anarchy, even by Underworld standards, and I chose not to stand idly by and watch my father's kingdom fall. My home overrun by those it was designed to contain. For now, I have taken in the souls of the Oudeis, but I will take in all that I can—souls from every field—if need be."

He shook his head, his signature sneer marring his face.

"How can a creature so steeped in darkness be so unaware when it courts her?"

"I am very aware of you," I replied, my voice sounding a touch too breathy even to my own ears. It undermined the sentiment I wished to convey.

"Because I am transparent in my actions," he countered, his eyes betraying him when they fell upon my lips for the slightest of moments.

"Hardly," I scoffed, though the word lacked my intended intensity. "You are transparent in your darkness, that much is true, but that is all. Everything else about you—your sullen, disgruntled nature, for instance—is secretive. Were you to give me five minutes and truthfully answer questions about you and your past—my mother—it would surely show just how opaque you have been with me since the moment we met."

"What I have and haven't told you has been in your best interest, new girl. I, unlike your precious father, have not failed you. Never forget that."

"I do not wish to be protected or coddled."

"Some things are best left alone."

"Because I cannot handle them?"

"Because they can be used against you and those you have come to care for," he explained, pulling away from me only slightly. "Just as I know your love of your father is being used against you now. You are simply unwilling to see it."

"So leave me to my fate, if you feel I am too stupid to be anything but a pawn in another's game. What you fail to see is that I am far more aware of what I am doing than you would believe. I am not fodder to someone else's agenda. I have my own, and I will utilize my skills as I see fit to fulfill it. If it proves my undoing, then so be it. Let me plummet, Oz. I neither asked for nor need your continued assistance," I countered, the heat in my words marred slightly by the slur with which I delivered them, my jaw still captured in his grip.

"No."

It was his only reply.

"No?" I repeated, wrenching my face out of his hand painfully.

"No."

I watched while his jaw flexed wildly, fighting to hold back an explanation that threatened to escape his mouth.

"Then you and I are at an impasse."

"Wrong again, new girl. Impasse implies that your will has anything to do with our interactions. That you have a say in the matter. What *you* continually fail to realize is that my presence in your existence is a constant—not something you can bypass because you see fit to. Like it or not, I am here. I will remain here. For now, you can consider me your safety net, though you may be loath to admit you need one."

"To what benefit of your own is your eternal presence?" I pressed, knowing that Oz had proven to be a self-serving individual in virtually every circumstance. Even when it appeared he was helping either me or my brothers, there was something in it for him. Always. I did not assume that his becoming Dark would offer any exceptions to this inevitability. If anything, it would likely only have made it worse.

My observation garnered his anger; his nostrils flared, and his wild eyes still glowed.

"I have my reasons."

With that, he quickly turned and stormed out of the room, slamming the massive wooden door behind him to punctuate his exit. Without the light of his dimly glowing eyes, I found myself alone in the darkness. I doubted that Oz would go far, not in light of his recent admission and his anger at my perceived stupidity. Most likely he would hover nearby, skulking in the shadows, waiting for danger to strike or for me to fall victim to my own error in judgment.

What he did leave in his wake was doubt, something I was terribly unfamiliar with. I did not want to give credence to his accusations, but I could not shake the feeling that perhaps he was not entirely wrong. That my previous ability to think rationally was being eclipsed by my rising emotions and that I was blind to it. If that was indeed the case, maybe having someone as cold, callous, and calculating as Oz watching out for me was not the worst fate imaginable.

Failing those who needed me, however, would have been.

25

"I would like to say good-bye to my—"

"You had your chance to do that, but instead, you vacuumed up an entire swarm of dead into your body," he snarled, walking a pace or two ahead of me toward the Great Hall and presumably the Acheron. "You squandered your opportunity, so don't whine to me that you didn't get to say good-bye to Daddy."

"I do not whine," I argued, spitting the words out with great disdain.

"Good. Don't start."

The halls were virtually empty as we made our way to the cliffs that the Acheron cut its way through. There was no Deimos. No Hades. No Persephone. Perhaps my taking in the Oudeis had created a peace of sorts in the Underworld already—at least for now. Persephone had said that she would find a way to restore my father's powers. I hoped she would do so in my absence. Perhaps if all was well soon, I could return to see her and collect on her end of our bargain.

Knowing that I was one step closer to getting my brother back and the answers I sought, if only somewhat so, quickened my pace. Even with the looming dangers that could be awaiting our arrival above, I still felt a small sense of joy deep in my heart. It made me certain that I did in fact hold my brother's soul within me. And soon I would get to see that joy in his expression once again.

It was not long before I could see our destination, the boys and Aery standing where they had been instructed to, waiting for our arrival. The Acheron was the final hurdle to be crossed before reaching the gate that divided the dead from the living—that which could not be crossed without one of the few who could freely traverse it. And with every step I took toward it, an odd pressure grew within me.

Unease.

Unrest.

Upheaval.

I flexed and stretched my fingers repeatedly, trying to distract my body from the dissonance that coursed throughout it. My efforts were in vain. Nothing could drown out the discord vibrating in every cell in my body.

Oz, eyeing my antics through his peripheral vision, stopped, turning his full attention to me. As the others continued on, he stared at me, assessing my actions with his piercing gaze.

"Something is wrong," he said, not asking but telling me so.

"I think I am anxious, perhaps. The feeling is strange, but I imagine this is what it would feel like."

"How exactly do you feel?"

"Fidgety. A growing pressure in my chest."

"Do you fear what is to come when you return to the world above?" he asked, still staring right through me.

"No. I do not think so."

"Of course you don't," he muttered. "You fear nothing—feel nothing."

"I feel," I refuted. "You acknowledged that yourself. I feel far more than you could fathom. Far more than you do, of that I am certain."

He thrust his shadowy features in my face, clenching his teeth so tightly that I could hear them grinding under the pressure.

"Then you know nothing," he growled, pulling away just as quickly as he had advanced. "Your nerves are getting to you, though I cannot imagine why. Perhaps you are uneasy about leaving Hades alone. That worry would not be misplaced. He is vulnerable here, as you said. Your harebrained idea of clearing the Oudeis may not have been so ill conceived after all. Not if you wish to see Hades alive again."

"Then we must not delay. The sooner we are out of this place, the safer he shall be."

His eyes narrowed.

"As you wish, *princess*," he mocked, sweeping his arm in a grand gesture while he took a reverent bow. His distaste for the name my father called me by was plain. Something else tainted his tone when he said that word. There was bite to it. I could not ascertain why.

I walked around him, giving him a wide berth. The others were off in the distance, already standing on the bank of the Acheron. They looked back at us expectantly, undoubtedly knowing that whatever discussion Oz and I were having was not a pleasant one.

"Problem?" Kierson called, starting to head back toward me as I approached him. His concern was plain, though it could not conceal the wariness that lingered behind it when his eyes fell upon Oz. Distrust of him was pervasive. Even Aery, infatuated though she was, seemed to navigate away from him whenever possible. Oz exuded a silent warning with his mere presence.

"No," I replied calmly, scratching my arm as I neared him. The nerves along my skin fired relentlessly, the sensation nearly maddening.

"You sure?" he asked, curiously watching me as I nearly tore my skin off, raking my fingernails viciously across my forearm.

"I seem a bit agitated. Nervous. I am sure it will pass once we are back in Detroit."

"Well, here goes nothing," Aery called, scooping Casey up and leaping over the raging river in one graceful movement. She returned immediately for Kierson, whose smile turned as mischievous as Aery's when she went to take his arm.

"I like this one," he whispered to me with a wink.

"I am not at all surprised," I replied, feeling Oz's dark form step closely behind me. Too closely. While I watched Aery guide Kierson safely across the perilous river, Oz dropped his mouth to my ear, whispering to me softly. His voice was seductive and terrifying.

"They are perfect for each other, are they not?" he asked, his breath hot on my ear. I nodded once as his arm snaked around my waist, pulling me uncomfortably tight against him. "Some beings are so suited for one another that their call will be answered, no matter what divides them—what stands in their way. It defies all rules. All natural law."

"All sanity," I whispered, not realizing the words were even a thought in my mind until they escaped my mouth.

"Sanity is overrated," he purred, squeezing me so tightly that I could barely breathe. "Time to go, new girl."

With that, he took to the air, swooping over the Acheron in seconds with the intent to place me down gently on the opposing bank. But as we reached the shore, something went wrong—terribly, inexplicably wrong.

And we were all about to pay for it.

26

I collapsed to the ground, my body limp and lifeless—paralyzed.

Kierson was at my side in a second, scooping me up in his arms while Oz hovered over us both ominously, dark wings still spread wide, sheltering me from an unseen danger. But there would be no protecting me from the danger that threatened. It was not possible. How could one protect me from an evil trapped within myself?

That question proved irrelevant far too quickly, for what I carried inside me soon escaped.

"What's wrong with her?" Kierson shouted, trying to hold me still while my body convulsed.

"Step away," Oz said, snapping his wings to their farthest reaches, punctuating his command. The shadow they cast blocked out what little light had been present. I could feel Kierson's hesitation.

Unlike when my gentle kiss sealed Oz's fate, passing a darkness into him that his soul could not withstand, the ghostly dead erupted from me as I lay on the ground, clutched in Kierson's arms, retching violently. I could not breathe while they purged themselves from deep within me, though I fought to do so with great effort. An unholy sound accompanied their liberation, announcing the event for all to hear—the jubilation of foulness trampled through my throat on its path to freedom.

"Get back!" Oz yelled over the commotion. This time, Kierson obeyed him.

Alone on the stony shore of the Acheron, I clawed at my throat ferociously, trying to abate the choking sensation I felt. My eyes bulged wildly. The veins in my face throbbed. I needed air if I desired to live long enough to undo the wrong I was in the process of doing.

When my torment subsided, I collapsed to the ground, greedy for air. My face down and sheltered with my arms, I could not see the magnitude of what I had unleashed. But once my lungs were filled enough for me to move, I pressed myself up and took stock of my surroundings.

Chaos did not begin to describe the scene.

Ghostly, transparent forms crashed upon our tiny group like a tsunami on a shore. The wave of attack was loud and immediate and punishing, scattering us in its wake. Disoriented, I searched the haze for the others. Casey roared his battle cry, and my eyes fell on him immediately, his form standing stoically yards away from me. Then, suddenly, he was silenced. A cloud of the dead engulfed him, cutting off his call to arms. I could see his mouth opened wide, suspended while the sound escaped him, but it was drowned out by the terrible screeching of those that had escaped. Those that I had released.

They moved with dizzying speed; their combined form was a foggy blur as they rushed around us. Most were headed for the gate. Others continued to encircle us individually, unable to resist the temptation we provided. Whatever traits they had possessed in life remained present in death. The most depraved of all wanted revenge and cared not who they rained it down upon.

"Pull together!" Kierson screamed. I frantically looked for him, finally catching a glimpse of him as he backed toward Casey, sword drawn. The fiery light that had been muted by the souls' presence flickered occasionally off the long blade—a beacon calling to the rest of our party. Trying to make my way to them, I watched as he and Casey came together, the two moving as though they were one. It was how they fought when together, how they had done so for centuries. But, unlike their past opponents, this time they fought the dead. They soon found that their efforts were futile. Every strike, every blow, was wasted, cutting through a misty nothingness. The souls could not be slain.

Looking on helplessly, I soon found myself adrift in that evil fog, wandering toward my brothers, though I seemingly gained no ground. Instead, I felt herded by the dead, led into isolation as though they were working as one, setting a plan in motion. My ability to see my brothers decreased as the distance between us grew. Aery was nowhere to be found. As for Oz, I wondered if he had left us to our fate when the maelstrom erupted. It was not as if he was above desertion. He had betrayed my brothers before, though never me. The fact that he might be willing to do just that in the face of the havoc I had unleashed was a harsh reality to swallow indeed. Despite my general cynicism where Oz was concerned, I could not deny that even I would not have thought him capable of abandoning me to that fate.

Perhaps it was a long overdue wake-up call.

When the souls had me completely secluded, no longer able to see those accompanying me back to Earth's surface, the swarm of dead surrounding me became all-consuming, their voices increasingly clear. Their message, however, proved disjointed and enigmatic. The sentiments they wished to convey came across in disconnected fragments, nonsensical in and of themselves. Though when my mind began to filter through the gibberish and piece it together slowly, one sentence echoed through my consciousness.

See his kingdom fall.

They were the army of darkness.

Once I had deciphered the phrase, it was all I heard around me, my ears ringing with its warning. I was entranced by the taunts of the damned, paralyzed by the implications if they proved true. In my stupor, I had not realized that their torture of me extended beyond the psychological until a repetitive, sharp pain nipped at my skin, slicing my clothes and body with razorlike teeth. Caught within the swirl of the damned that enveloped me, I could not ascertain how it was happening. The dead had no solid form. No vehicle through which to impart that kind of torment.

Searching the cloud around me for answers, I saw something—an inky-black blur slicing through the fog. With every pass of what appeared to be a ghostly blade, the terrorizing mist thinned. The souls were disappearing.

I squinted in an effort to see what was happening—who wielded this weapon of death—but I still could not discern who fought the mass of dead so fiercely.

Until he spoke my name.

"Khara!" Oz shouted, clearing my head. "For fuck's sake, collect your brothers and take them back to your father. Now!" I stood unmoving, still searching for his form amid the clearing haze. Suddenly, a blinding light cut through it, becoming ever brighter as he stormed toward me. I lifted my arm to shield my gaze from his blazing white orbs as they approached. "Get Kierson and Casey across the Acheron or your brothers will perish," he boomed. "You have already lost Drew. Would you risk the others? Would you risk yourself?" His voice was not his own. It was cruel and dark and motivating. And it snapped my attention back to those the dead had alienated me from.

"I cannot cross it," I shouted, my eyes closed and averted from the piercing light radiating from his own.

"Aery is waiting on the shore," he growled. "Go. Now. I will not suffer your insubordination."

With the turn of his head, my eyes gained reprieve from the punishing brightness and slowly opened. Once they adapted to their surroundings, I could see Oz, slicing through the terrible evil engulfing us with his broad wings. With every pass, he cleared a path through the dead, their transparent forms disappearing into the ether. He brought true death with his darkness. A death that did not end with a place in the Underworld. It was then that I truly understood why the Dark Ones were so feared.

Not even my father could eliminate a soul completely.

Wishing to avoid Oz's wrath, I did as he bade me and set off toward my brothers, or at least in the direction I thought them to be. There were still myriad souls circling me, though they were dropping quickly. Some seemed to be attempting to escape, hurrying toward the gate, while others remained undaunted in their attack. It appeared that I could not be harmed by them, which made me question their motivation. But when I was able to locate my brothers at last, I better understood the damned's reasons for staying.

Casey and Kierson were not faring well at all under the siege of the dead.

Instinctively, I ran toward them, screaming their names. When I could see them more clearly, I knew that something had gone terribly wrong. Casey's ears were bleeding; a thick reddish-black substance ran down his neck. He was barely able to stand. Kierson had his arm wrapped under our failing brother's shoulder, though he, too, was succumbing to the torment of the damned. Blood hemorrhaged from his nose at an alarming rate, and his gait faltered with every pass of the swirling haze. I heard him scream against it, which seemed to deter the assaults on the duo, if only for a moment. If Oz could not get to them quickly enough to slay the souls, or I could not help them get to Aery and across the Acheron, I feared that they would go mad or be lost. I deemed neither outcome acceptable.

Amid the chaos, I tried to focus, thinking of how I had cowed the souls that ran amok when Oz and I arrived in the Underworld. Whatever power I had exerted over them should have, in theory, extended to the souls now attacking us as well. I tapped into my frustration, my fear, my doubt. I brought myself to the mental place I occupied when I could not find my father. When I feared he was dead.

And then I screamed. The shrill cry of despair muted the souls that surrounded us. Just as it had before, it paralyzed the dead. I slowly turned, taking in their ghostly, slack expressions before I ran to my brothers, hooking Casey's other arm up over my shoulder to aid him. He was barely ambulatory.

"What . . . was that?" Kierson wheezed, staggering forward as he tried to carry the rest of Casey's weight.

"Something I have done before," I said simply, guiding us toward the shore, which I could now clearly see. As we neared it, I hazarded a glance over my shoulder to find Oz easily picking off the dead one by one. He was taking his time now, taunting them as they had my brothers and me. The sheer rapture he found in the elimination of the enemy was awe-inspiring. His eyes glowed with delight.

Returning my focus to the task at hand, I led us the rest of the way to Aery, who stood at the water's edge, awaiting our arrival. She looked rattled by what had just broken out around her.

"I will take him first," she called out, reaching for Casey. With a delicate, graceful leap, she bounded over the vast river, gently placing Casey's tortured body down on the opposite bank. She returned in the same manner to collect Kierson, then delivered him to the other side. When it came time to get me, she looked across the Acheron, a nervous smile overtaking her countenance. "I think you have your own ride," she called across the river.

I turned to find Oz running across the barren ground toward me, wings spread fearsomely around him. There was not a stray soul to be seen in his wake.

"That seems a rather handy trick, new girl," he said with a smirk. "Not that I required your help."

"I did not do it for you," I informed him, bringing my attention back to the wounded warriors across the river. "I did it for them. This was an evil they could not fight. Could not slay. They were not meant to fight that which populates the Underworld. Not even Casey, who was born of it."

"Surprising, isn't it? To see the weakness in those you deem so capable."

"I want them home. Now. They were not meant for this place. They are not like you and me in that regard." My voice was neutral and controlled, but I felt anything but. It was unnerving to see my brothers rendered so helpless by those my father had contained and ruled. In my mind, I had built them up, just as Oz had implied. I thought them invincible, even if I knew that to be false, excepting Sean. It made me wonder how he would have fared under the same assault. Would he have faltered or remained undaunted?

"And I will return them. But first, we must find Hades. The Fields of Oudeis have fallen. I dispatched the souls that were unable to avoid the temptation you and the boys presented, but countless others escaped."

"What will become of them once they set foot above?" I asked, knowing that his response would not be good news.

"I do not know. This mass exodus is unprecedented. Only Hades may know what the ramifications of his failure could be."

"I am the failure," I countered, watching Aery head off toward the Great Hall with Casey in tow, leaving Kierson lying on the opposite riverbank. "This was my doing. I let them out."

"Was that your intention? To release them once we crossed the Acheron?"

"No."

"Then it is not your fault. Something about this does not sit well," he rumbled. "We will soon find out what."

"Wait!" I shouted at Oz, catching his forearm in my hand. I swallowed hard against the words I did not wish to utter. "Drew . . . did you see him? Could you make him out amongst the others?"

Oz frowned.

"No."

"Is he—"

211

"I don't know, but I can't imagine that he would have stayed behind to be slaughtered."

"Drew would have seen our brothers and me and come to our aid."

"Possibly. But Drew also wanted a way out of the Underworld at any cost—badly enough to risk his soul to the Oudeis in the first place," he rebutted, though his argument lacked the conviction I was hoping to hear. "Regardless of what may or may not have happened to him, we can't sit here and speculate about it. We need to go to your father. Now." There was a harshness to both the set of his eyes and his tone that snapped me back to our reality.

With that, he snatched me up in his arms and flew us quickly over to Kierson before releasing me in order to grab my brother roughly off the ground. I then let my wings erupt from my back and took flight next to Oz and Kierson. While we continued our flight back to the Great Hall, Oz said nothing more. He often had proved dangerous when silent; undoubtedly, he was mulling over the multitude of errors that had occurred leading up to this inconceivable breach. I used the quiet to contemplate just how I could tell my father that my doubt in him had led to the pandemonium I created. The mess he would have to clean up.

There was no other option in the matter. Hades would have to return to Earth with us, a journey he had made only a handful of times in his existence. But I saw no way around it. He needed to corral those he commanded and return them to the Underworld—providing he could.

The King of the Dead was losing control of the Underworld, just as Persephone had warned. Could his crumbling throne be salvaged, or was this truly the end of an era? The end of his reign?

Would I see his kingdom fall?

27

The air in the Great Hall had shifted. The change was barely perceptible; the others did not seem to notice. But to me it was unmistakable. I feared I had set something in motion, though I was loath to admit it. And that was precisely what I had to do: tell Hades that the most terrible of his charges had been let loose upon the world. Again.

I did my best to maintain a modicum of calm while I quickly made my way on foot through the labyrinth of corridors in the Underworld. I needed to locate Hades; a plan had to be made as quickly as possible and enacted without hesitation. The longer the evil I had released lingered in the world above, the more havoc it would create. I did not envy my PC brothers there, neither the ones I knew nor those that remained unknown to me. The task of maintaining the balance between the human world and ours had just been made astronomically more challenging. My ineptitude had failed both them and my father.

When I finally saw Hades emerging from one of his many private rooms, I lowered myself to the ground and ran toward him. Oz and the others were not far behind.

"Father!" I called, an uncharacteristic unease tainting my tone.

"Khara. What's wrong? You look unwell," he replied, his eyes filled with concern. His expression was wildly appropriate, though for reasons he did not yet know.

"I have done something. Something unthinkable . . ."

"Tell me, my princess. What could you have possibly done to warrant such distress? I have never seen you like this."

"The Fields of Oudeis," I started, watching his concern bleed to horror before I could relay my misguided actions to him. "They are empty."

"Empty?" he echoed, his voice a whisper while he looked past me in the direction of the realm I had unleashed on the world.

"Yes. I released those that reside there."

"What?" he choked out, disbelief contorting his features. *"Why? How?"*

Oz stepped closer to me, flanking me on my right side. Tension rolled off him, his obsidian wings fluttering minutely while he wrapped them around behind me.

"Your power . . . I knew it was failing you," I said plainly, hiding the surge of guilt that tried to claw its way onto my countenance. "I thought that, if I could contain those that would threaten you most, it would buy you the time to regain all that you have lost."

His eyebrows rose high, creating creases in his forehead before they slammed down, furrowing as he glared at me. There was hate in his stare. A murderous look I had seen him turn on many over my time with him.

But never on me.

"Khara!" he roared, forcing me back a step into the black down of one of Oz's wings. It held me steadfast when I wanted to escape. Never in all my life had I wanted to flee anything—a situation, a battle—but especially not my father. Standing before him, facing the brunt of his rage, I wanted to be anywhere but here.

"I feared what would happen—"

"You have undermined both me and my authority!" he screamed, pressing toward me.

"Your authority is failing. You know this. I know you do," I argued, my voice faltering minutely. Perhaps it was only noticeable to me.

"Silence!" I flinched at his order. Emotions rattled through me, their disharmony making it hard to focus—to think. "I will not suffer your excuses. You betrayed me. You . . . my princess. My beloved one."

I swallowed hard against the sadness that threatened to escape me at his accusation.

"Father—"

"*No!*" He lunged at me, pointing a finger heatedly in my face. "I am *not* your father. That is abundantly clear. No child of mine would ever presume to conspire against me as you and your pet have," he snarled, turning his hateful gaze to Oz, who remained still at my side. But his stillness was a ruse. I could feel his body coiling, preparing to attack Hades at any moment. Having seen the death he brought to the souls that had attacked us only moments earlier, I did not wish for his retribution to befall my father—even if Hades claimed he was my father no longer. His words were spoken out of anger. He had not meant them.

That is what I continued to tell myself.

"He has tainted you. Poisoned you, just as I warned he would." I looked on helplessly as the man I had been closer to than any other being turned on me in an instant. "Get out," he growled. "Take your brothers and this thing with you, and get out."

"No," I rebutted weakly. "You need me. We will fix this."

"I need no one."

"Watch yourself," Oz warned, still motionless behind me. "Continue on like this and you will have no one. And where will that leave you, I wonder? Perhaps I'll do as you ordered and take Khara and the others out of here, leaving you to your fate." I turned awkwardly to look up at Oz's face, as his jaw tensed fiercely. "You seem terribly keen on the idea, Soul Keeper. I wonder, will you keep Persephone at your side as everything you know—everything you've ever loved—comes crashing down around you? Upon you?" Hades' chest pumped wildly, his temper rising dangerously high at Oz's words. "Well, I guess not everything you ever loved," Oz continued, taking one purposeful step forward toward the one I had always called Father. "Because I'm getting her the fuck out of here."

Before Hades could rebut, Oz turned on his heel and stormed out, whisking me up in his enormous wings as he did. They sheltered me and prevented me from looking back at Hades. I do not know what I would have expected to find in his expression other than anger and resentment, and I was better off not having that memory etched into the back of my mind.

No apology I could offer would have erased his loathing, that much I knew. Treachery was the highest offense in his eyes. And in his eyes, that was precisely what I had just committed.

Kierson and Casey fell in silently behind us and followed Oz as he stormed away from Hades, ushering me back out the way we had come. It was unlike them both to be so quiet, but, after Oz's parting words to Hades, what was left to say? They were still getting what they had ultimately wanted the whole time—my departure from the Underworld. But even they had not wanted it to come at such a heavy price.

When we passed Aery, who had apparently been waiting for us down the corridor, she looked torn. Hades had always been good to her. She was one of his favorites. Since she was not directly involved in the events preceding the escape of the Oudeis' souls, I could see the debate that waged in her mind as it played out in her features. If she aided us in our return, would she then be a party to our crimes? Would Hades ever allow her to come back home?

The irony was that if things continued to collapse, there would not be an Underworld to come back to at all.

Regardless of the risk to her future, she accompanied us, and when we reached the bank of the Acheron, she looked over to me and gave a wan smile. The heaviness in her gaze was impossible to ignore.

"Are we doing the right thing?" she asked quietly.

"We were given no choice," I replied simply. Hades had made his desires abundantly clear. We were not welcome there any longer. "You, however, still have time to make yours."

With lips pressed tightly together, she nodded in resignation.

"I will go with you, but I cannot carry them both at once," she said, her eyes darting back and forth between Kierson and Casey. Kierson looked much more himself than he had earlier, but Casey was still struggling to recover. I was concerned about him. By then, he should have been doing better than he was. The wary look in Kierson's eyes told me he thought the same.

"I will take them," Oz declared, making his way from my side to that of my brothers. Kierson tensed slightly. Casey growled. I think it took what small reserve of energy he had to do so, but that was my dark-hearted brother. He would fight until he could fight no longer. A true warrior, though misguided on this occasion. Oz was not the enemy.

My father was.

"Let him take you, Casey. You have my word that his intentions are pure." Kierson stared at me as though I had lost my mind. "Perhaps 'pure' was a poor choice of words."

"Ya think?" Kierson replied, shifting his gaze to his black-winged escort.

"Scared, are we, Kierson?" Oz taunted. It reminded me of his incessant teasing at the Victorian.

"Fuck you, Oz. Let's just get this shit over with."

"This shit is just beginning," Oz corrected with an evil smile. The faintest glow came from his eyes as he did. "The real fun begins when we set foot in Detroit."

"Is that where we are to go first?" Aery asked, mild confusion in her voice.

"It's a beacon for evil beings. They will go there first, though only few will stay. If you wish to stop them, then we have no time to waste."

"I will follow your lead," she said, placing her arm around my waist.

"You all will," he replied. "Or you will all die, and not by my hand. Hades' ignorance or arrogance—I cannot decide which it is—has indirectly let the most lethal souls the world has ever known loose on Earth. Souls that the PC are ill-equipped at best to deal with. And if, by some unfathomable means, those souls can become corporeal again . . ."

"We'll have a motherfucking shitshow on our hands," Casey uttered, breathing hard after the words—and the strength he mustered to speak them—left his body.

"Precisely. A shitshow that none of you want to clean up. I'm not even certain you could if you wanted to." He muttered that last sentence under his breath, as though he felt an ounce of concern for my brothers and what they were about to face. "But a way to clean this mess up will need to be found, and soon. So, with that in mind . . ." Oz drawled, his gaze drifting off toward the physical gate between the dead and the living. "Shall we?"

Without awaiting a response, he snatched up the brothers in a flash and flew toward the exit at a dizzying pace. Aery sighed heavily beside me.

"I hope he knows I can't possibly keep up with him if he insists on showing off the whole way there," she lamented. "Come on, Khara. You know the drill."

I did indeed.

I bent over slightly and snaked my arms around her neck from behind her, clinging to her back. Her fragile-looking, transparent wings stuck out from her sides. Her wings attached far differently from mine. They were positioned more laterally, allowing for someone of my build to easily lie between their insertion points without obstructing their motion.

"I'm glad I wiggled my way out of that one," she said with a wink. "Your brothers are heavy!"

"Hopefully I prove to be a lighter, more comfortable passenger for you than they," I replied, my hair flying wildly around my face while her delicate wings fluttered at a hummingbird's pace. Aery was a study in contradictions. Everything about her spoke to her weaknesses—her petite frame, frail-looking wings, and childlike innocence—but they were a ruse. She was strong, fierce, and far more deadly than many would have imagined. More so than many would give her credit for. I had seen on only two occasions what she was capable of, and it was unsettling to say the least. She would be an asset to us once above if she was able to wield her abilities against the souls we released on Earth as she could in the Underworld. If not, she would likely stay and observe the surrounding chaos anyway. She did as she pleased, from all I had experienced, except when working under the direct orders of my father. And without him around, there was no telling what she may do.

Thankfully, she had always taken a shine to me. Something about my unfazed demeanor intrigued her, as though she was trying to find a way into my mind to see what drove it. Historically, her efforts had been in vain. I wondered if my new preponderance of emotions would one day prove advantageous to her in her quest.

I remained quiet for the greater part of our journey so as not to unwittingly unveil some piece of information—some insight—that she could later use against me. Perhaps I was being unfair to her. Though mischievous, she had always been kind. Unfortunately, kindness does not imply loyalty. And, with nymphs, that latter trait could be easily bought. Knowing this made submerging her in the various evils of Detroit seem ill-advised, and yet it was still the plan. With luck, she would either be of use to us or, if not, would willingly return to the Underworld, hoping to evade any repercussions from my father.

By the time I could see the distant Detroit skyline, only one thought plagued my mind. If we were not to have the aid of Hades' knowledge and power to collect the souls I had let loose, was it even possible for us to return them to my father's realm? When he had so quickly ordered me out of the Underworld, he said nothing about coming above to address the pressing matter. Perhaps his first concern was stabilizing what remained of his kingdom. Perhaps he did not wish to abandon Persephone to an unknown fate by leaving her behind with the threat of upheaval looming. Perhaps he truly wished to be rid of me and was leaving me to my fate. His most recent reaction to my departure could not have been more different from the last.

"You really called this place home, huh?" Aery yelled back to me, disbelief polluting her normally cheerful tone. "It's a wasteland of ugly."

"Detroit is an acquired taste of sorts. But it does leave a strong impression."

She laughed.

"That might be the euphemism of the century, Khara. I'm guessing the light of day does nothing to improve it."

"You would be correct. The dark of night suits it best."

She laughed again.

"Kinda like you," she said more quietly, though her words trailed back to me. Then she dove hard and fast toward the ground. The decaying neighborhood that was home to the Victorian drew ever closer. I was nearly there.

That realization was a double-edged sword.

While I felt a certain relief at my return, the old yellow house would not hold the same sense of warmth that it once had. Drew's absence would leave an undeniable void—one that could never be filled by anything other than his return. And I feared that possibility was not meant to be. Though Persephone and I had succeeded in pulling Drew's soul into me, he was no longer there; he had been released with all the others when I crossed the Acheron. Without his soul contained within me, there would be no chance for Hecate to pull it forth and restore him to the world above.

That chance was lost forever. At best, we would find him eventually, wandering the Earth, then return him to the Underworld. At worst, he had already fallen victim to Oz's absolute death. Either way, I had squandered the only opportunity I would ever have to bring him back.

As I set my feet down in the yard that Drew would never see again, a tear ran down my cheek.

28

I stood outside the Victorian, a wash of emotion flowing through me. It could not have been more different than when I originally arrived there with Kierson and Drew. Then, I had felt nothing but acceptance. Now, I felt little more than a deep sense of loss. The twinge of anticipation I had hoped to feel when I looked at the building's weathered yellow exterior was absent. There was no warm invitation beckoning me inside.

It did not feel like home.

Suddenly, the front door opened, pulling me from my dark thoughts. I looked up to see Pierson leaning against the door casing. His normal air of superiority and arrogance had been replaced with one of surprised awe. And I would soon see why.

"Pierson," I called to him, attempting to break whatever spell he was under.

"How did you do it?" he asked, his voice still distant and detached. "I cannot figure out how you did it."

Our entourage still stood in the front yard, exchanging curious expressions. There had been no greeting. No chastising remarks regarding my selfish departure to the Underworld. Instead, he stood there, the vacant expression on his face looking foreign and off-putting. His behavior was utterly out of character. What had happened to him during our collective absence? I feared the answer to that question was far more ominous than any of us would have bargained for.

"Do what, brother?" I asked, stepping forward delicately as though any sudden movement would startle him—break him somehow.

My advance garnered his attention; his dilated eyes focused on me in a more lucid manner. The anxiety I had not realized I was experiencing abated slightly when he scrutinized me more acutely. With every step I took toward him, he seemed to come back to himself.

"Come see for yourself," he said, his voice sharp and familiar.

But I did not need to go far. The subject of his incredulity stepped out onto the front step, unveiling himself to me and the others. It was then that I completely understood what Pierson was so unable to wrap his analytical mind around. Drew shouldn't have been standing there. He had been lost. Damned.

"Drew," I whispered, my voice small and meek. His eyes darted from Pierson back to me, utter confusion marring his features. Once again, my brother did not recognize me. "All is well, brother. You are home now."

"I felt something brush against the wards," Pierson started, "and I came outside to find him standing in the front yard, just as you stand here now. He did not know me or where he was or why he was here. He just stood there, vacant and lost."

"He will be all right," I explained, moving toward them, excitement overtaking me as I did. I could not suppress the growing elation that I felt. He was physically restored—an exact replica of what he had been before his untimely death. I may have let the worst of the damned escape, but, in doing so, I inadvertently accomplished the very thing I had sought to do since I had first realized that Drew had succumbed to some formidable power above. If the release of the damned was the price required to free him, then it was a price worth paying in my eyes. "He suffered the same loss of identity when he arrived in the Underworld. It will wear off gradually. It should only be a short time—maybe hours—before he will start to piece things together."

Just before I got to the foot of the front steps, Pierson's hardened and questioning gaze stopped me short. Something was brewing behind those light blue eyes. Pieces of a puzzle were being linked together, and the ultimate picture they created was not a favorable one, judging by his expression.

"What?" I asked bluntly, unable to fathom why Pierson was unexcited by his brother's return. "What is vexing you?"

"Do you know how Drew has returned here?" he inquired, his tone one of interrogation.

"I released him. I released all who called the Oudeis home."

"When?" He barked the question like it held answers far beyond my comprehension.

"I cannot be certain—an hour ago. Maybe two. As soon as we realized what I had done, we returned here."

His expression soured instantly.

"Khara. Drew has been here for no less than a day."

Time stopped.

The weight of his words and the implications that accompanied them tore through me. I had not been the one to return Drew. Hades had been.

He—his powers—had not failed.

"That cannot be—"

"And yet it is," Pierson interrupted sharply. "His memory has not improved over that time. He is as he was when I found him. He remembers nothing of his former life. His title. His family. His history. It is all gone."

My heart sank; the cautionary words of my father ran through my mind. *There is always a price to pay with magic.* Drew may have indeed been reborn, but reborn to what degree of his former self remained to be seen.

Unable to hide my sorrow at this revelation, I turned wet eyes to the shell of the noble brother I had known. I was met with a look of confused concern.

"I should know you. . . ." The look of concentration on his face only deepened the sadness I felt. It was as if he was willing himself to remember something that was so clearly lost to him—maybe lost forever this time—just to ease my pain.

I felt Kierson and Casey flank me on either side, the three of us looking up to our bygone leader. Whatever crisis we had returned home to address would wait. The crisis standing before us was far more pressing in our collective eyes.

"I'm Kierson," Kierson offered, extending his hand toward Drew slowly and cautiously. Drew looked at it strangely for a moment before taking it.

"Drew, or so I am told."

"Khara," I said, taking Kierson's lead and reintroducing myself to our reborn brother. "I am your sister. Your only sister."

When it was Casey's turn to speak, he did something wildly unexpected. Startling us all, he pulled a blade out from his sheath in a blur of motion and lunged at Drew. Before any of us could intercede, Drew had disarmed him and pinned Casey to the ground, his own blade pressed tightly against Casey's throat.

"Glad to see you haven't lost everything," Casey said awkwardly, doing his best not to disturb the sharp edge digging into his neck. "I'm Casey."

Drew blinked heavily before pushing away from his near-victim, stepping back while he dropped the weapon to the concrete step.

"How did you—" Drew started before Casey interrupted him.

"I had a hunch," he replied as he slowly stood up. The act of doing so highlighted the fact that he was still not fully healed from our attack at the Acheron. Still, his weakness clearly did nothing to stave off the usual aggressive tactics he employed to make a point. "What would be the sense in returning a worthy warrior to the world above if he didn't retain *any* of his former self?" His argument was hard to find fault in. "Drew may not know who the fuck we are or who he was, but he sure as hell knows how to fight. Whatever DNA for ass-kicking he had is still intact." Casey turned his maniacal smile to our disoriented brother. "Maybe he'll be even better now that his good-little-soldier tendencies have been erased."

"Not all," I said, the words escaping me softly. I could not shake the sense of familiarity I perceived in Drew when he tried to remember me. It was as if my sadness pained him more than it had me and he would have done anything within his power to abate it. That was the Drew I knew. The Drew he had proven to be time after time. Perhaps that part of him was somehow ingrained enough to have endured his rebirth; the thought brought a smile to my lips.

Then it quickly fell.

I looked over my shoulder to see my father walk up to the yard before he stopped beside Oz. Both stared up at the entrance to the Victorian. Hades looked shocked. Oz looked amused.

"I cannot believe it," Father said under his breath.

"Oh, you'd better believe it, Soul Keeper. Shit has just gotten really, really real." Hades turned to assess Oz's profile. "Nice of you to finally show up, by the way. I was wondering when that was going to happen."

"Because releasing the contents of the Oudeis was not *real* enough for you, Dark One?" Oz shrugged Gallicly, dismissing Hades' question. "As for my whereabouts, I had things to handle before I left the Underworld, not that it is of concern to you."

I watched the two of them silently, looking on from the shelter of the Victorian. The circumstances under which I had left the Underworld made Hades' arrival uncomfortable for me. It also brought something to light that I previously would not have believed. He had come above with such ease that I could not fathom why he had not come looking for me when I had been abducted—unless I was not a high enough priority to warrant it. The way he cast me out was so unexpected and harsh that it made me further question if his previous pretense of love had been nothing more than a ruse. My chest tightened so violently at the thought that I grabbed it, pushing down on it forcefully and drawing attention to myself when I did. Attention I had wanted to avoid.

"Khara," Kierson said softly, putting his arm around my shoulder. "What's going on?"

"I had a pain—it is nothing," I explained, removing my hand from where it had rested over my heart. Then my eyes betrayed me, glancing over to Hades, who remained at Oz's side. Catching my eye, Hades frowned.

"Hades," I said, acknowledging him coolly.

"Khara." The chill in his tone was unmistakable.

"Perhaps we should take this inside," Pierson prompted, glancing at Hades before looking down the street through the run-down and abandoned neighborhood. He led the way with Drew falling in line behind him. The rest of us followed into the foyer and directly through to the living room. Being there evoked a sense of nostalgia in me.

Hades, however, seemed to lag behind, taking in the humble yet once-stately dwelling.

"This is where you stayed in your absence?" he asked incredulously.

"Yes. My room is in the basement."

"The *basement*?"

"Total downgrade from the Underworld, I'm sure," Oz sneered, taking his rightful perch on the staircase, just as he always had. Seeing him there was so familiar and yet also not, given the changes he had undergone.

Hades did not reply to Oz's retort, finally entering the room, though his distaste for his surroundings and my winged companion was quite plain on his face.

Ignoring the devolution of the situation, Pierson continued with the business at hand—just as Drew would have done, had he been his former self.

"You spoke of the Oudeis, Khara . . . that you freed those it had contained and that this was why you have returned so abruptly. I know not of this. What are the ramifications of this act?"

While we all settled into various spots around the room, I attempted to explain.

"There are various realms of the Underworld," I started, shooting a wary glance in Hades' direction. "In short, I released the souls that were relegated to the most isolated of these realms into the world above. The worst that the Underworld has to boast."

Pierson's eyes widened before narrowing astutely.

"And now it is our job to round them up and return them." His words were not a question.

"Precisely," Hades concurred on my behalf.

"And you are the great ruler of the Underworld," Pierson stated, turning his attention to Hades, who stood behind the sofa, his back to the foyer and also to the staircase where Oz sat.

"I am."

"I've studied much about you over the centuries."

"Have you?" Father replied, his tone curious but cautioning.

"Khara has said that you do not come above often . . . at least not in her time with you."

"True enough."

"But from what I know of you, you used to return with great regularity. You did so under a veil of magic that offered invisibility." Hades was silent. "But if you truly are the King of the Dead, then you should not be visible to me. This poses a conundrum. Either you are not who you say you are, or your powers above are virtually nonexistent." There was no threat in Pierson's tone. No accusation in his words. As was so typical of him, he had simply made an observation based on the facts as he knew them. And he knew many.

A deafening silence hovered over us until Pierson saw fit to continue.

"I find it unlikely that you are not who you claim to be, so the only conclusion I can draw is that you are, for whatever reason, without the Unseen ability that you used to possess, which leaves me to question why it is that you have come here at all. If you no longer can wield magic above, what assistance can you offer in the capture of the souls that have been released?"

"Your brothers seem to all be afflicted with the same boldness," Hades said, his deep voice booming above me while I remained seated on the couch before him with my back facing him.

"Pierson lacks the tact necessary to survive in the Underworld, but it is not a show of disrespect," I said to Hades. "This world, as he sees it, is ruled by the binary of truth and untruth. He feels no need to paint it as anything else. Do not be offended by his approach."

"All I am trying to ascertain is what good you will be to us when we endeavor to round up those that have been let loose," Pierson volunteered.

"My power that you question is not a concern in this matter. I come to you visibly because I no longer require the magic I once did for survival. Going Unseen was a precautionary measure against the gods. They are no longer a threat to my safety, so I choose to forgo the once-necessary precaution," Hades answered in a rare moment of disclosure. "As for how I can assist in rounding up those that are loose, I know virtually everything about those that resided in the Oudeis. If you wish to catch them, you will need me to brief you first." Hades came around from behind the couch to stand before Pierson, who stood stoically before the wall of windows that lined the far side of the room.

"Know thy opponent," I said plainly, drawing Hades' attention.

"Yes," he agreed tightly.

"Then you and I shall go to the library upstairs where we can sit and draft a plan of attack based on the knowledge you have regarding those that have returned to Earth," Pierson suggested, making his way past Hades. He looked back to my father, then gestured to the stairs that Oz occupied. "If you would follow me."

Hades was not accustomed to receiving directives, but he reluctantly fell in step behind my brother, moving around Oz's ominous form without acknowledging him as he climbed the steps past him. As I watched them go upstairs, my eyes drifted back to Oz, who sat staring intently at me. He did not look away when I caught him doing so.

"The rest of you need to get ready," Pierson added before he disappeared to the second floor. "We will have a war on our hands; that is for certain. The task of collecting those that have been reintroduced to the world will not likely be an easy one."

"How are we supposed to find something we can only sort of see?" Kierson asked. It was a valid question and not one that had yet crossed my mind. Thoughts of Drew and his new, reborn state still plagued me, cluttering my consciousness with matters that could wait until the dead were dealt with.

Kierson's question was met with silence from the floor above. Then Drew's voice managed to break that silence, our collective attention snapping to where my reborn brother stood.

"Surely if you let them out, Khara, there is a way to return them through you," he said. There was a hint of frustration in his voice, though his expression showed his continued confusion regarding the matter at hand.

"I'm sure there is," Kierson replied in earnest. "But that requires us figuring out how, and fast. I'm not so sure that's going to happen."

"Your pessimism certainly isn't going to help," Drew retorted. That brought about a strong sense of déjà vu, which I welcomed. It reaffirmed my suspicion that he still possessed inherent traits that he would never be rid of. "Khara, do you remember anything about how you collected the souls of the Oudeis in the first place? What happened? How you felt?"

"For the greater part, yes. I do."

"Do you think it's possible that if we recreated that same situation, you could do it again?"

"Perhaps, but removing them from the Oudeis required necromancy, a skill that none of us here possess, and it was by Persephone's hand that they were directed into me. There is no way for her to join us and aid in this endeavor. She is bound to the Underworld eternally now."

"So you're saying you can't just do whatever it is you did before and hold them inside yourself until Aery can get you back into the Underworld?"

"It seems unlikely, Kierson," I said with a furrowed brow. His mention of Aery brought my attention to her absence for the first time since our arrival. "Especially given that she is gone. That would make the latter part of your plan somewhat challenging."

"She said she had to return below. That there was something she needed to check on, but she's coming back," he responded rather adamantly. "She wants to help."

"I got Khara to the Underworld the first time," Oz rumbled from the stairs. "I'll get her there again. Don't worry about shit that is already handled. Worry about the shit you have no clue how to deal with for now, like finding the souls on the lam."

"Isn't that where you come in?" Casey sneered from where he lounged on the couch. "Didn't you argue not so long ago that you were the expert tracker of the dead, not me? That their souls screamed to you? Oh, wait. Maybe that was before you sold your traitorous soul for a pair of shiny new black wings." Pushing himself off the couch, Casey meandered his way over to Oz, taunting him by flapping his hands mockingly along the way. "Shit, who knows. Maybe you still can track them. Depravity does tend to attract depravity, does it not? And you're about as depraved as one can be, so I imagine that you could find these escapees without so much as breaking a sweat if that is indeed the case."

"You say depraved. I say upgraded," Oz rebutted, a look of dismissal on his face. "But if you're hoping that I am somehow your ticket to finding these souls, try again. I can't track them."

"Can't or won't?" Kierson boldly asked, his tone accusatory.

"Doesn't matter, Kierson," Casey interrupted. "The dead still call to me."

"Fantastic. That means it should only take what, maybe a century or two to actually collect them, based on your stellar performance last time with the Stealers?" Oz mocked, uncurling himself from his station. He loomed above us all, several steps up the staircase. Even without his vast wings visible—they were fully retracted for once—his presence was intimidating. "Maybe Hades really does have a shot at figuring out a way to find them if those are the time constraints he's working under."

Unfortunately, Casey was one who would not back down. Ever.

In the blink of an eye, Casey launched himself across the room at Oz, a familiar scene playing out before us all yet again until it was stopped short. He was still weakened by the attack at the Acheron, but he did not care.

"Stop!" Drew shouted from the far side of the room. When Casey froze on the spot, even Drew looked startled by the abruptness with which he halted. He had no idea of the commanding power he could wield.

"He may not remember fuck all," Oz laughed, "but the kid still has his mojo." He was clearly amused by the situation and prepared to take full advantage of Casey's verbally imposed imprisonment, advancing on him slowly. Teasingly. In the presence of the Dark One, Casey's anger never faltered, though he remained frozen by Drew's command. "I'm not sure what you hoped to achieve by attacking me, Casey, but you would be wise to remember that I am no longer the fallen one who used to live upstairs and fuck everything in sight. I owe you nothing. I am not your friend. I am far from your ally. And if your mission to rectify this shitshow relies on me in any way, consider yourselves fucked. I have one purpose here, and one purpose only."

"And that is?" Drew asked, striding toward Oz, whose attention snapped to the one he clearly perceived as an incoming threat.

"None of your business, that's what it is."

It was then that Pierson quickly descended the stairs, my father close on his heels. He had learned something already. Something he deemed worthy of sharing.

"We've mapped out who the greatest threats are and where they would most likely be heading," he announced as he rounded the newel post to join us in the living room.

"Did you account for all the souls I eradicated in the Underworld?" Oz drawled. "I must have taken out a few hundred on my own."

"Since we have no way to ascertain who your kills were, we're sticking to my plan. There is still much to research to be certain that we will succeed in the capture of those who escaped, but this is a start. A solid one. And, given who some of the potential escapees are, time is of the essence. We must split up if we wish to succeed. We will form three groups. Casey can track the dead and should find this task easier when provided with the information Hades and I have compiled. He and Drew will work together. Hades and I will join forces, leaving Kierson and Khara to pair up. Each team will have assigned targets—emphasis on the plural, though I have ranked them in order of importance. I have also divided them into regions so that there is less ground to cover while hunting them."

"Um, Pierson?" Kierson called out, his tone laced with uncertainty. "I like this plan and all, but what exactly are we supposed to do with a bunch of disembodied souls once we do find and subdue them, assuming we can subdue them at all?"

"Drew should be able to command them. Hades believes he and I can use magic to entrap them, if only temporarily," Pierson explained plainly.

"Right, but what about Khara and me?"

I looked up at Kierson to find worry etched deeply into his expression.

Pierson's countenance soon matched that of his twin's. "We can only hope that Khara will be able to replicate what she did when she aided in the evacuation of the Oudeis."

"That's a big fucking chance to take. What happens if she can't do what you're proposing? She could be slaughtered!"

"As could you," I said, addressing my overprotective sibling. "Which is why I think I should hunt them alone. You should join Casey and Drew. I created this debacle, and I will face it. If my death is brought about in the process, then so be it."

Kierson rolled his eyes dramatically.

"Why can't death scare you even the tiniest bit? Please? It would make my life so much easier if it did. And you're fucking nuts, by the way, if you think I'm leaving you alone."

"I will go with her," Drew said, distracting Kierson from his lamentations.

"No," Kierson argued. "I would feel better if I was with her—you know, given your memory situation and all."

"And if you can do nothing to stop them?" Drew volleyed, his tone flat. It was a stark contrast to his former concerned self. His desire to keep those around him safe was still inherent in his actions, but the loss of emotion in his words was unsettling to witness. It caused an ache in my chest that made me second-guess my decision to bring him back, though only for a moment. It also removed that brief sense of hope that I had entertained when I first caught a glimpse of the brother I had known.

While I pondered Drew's rebirth, Kierson ruminated over Drew's request, ultimately coming to the conclusion that Drew was right, though he admitted this grudgingly.

"Fine," he snapped, storming out of the room and into the adjoining kitchen. "But you'd better hope your powers don't fuck up somehow and get her killed, because I will send you back to the Underworld myself. You understand me?" The crashing sound of a table being overturned punctuated his remark.

Drew's earnest face turned toward me, offering me what little comfort he could.

"I will not fail you."

"In that, I have no doubt."

"Then it is settled," Pierson said, taking control of the situation once again. He handed each pairing a sheet that listed the names, estimated locations, powers, predilections, and weaknesses of those we hunted. It was a long and interesting list indeed. Drew looked over my shoulder, reading our list with me. Silence filled the room while the others took stock of which souls they would be responsible for removing from the earthly realm. It was in that silence that I had a thought. Perhaps an epiphany.

"Could we not just kill them?" I asked, remembering how easily Oz had slain those attacking us on the shore of the Acheron. My brothers were unable to fight them below with earthly weapons, but if it were possible that being above was an advantage for the PC—that being on Earth would somehow make their weapons effective—then maybe the tables would be turned in our favor. Smiting those that had escaped would be the quickest way to rid the Earth of them. Perhaps, if our efforts proved as effective as Oz's had been in the Underworld, they would be wiped from existence entirely.

Hades took a deep breath, sighing heavily in response.

"I fear it is not so simple."

"Why not?"

"Because souls that escape the clutches of the Underworld are impervious to the weapons of man—even those of my kingdom. The conditions under which they now live preclude them from being put down as they had been before."

"So if it comes to a fight?" Casey asked, clearly seeing the subtext of my father's statement.

"There won't be a fight at all," he said plainly. "There will be you losing. There is no other possible outcome."

Casey's evil grin spread widely across his darkened expression.

"We'll see about that, Soul Keeper," he said with a snarl. "Maybe it just takes someone of the Underworld to put them down, and I can't think of a better person to try that theory out. They're on *my* turf this time. . . ." He methodically wiped one of his blades back and forth across his pant leg, itching to begin this battle, even if he might prove the underdog. Ironic that he believed me to be the crazy one.

"But Oz can—"

"Not stand listening to all this fucking talk much longer," he interrupted, shooting me a scathing look across the room. "Are we doing this or not?"

"We?" Casey asked, quirking his brow menacingly.

"I said I couldn't track them. I never said I wasn't tagging along for entertainment value."

"I have contacted Sean about this," Pierson volunteered, ignoring the tension between Oz and Casey. I, however, was left questioning why Oz had silenced me so abruptly. If I could find out, I planned to. "He is amassing an army of the PC to join us, but this endeavor will take time. Time we may or may not have, so I believe it is in the collective best interest for us to head out. Now."

Without any further argument or distraction, my brothers went about collecting all that they would need, stashing cell phones securely away and strapping copious weapons to themselves, handing me sparingly few. They had seen my ineptitude with them before. A blade was all I could safely wield, and, if Hades' words were true, weapons would do little if it came down to it, so there was little need for them at all, really. For the boys, it was a matter of comfort. They felt complete with weapons at the ready.

While they rushed about preparing themselves, Oz sat on the stairs, staring at me intently. When Pierson was satisfied that we had all that was needed, he gave the go-ahead for us to leave. I made my way to the front door of the Victorian, following behind my family, ready to right my wrong.

Then Oz's voice in my ear stopped me cold.

"You didn't think you were leaving without me, did you?" he whispered. "You and I move as one, remember?" Every hair on my body stood at attention, but the feeling was not entirely disagreeable. "And as for what I did back in the Underworld . . ." His voice was so low and faint that I strained to hear his warning. "That is something we will keep between you and me."

I said nothing in response. It took me a moment to recover from my traitorous body's response to his proximity; only then did I continue on my way out of the house. The others had already filed into the night without us.

I was in no way surprised that Oz was coming with me. To have expected a sudden change in that regard would have required either naïveté or stupidity on my part. I possessed neither, as far as Oz was concerned. But his need to keep secret his ability to take out those that we hunted was a twist that I had not foreseen. For the moment, I chose to comply with his demand.

But I made no promises for the long term.

"So are you telling me that you will not assist in our endeavor to either detain or eliminate the souls? That you are simply coming along as my chaperone? Again?" I asked, my words curt and heated. They failed to have the effect that I sought. Instead, they amused him greatly.

"I will keep you from falling victim to your own lack of judgment," he replied tightly. "Had I been present the last time that occurred, you would not be in this predicament now." As we joined the others in the front yard, he plucked the paper that Pierson had given me from my hand, and a wicked smile spread across his face when he read it. "I was hoping there'd be more . . ."

Again I remained silent, unable to agree with his sentiment. I knew exactly what we were about to hunt down. The thought of facing the beings I had released at the Acheron was not especially inviting. And yet it was what we had to do.

There would be no rest for the wicked.

29

With the cover of night tucked around us, Oz suggested that we fly to our destination. He seemed familiar with the location, which was fortunate, given that I had only spent time in two places on Earth and Drew had no recollection of anything. For a moment, it made me grateful for his unwavering commitment to accompanying me.

"I'll take Drew," he told me, snapping his wings out to their full breadth. Mine were still hidden beneath my skin, since Aery had brought me all the way back to Detroit. I had not chosen to force mine to emerge along the way. Standing before Oz and Drew, I focused, demanding my newfound appendages to break through. It was still a painful process, but in less than a minute they were free. While I stretched them, testing each cautiously, I saw Drew reach for the tip of my left wing, a curious expression on his face.

"So strange that something so large can be hidden in someone so slight," he observed, slipping a feather gently between his fingers.

"When I last saw you, I did not know how to hide them away. I had only just gotten them," I replied gently. "Perhaps there will come a time when you will remember that night."

Oz's dark form suddenly loomed over my brother and me, disturbing our conversation.

"If you two are finished, it's time to go." He looked at Drew, who had released my feather but still stared at the mottled-gray wing as though it perplexed him. It was strange that the sight of Oz's wings did not give him a second's pause. "Let's go, amnesiac," Oz called amusedly. "You should make for amazing conversation along the way."

"Where are we going?" I asked.

"How about you just try to keep up," he challenged, his familiar hubris still firmly in place. Not allowing me a chance to retort, he snatched Drew up and took flight; the cloud-covered, moonlit sky created a hazy background that was nearly blocked by his ominous silhouette. Seconds after he took flight, I followed.

The view from above was greatly obscured by the low-lying cloud layer, but an occasional break in the haze gave us a glorious view of Detroit. Its downtown lights sparkled brightly. As we flew east, I felt a slight pang of longing—a longing to stay behind. Detroit had quickly become part of my life. It was a symbol for who I had become and the family I had discovered—I was part of the PC. But my father's kingdom represented the other part of my life. The part where I had been a princess of the Underworld. The part that no longer existed.

As I climbed higher and higher, ascending to the safety and cover of the thickening clouds, I heard the scream of a female. An unholy, ear-piercing cry that rang out through the night so clearly that it seemed as though whoever had released the sound had done so from beside me. Without thought, I dove toward the Earth below. Toward the outskirts of Detroit. Again the shrill cry cut through the noisy air rushing around me while I careened toward a familiar part of town. I was nearing the Heidelberg Project and the seedy neighborhoods that surrounded it.

But the sudden silence that greeted me once I hovered just above the abandoned homes thwarted my search. No longer able to follow the ominous call of pain and torture—sounds I knew very well— I could not locate the victim. Why I felt compelled to find her in the first place was strange enough, but my desire to track her only increased as the quiet drew on. There had been an inhuman quality to her cry. After landing quickly, I found myself running through the deserted urban area. I rushed past boarded-up houses and empty lots, populated only by the rubble of what had once been stately homes. I had no idea where Oz was or if he had even realized I was no longer following his lead. I did not care. My mind was consumed by my need to find the owner of that tortured scream and aid her.

If I could not do that, then I would bring her assailant to justice—providing I could find him. That was the way of the PC, and I was one of them.

As I weaved my way through the deteriorated streets and downtrodden alleyways, a rustle of leaves from a copse of trees at the end of a vacant lot attracted my attention. Approaching cautiously, I listened for further indications that there was indeed someone there—perhaps multiple someones. All I heard was the occasional snapping of twigs and a wet feeding sound—one that a predator would make while gnawing on its prey.

Despite the fact that it was nighttime and there were a multitude of nocturnal animals capable of making the sounds I heard, I approached, unable to shake the feeling that something was amiss. The closer I got, the more I felt compelled to continue on.

When I finally arrived at the trees, I instinctively drew my blade, though I was still unsure what awaited me. Father had said that earthly weapons would do nothing against those that had escaped. He had seemed so convinced of that fact, but when I stepped closer, pushing just past the layer of brush, I was far less certain. The eyes of the one I found hiding in the shadows turned to lock onto mine, and my need to bury the dagger hilt-deep into him was all-consuming.

I was willing to test the accuracy of Hades' claim.

30

"You," he sneered accusingly, looking over his shoulder at me as I approached him. His eyes were wild. Rabid. Feral. As the blue light of the full moon shone down upon us through a crack in the clouds above, I took in the grisly sight. The face that glared back at me was familiar. I had seen pictures of the statues erected in his honor before; the likeness was undeniable. Hermes. Messenger of the gods. Conductor of the dead.

Persephone had been wrong about the fate of the fallen gods.

Undaunted, I stared at the former god before me. His legendary boyish handsomeness was marred by the blood he had streaked across his face when he wiped the back of his arm along his mouth. Rising slowly, he turned his gore-covered, naked body to face me. When my eyes met his, I saw no semblance of sanity in his gaze.

I took in the sight of a mangled corpse lying at his feet, quickly realizing that there was no semblance of sanity in his actions either.

I was transfixed by the sight of her. Her blood-soaked hair was matted to her ghostly pale face. Her dull, dead blue eyes stared back at me hauntingly. Her agony may have been over, but the evidence of it lingered.

The devilish smile that had overtaken his countenance was quickly left behind when he threw his head back and laughed maniacally. Stunned, I looked on, not quite processing the macabre scene that lay before me or what it implied. Hermes, the cunning god of flight and former guide to the Underworld, stood before me, and he was very much corporeal.

"You know who I am," he said, sounding rather pleased with himself. Vanity was only one of the many sins the gods often fell victim to. "But do you know what I have done?" A challenge was contained within his words. He wished to play a game with me.

"You have murdered that woman," I said plainly, unwilling to give him that which he desired: a reaction.

"Not a woman," he corrected, stepping aside just enough for me to see how diminutive the victim's body was.

"A child," I whispered, focusing more intently on her face. How I had initially missed the fact that she was so young was beyond me. Perhaps the state of Hermes had distracted me. Now seeing her—her life so violently cut short—I could not suppress the anger I felt at this revelation.

Hermes' sharp, caustic laughter rang out through the city, raising the tiny hairs on the back of my neck. His sadistic smile widened.

"A *virgin.*"

That word rang through my mind, a loud, screaming warning. Again, I looked beyond his naked form to the dead child at his feet. She had been utterly disemboweled. He had drunk of her blood.

A sacrifice.

A sacrifice to the crazed god himself.

The smug look of satisfaction that appeared in his eyes when he saw my realization of what he had done was sickening. But before I had the chance to challenge him, the hilt of my blade still uncomfortably pressed into my palm by the force of my own grip, a voice came from behind me.

"Hermes," Oz boomed, immediately drawing the god's sharpened gaze away from me. Recognition flashed in his eyes for a second, forcing him into a defensive stance. Whether it was recognition of Oz himself or the Dark One he had become, I could not be certain.

What I could surmise was that Hermes was afraid of the approaching angel. And he was wise to be. "You cannot be here," Oz said.

A growl escaped him when Oz unfurled his wings to their full span, darkening the night's dim light. His features twisted into a savage expression, his bloodstained lips curling into a menacing snarl. No longer the impishly handsome being he had once been, Hermes was ruled by survival. And Oz appeared to threaten that survival.

"I can be anywhere I please now," he snapped, bloody spittle spraying wildly as he spoke. "Be sure to tell that to the King of the Dead. He rules me no more."

Oz stood strong against the crazed god.

"You cannot be here," he repeated, taking a step toward him. "You made your choice when it was given. It is time to return to the Oudeis and pay your eternal penance."

"My debt has been paid. I have been reborn now, and there is nothing you can do to change that." He leaned forward, whispering in a conspiratorial manner while the moon shone in his impossibly wide eyes. "You are too late."

"What he says is true," I told Oz, who was now standing at my side. "He appears to have regained all that was taken from him, cementing his reincarnation by means of that sacrifice. A *virgin* sacrifice."

Cold, empty eyes shot toward me; Hermes assessed me as though I had finally said something interesting. He cocked his head, his eyes darting from Oz to me and then back to Oz again. His mind was not right.

"Intriguing," he purred, sniffing the stale air as the wind picked up and began to swirl around us. "I think your evening is about to become a touch more surreal than it already has been. I shall take my leave now so that you might enjoy it." His enigmatic words presaged his exit. He then leapt high into the night sky on winged feet.

"Stop!" Drew shouted from behind me, startling me slightly. I had forgotten that he would have accompanied Oz.

Hermes looked down at us, hovering for a moment. The wicked smile on his face told me all I needed to know.

"Your powers carry no weight over me, warrior," he declared, turning his attention to the dagger in my hand. "Nor do your weapons. I cannot be stopped. *We* cannot be stopped."

"I can stop you," Oz drawled, unable to suppress the joy that knowledge brought to him.

"Perhaps another time, Dark One," Hermes replied before disappearing in the blink of an eye. One moment he and his winged feet hovered in the air above us, the next he was gone. I turned to see the most grim of expressions on Oz's face. It was laced with a note of surprise.

"I didn't see that coming," he uttered under his breath.

"He must be stopped," Drew said, approaching the remains of the young girl with reverence. He had always been sympathetic to casualties of war. It was a part of his existence that he had not made peace with. Not that I had witnessed. It seemed that, even reborn, he still was unsettled by it.

"He will be," Oz growled in reply, looking off into the night sky as though it would provide him with the answers that we so clearly lacked. "But first we must alert the others. There's been a change of plans." He stalked away from my brother and me, heading toward the decrepit homes that lined the abandoned street. Drew and I exchanged a brief look of confusion before we followed the black wings in front of us. When I finally caught up to their owner, I carefully walked around the outstretched appendages so I could talk to Oz face to face.

But he was already talking to someone else.

"Yeah. We need to meet," he barked into his phone, still striding through the neighborhood. "We need to talk to Hades. Now." A brief pause. "I don't give a fuck where you are or what you're doing. Get back here. This can't wait. And call Pierson, too, but don't tell him what it's about." Another pause. "Fine. The Heidelberg Project. Be there in ten." Then he hung up the cell phone and shoved it into the back pocket of his jeans.

"Kierson?" I asked.

"No. Casey. He's getting the others," he replied, staring off into the distance while he continued to storm toward our destination: the Heidelberg Project. The eerie neighborhood seemed to be the regular setting for this group's midnight meetings of the minds. It was a strange and macabre place to carry them out.

"What of the girl's body?" Drew asked, now flanking me on my right.

"Leave it for now. Pierson will take care of it once I have a little chat with the ruler of the Underworld," Oz said sternly.

"You are concerned about Hermes," I observed.

"I don't give a shit about Hermes or anyone else that escaped. What I do give a shit about is why his name wasn't on our list. No mention of the gods was made whatsoever."

"You think Hades has withheld information."

"I know he's withheld information. He's hiding something," he corrected, grinding to a halt while he fixed his piercing gaze upon me. "And I want to know what the fuck it is."

"And you think he will just tell you?"

"I sure do."

"How can you be so confident?" Drew asked from beside me. It was the question I felt compelled to ask Oz myself.

"Because," he said, turning his malicious smile to me. "Her life depends on it."

"Were you not there when Hades disowned me? I hardly see how I could be used to leverage him into doing anything at this point."

Oz shook his head condescendingly before walking away into the night.

"It's a good thing you have me around, new girl," he called out, not bothering to look back. "It really, really is."

After exchanging dubious expressions, Drew and I picked up our pace in order to catch up to the Dark One again, who led the way to the Heidelberg Project. His arrogant swagger never faltered. I could make no sense of his current confidence; it seemed unfounded to me. But, as was always the case with Oz, there were truths that ran deeper than I knew. Knowledge I was unable to extract. He was a veritable safe of secrets, and I wondered if there would ever be a way for me to crack it open to study its contents. Resisting him proved unhelpful in that endeavor, much as with Deimos. Perhaps those two were far more alike than even I cared to admit. But it begged the question: If giving in to Deimos had worked in the past, would doing the same with Oz yield similar results?

If I survived the night, I was determined to find out.

31

It was not long before we found ourselves huddled in front of a three-story home I remembered from my last time in the Heidelberg Project, completely covered in what appeared to be dismembered doll parts. Then, it had just seemed odd. Now, after seeing the body that Hermes had just mutilated, the sight of the building was both macabre and unnerving. Casey and Kierson arrived moments after we did, pulling up in the familiar black SUV. Not long after that, Hades and Pierson suddenly appeared from around the side of a burned home down the block.

"So, what's this all about?" Kierson asked, surveying our surroundings. "Casey wouldn't tell me."

"Casey doesn't know," Oz informed him, his eyes fixed on the approaching pair. They narrowed in on Hades in particular. "But the Soul Keeper does, don't you?"

"Know what?" my father asked, annoyance tainting his words. "We are wasting time. Perhaps you care not for the balance between the living and the dead—the supernatural and the mundane—but both the PC and I have a responsibility to uphold, so I will ask you this only once. What is all of this about?"

The white of Oz's teeth flashed in the moonlight.

"*Hermes.*"

I looked to my father to find him staring back at us impassively, something missing from his countenance, something that was very present on the faces of the others who had not encountered the god. Surprise. Shock. Disbelief. I found none of those emotions in the depths of my father's eyes.

I did not believe that to be coincidence.

"I descended upon him only blocks from here, though I can see in your eyes, Father, that this news is not entirely unexpected to you." My tone held the slightest accusatory note. He did not flinch under the weight of my words, but his silence was all the affirmation I needed. "Should we assume that there are other gods freely roaming where they should not be?"

His expression tightened minutely.

"Yes."

The others became eerily quiet while Hades and I spoke. The growing tension between us was uncomfortable indeed.

"Why did you not tell us this when you arrived? While we were preparing to hunt down those whom I had freed?"

"Measures to rectify the situation were taken immediately after learning of the foolish stunt you pulled."

"*Measures?*" I asked incredulously. "Whatever measures you have taken have proven insufficient, Father. There are the remains of an eviscerated child where I encountered Hermes that attest to that fact."

"You mean to say that he—"

"Sacrificed a child—a virgin—and drank her body dry?" Oz interrupted, his eyes burning with a narrowly contained rage. "Yes. He did."

My father paled slightly at the news, his bravado faltering.

"This cannot be . . ." he muttered to himself. The disbelief I had hoped to see when he learned of Hermes' existence now contorted his features.

"And yet it is, Soul Keeper. The question still remains: What do you intend to do about it?" Oz taunted him while Hades fought to process the information given.

"You are saying that he has regained his *powers* . . . that he is corporeal? Reanimated?"

"Fancy flying feet and all," Oz quipped, feigning levity. Though he continually professed that he had no vested interest in the outcome of my indiscretion, he seemed extremely agitated by my father's oversight and inaction. I could not for the life of me understand why.

When Hades finally processed the implications that were undoubtedly running rampant in his mind, his look of disbelief bled into one of anger. Anger he chose to project onto the group or, more pointedly, at me.

"Then we are running out of time more quickly than expected," he said, disdain rolling off his tongue with every word.

"Had we known what we were up against from the beginning, perhaps we would not have found ourselves in this position," I offered in defense.

"How dare you scrutinize the methods I choose to employ!" he roared suddenly, his anger erupting. "The methods necessary to clean up the mess that you yourself made." He scowled at me as though I were a child who had once again disappointed him. Perhaps that was precisely how he viewed me. There was such hatred in his eyes. Hatred that I had never before witnessed where I was concerned—not even when I reported to him what had happened to the souls of the Oudeis. Previously, he had always been a doting father for as long as I could recall. How one mistake unraveled it all so quickly was still hard for me to process.

Could my recollection have been so inaccurate? Was it conceivable that his outward affection had long belied an inner resentment that was so impassioned that, once released, it became undeniable? Or was one act, albeit a treasonous one, enough to nullify the unconditional love that he had always shown toward me?

Composing himself only slightly, he continued to berate me before my brothers, his voice echoing through the crisp night air.

"You are the reason they are here. Not me. You and your lack of faith combined with your lapse in judgment have led to this, Khara. If you have such little faith in my efforts to eliminate the threat the released gods may pose, tell me this: Why do you presume that any of you can reverse this debacle and send them back? If Hermes has already secured his stay above through sacrifice, who is to say that the others will not have already done the same?" I stared at him mutely, unable to supply an acceptable answer to any of the questions he posed. His argument was convincing. "You have unleashed an evil on this world that it will not survive."

"That was never the end I meant to see. I did what I did only to protect you," I replied, the detachment in my voice belying the true emotion behind my words. If he was truly going to cast me aside, then I wanted to at least be permitted the chance to explain the rationale behind my actions, though it would change nothing. "Persephone came to me, beseeching me for my help. She was confident that if I could keep the darkest souls of the Underworld at bay until your power returned to full strength that it would ensure your reign as well as your safety. We knew nothing of the former gods residing in the Oudeis. In fact—"

"My power is perfectly intact," he fumed, cutting me off.

"Persephone seemed far less confident in that truth than you, Father."

"So you would blame your mistake on her?"

"No. I do not seek to lay blame; I only wish to explain the reason why I did what I did," I said calmly, his erratic and harsh behavior toward me unnerving me as I spoke. "We succeeded in our endeavor—for me to ingest the damned souls—but neither she nor I could have possibly foreseen what would happen when I crossed the threshold of the Acheron, nor could we have known that there were former gods rotting away in the Oudeis. Persephone said the gods were gone . . . that they had suffered a true death at the hands of the Christian God—"

"Then she has been misinformed," he growled, cutting me off. "But regardless of the inaccuracy of her statement, both of you knew just how depraved the souls of the Oudeis are. Any reason why you would ever seek to remove them from their punishment is nothing short of insanity. There they were locked away, Khara. But here," he gestured, highlighting the morally questionable city around us, "they are free to feast." His expression hardened as his eyes went cold and distant. "You do not know what it was like when the gods roamed free, all-powerful—their actions without recourse. This world has been a better place in their absence. It should have remained that way."

"Hades," I replied, my words sharp and curt. "They would have escaped with or without my unwitting assistance. The walls between the damned and those who keep them at bay were failing—likely they still are. Whether you are unwilling to see that as truth or you are simply loath to admit it, I am certain that some part of you is not ignorant of the fact. If I myself could feel the fading magic when I crossed through the veil of the Elysian Fields, then it was only a matter of time before the souls they contained noticed when they decided to press against it."

I could see him tense when I delivered what I believed to be the slap of reality he sorely needed. In all my life, I had never seen anyone speak to him the way I just had. It was in that moment that I realized it may have been possible for even me—the one he used to call princess—to push him too far. However, before he had a chance to react, Oz was there, standing between us as though I needed saving.

"This is hardly the time to argue who is to blame for this, Hades," Oz growled, his wings spread wide to intimidate my father. Since they blocked my view, I could not see if his effort to do so was successful. All I heard was the rumble that escaped my father's chest. "It is done, and now, because you have chosen to withhold pertinent information, the situation has escalated. Quickly. So tell me, Soul Keeper, how did you intend to collect the escaped gods?"

I ducked under his wing to see Hades' expression tighten.

"He sent me," a dark and foreboding voice called out from behind us. It sent shivers down my spine. We all turned to find Deimos approaching, his body strapped heavily with assorted weapons. Weapons I had never seen before. Weapons that were not of this world. They were not of my father's, either.

"I see you've done an excellent job," Oz mocked, his wings twitching ever so slightly.

"I have taken out two already, Dark One," he retorted, pointing to the drying blood on a long, iridescent-white blade that was slung over his shoulder. "How many have you sent back?"

"Souls or gods?" Oz asked, seeking clarification. "I just want to be clear so I can keep the scoring fair. If you want a little friendly competition, I'm happy to oblige."

A sadistic smile crept across Deimos' face, but nothing about it indicated that he found Oz's taunting to be humorous.

"Either."

"Then the answer is too many to count, but I can wipe the slate clean and start over. It'll give you better odds."

"No need. Keep your advantage. It will not last long."

"How do we kill them?" Kierson asked bluntly, interrupting the posturing between the terror-inspiring son of Ares and the Dark One. "I mean, if the gods, maybe even the souls, are corporeal again, shouldn't we be able to take them out?" He looked around at the other faces in the group, his earnest expression forcing a tiny smile from me. In all that had transpired, Kierson, my most easily distracted brother, had not lost sight of the task at hand.

"You will need these," Deimos said condescendingly, indicating the weapons he carried, "if you want to kill anything, soul or god. And there is no guarantee that they will work in your hands, but it is better than going into battle against them virtually unarmed." His comment garnered a snarl from Casey, which only fed Deimos' arrogance. "It will not matter if they have been reanimated or not. In the right hands, these blades will smite them."

"Then stop fucking talking about them and hand them out," Casey growled, staring Deimos down as though he posed no threat to him. His fearlessness knew no end.

Perhaps it was foolishness instead.

Deimos cast a glance at Hades, who nodded once, his irritation with the situation still plain. Deimos then quickly dispersed his various daggers and swords to the brothers. He made quite a show of denying Oz a weapon.

I, too, was left empty-handed.

"Shall I use my bare hands to send them back?" I asked Hades, resentment bleeding into my tone.

"Deimos was told to scrounge up what he could find to equip your brothers with the necessary implements," he said flatly. "That was part of my plan, which you find so objectionable. I said nothing of it earlier because I had hoped that Deimos would be able to discreetly take care of the situation, but it is now clear that it has escalated too quickly for even him to defuse it in a sufficient period of time. Bringing weapons to your brothers was Plan B."

"It matters not. I will do my part without one."

"You will go back to the Underworld and wait," Hades said abruptly, looking off into the distance, his eyes trained on the sky. "I think you have done quite enough already."

"Khara," Pierson called, breaking the mounting tension between my father and me. "The body . . . where can I find it? I need to dispose of it."

"I will take you there," Drew replied, heading off in the direction we had come from earlier. Pierson gave me a tight nod and followed behind him, giving Deimos a wide berth.

"We should head out, too, Casey," Kierson said, his mannerisms displaying his discomfort with the situation. "Maybe we'll feel better after we get to kill some of these fuckers."

"I couldn't agree more," Casey drawled, his eyes slowly passing back and forth between Hades and his second in command. "You gonna be all right if we go, Khara?"

"She's going to be just fine," Oz answered, moving closer to me.

"I am always fine, Casey, or have you forgotten?"

"Right," he sighed. "Try to keep the batshit under wraps while we're gone."

With that, he and Kierson started off, making their way back to the Suburban. Where they were headed, I did not know. But I hoped I would see them again. The pressure in my heart would not likely abate until I did.

As soon as they were out of sight, the infighting resumed.

"You, Dark One. You will take her back to the Underworld. Now!" Hades barked, the lines of stress deeply etched into his face. He looked older. Haggard. No longer the image of stateliness that I had always remembered. "And you, Khara. You will remain there and await my return. Once I am back, we will decide upon a punishment befitting of your crimes."

Oz met Hades' order with defiant silence. It was clear to me that he had no intention of doing as he was ordered.

"I will return her," Deimos offered, an undeniable glint in his eyes as he spoke. His enthusiasm for the task did little to settle the mounting fear I felt in his presence. "I will keep her there until you return."

"Not a fucking chance," Oz growled. "She stays with me."

"I need you here," Hades told Deimos.

"He cannot be trusted with her," Deimos argued, forgetting himself for a brief moment.

And that was when I saw it—the faintest flash of concern in Hades' eyes. He did not want to send me back to the Underworld alone with Deimos. Oz's plan had worked. As far as my well-being was concerned, there remained a seed of doubt in his mind regarding his next in command.

Knowing that also made another point clear: Hades had not written me off as entirely as I had presumed. He was angry, yes, furious even, but he had not cast me away from his heart. His doing so publicly was for show. Perhaps all of his misdirected rage was.

"Leave us," Hades commanded. When neither Deimos nor Oz moved, Hades took me by the arm roughly and guided me down the street away from where the two dark and ominous warriors stood steadfastly. When he seemed satisfied that we were far enough away, he lightened his grip on my arm but continued walking briskly into the shadows cast by the vacant homes. "You must listen to me, my princess," he said softly, looking over his shoulder toward the looming silhouettes of Oz and Deimos. "You must go. You are not safe here."

"Will the Underworld be safer, given your absence?" I challenged. "Would I be safer in Deimos' care?" His lips pressed together, forming a grim line of understanding on his face.

"What would you have me do, Khara? Leave you here defenseless? I failed you once. I will not fail you again."

"You fail me only by your lack of confidence in me, Father. I am not defenseless. I can aid in this endeavor. You must let me show you what I have become." My uncharacteristically pleading tone echoed softly around us as I argued my case. It was plain in his wizened eyes that he did not want to concede, but he knew that there was no other option. He would not send me back with Deimos, and he could not force me back with Oz, who was unwilling to return me. Whatever Oz's plan was, it did not involve taking me back to the place where the Dark Ones had so easily found me.

"You possess Ares' stubbornness," he replied with the faintest of smiles. "It may be the only trait you inherited from him."

"When all of this is over, you can tell me all about him, and I will determine if your assessment is valid. Until then . . ." I paused, looking away from Hades. My gaze fell in the direction of Oz and Deimos, who stood nearly nose to nose. A battle was brewing between them, and it was one that we could not afford. We needed them both if we were to succeed in our mission. Without thinking, I started down the road toward them. Just as I did, their collective attention snapped to me. Even in the darkness of night, I could see the shock on their faces; the two of them simultaneously charged down the road toward me.

But they did not make it that far.

Instead a blinding bolt of lightning shot past me, the heat of it searing the flesh of my arm through the fabric of my shirt. It landed directly between Oz and Deimos, the force of the blast knocking them both off their feet, separating them by several yards when they finally came back to the ground. Neither of them moved.

Panic. That is what I felt as my throat tightened and my heart raced. My mind reeled, indecision paralyzing me momentarily. I, too, did not move. Not until I heard a threatening voice call to Hades. It held too much power in it. Power it should not have.

I carefully turned to look over my shoulder, uncertain what awaited us. With my worst fears affirmed, I stared down the street in awe of the glowing form standing in front of Hades. In front of my protector. My father.

The mystery of Zeus' whereabouts had been solved.

He was very much alive. Very much corporeal. And very much in full possession of his previous powers.

Powers he now aimed at my father.

32

Too many thoughts cluttered my mind at once.

The one that seemed most significant, however, was that Hades was in danger. So, without further analysis, I acted. I shouted his name while I hurried back to where he stood, glancing over my shoulder at the two bodies that remained behind us, still on the ground. They would be of no use in this fight.

Perhaps ever again.

"Father!" I called again as I watched Zeus loom above Hades ominously; he was the larger of the two brothers by a sizable margin. His aura of white became harsher to my eyes while I approached, and I sheltered them with my arm as best I could, all the while trying to focus on the brewing standoff. Hades stood stoically before his brother. His bravery was noteworthy, but it was clear that, in a fight, he would be bested by his larger, stronger, and more powerful sibling.

Hades turned sympathetic eyes to me briefly before returning his hardening gaze to Zeus.

"I knew you would come," he said, staring down his formidable brother.

"Good. I would not wish to hear you crying ambush before I choke the life from your body," Zeus retorted haughtily.

"Is that what you think is going to happen, brother?" Hades asked. I came to stand beside my father, glaring at Zeus as though I had nothing to fear. But I knew otherwise. Both Hades' and my lives depended precariously on Zeus' actions, and judging by the look in that god's eyes, he was out for blood. Blood that would easily spill. "What do you stand to gain in this, other than the revenge you clearly seek?"

Zeus scoffed arrogantly, as only one who had ruled the world at one time could.

"*Everything.*"

"And yet you will get nothing," Hades retorted. Father did not falter under the threat of death. Instead, he expertly bluffed, conveying an air of confidence regarding his argued advantage in the situation. An advantage he did not possess. "You are a fool if you think otherwise. All you stand to accomplish here today, Zeus, is a more painful imprisonment than you were first subjected to. You have escaped this time. You will not again."

"I will not need another chance," he replied with unmistakable malice in his voice. He then turned that hatred toward me. "And you . . ." His voice trailed off while he organized his thoughts. It was clear that he had a point he wished to make, and he wished to make it with precision. "You provide me with a conundrum. I could use you, but your allegiance to this disgrace," he said with disdain, indicating Hades, "presents a problem. The question is whether or not that hurdle can be overcome." I stared at him silently. "If yes, then I shall have to rethink my initial plans. If no, I will go forward as I intended."

His hazy, pale blue eyes bore into mine, looking for the answer he sought. The one I was unwilling to give. His whole being glowed more brilliantly as his irritation with my insubordination grew. It only fueled my silence.

"I see," he drawled. The disappointment in his tone was plain. He had hoped to acquire me—to use me as a pawn in whatever maniacal plan he had concocted—though I did not know why or how. What I did know was that I had no intention of siding with him. Hades had indeed proven loyal to me, just as I had hoped he would be. I would not betray him.

"She will never choose you," Hades said confidently. "She, unlike you, possesses a strong sense of family, which has only strengthened as of late."

"Then she will die," he said quietly, leaning in toward his brother conspiratorially.

"I would not count on that," called a voice from far down the street, where Deimos and Oz had been incapacitated. Every hair on my body stood at attention at the sound of it.

"I wouldn't either," shouted another, more welcome voice.

I looked back to see Deimos and Oz rushing toward us. The vengeance in their eyes was evident in the darkness Deimos possessed and the glowing white of Oz's form.

Zeus growled behind me, and I could see the light emanating from him more brightly. Suddenly, I was surrounded by it, a high and vast bubble of constantly moving lightning that caged Hades, Zeus, and me inside it. Oz and Deimos crashed into the protective electric field. Deimos dematerialized on contact, his body fading from solid form to a ghostly, immaterial presence in a split second. Then he disappeared entirely. Oz, however, did not. He stood steady, pressing against the flashing barrier, the pain it caused him evidenced by the grimace he wore.

But he pushed on regardless.

Thunder boomed around us as Zeus' anger rose, the cacophony of it drowning out Oz's cries. I could see Oz's mouth moving—the muscles in his neck strained while he fought against the electrified wall—but I could not hear him. The only sensation I experienced was the thrum of electrical energy that passed along my skin while the lightning danced continually around us. I felt as though it was charging me, fueling my own anger.

"Tell me what you want," I demanded. The quirk of Zeus' brow demonstrated his intrigue. "You said that I may side with you. I want to know what is in it for me."

Inside our flashing bubble, with thunder clapping loudly around us, Zeus roared with laughter. Hades, however, flinched at my words, though his reaction would have been imperceptible to anyone but me.

"I want to rule," he said plainly, as though that answer was nothing short of obvious. "More specifically, I want to rule the Underworld, though my aspirations may become loftier over time. And you could help me."

"How?"

"I have learned of what you can do. Do not think that the Oudeis is so estranged from the other fields. Well, it *was* . . . until you came along. Or, better yet, until you were ripped from the Underworld. There was a palpable shift in the air, you see. Things became rather interesting in your absence. And now, they prove even more interesting in your presence." He leaned toward me conspiratorially. "I have you to thank for my freedom, do I not?" I met his question with my silence. "I wish to repay you for this courtesy you have done me."

"You wish to control me," I rebutted. The energy around me pricked my skin painfully.

"I will control all eventually. But you would be in a far more enviable position than others if you join me willingly."

I stared at him, truly taking in his regal glory. But there was an edge to it—a madness—that simply could not be denied. I had no intention of becoming a tool for him to use, especially since I did not understand how he would use me. What I did know was that Oz had forewarned of this—that once word got out about my status as an anomaly, the greatest evils would seek to either wield or destroy me.

I would settle for neither.

"On that point, we shall have to agree to disagree," I replied acerbically.

"Then you die," he said suddenly, lifting his arm, which was ablaze with white-hot fire. Before I could react, he blasted me directly in the chest with a bolt of lightning, sending me hurtling through the air until his electrical cage abruptly stopped my flight, my back slamming painfully against it. The fiery blast ran through my body and caused indescribable pain. I convulsed violently, still pinned to the electric wall behind me by Zeus' bolt. My screams nearly drowned out Hades' wails. I fell limp to the ground, the smell of charred flesh offending my nostrils.

In my peripheral vision, I could see Oz thrashing against the charged bubble that enclosed me, his fists pounding it in futility. Painfully, I let my head loll to the side to see him. He stilled instantly. Through barely open eyes, I watched while he pressed his palm against Zeus' cage of lightning. Had it not been there, he would have reached my face. That gesture was the last thing I saw before my vision doubled, then blurred, then blacked out entirely.

My heartbeat slowed.

I was dying.

For a moment, I could hear Hades' distant voice, his cries signaling the bereavement he felt at the loss he was only moments away from suffering. Then everything fell silent. With my father's sorrow no longer the melody signaling my end, I waited for death to take me in its arms and deliver me to my home.

But death eluded me.

My mind had been drifting off into a dark and inviting place when the implications of Hades' silence jostled it into alertness. Hades would be the next to fall at the hands of his unstable sibling. That unacceptable fate was enough to pry me from the throes of death.

I would not fail my father again.

I had not realized that my breathing had stopped completely until my body, unwilling to march into death without a fight, shot up off the ground, gasping for air. Still in distress, I tried to focus my eyes on Hades, to see if Zeus had indeed killed him. He had not. Not yet. He was enjoying torturing him far too much to end it quickly.

As my senses returned to me and my rage grew, I became acutely aware that I was glowing. Not a faint aura of leftover static. Not a dull haze surrounding me. I was as blinding as the bolt of lightning that Zeus had throttled me with. The thrumming sensation that coursed through my body felt foreign and uncomfortable, like it didn't belong there. Like it was trying to escape.

Zeus had turned his back on me, presumably because he thought I was dead and no longer posed a threat. Struggling to stand as quietly as I could, I looked past Zeus to see my father's eyes as he knelt before his brother. They were empty. Defeated.

My rage boiled over.

Zeus drew his arm back dramatically, and I watched as it started to glow more intensely, its incandescence increasing with every second until it was a blaze of white-blue fire and spark, waiting to escape its corporeal confines. Ready to deliver the killing blow, Zeus taunted Hades one last time.

"Any last words you'd like to share before I wipe both you and what is left of your pathetic army from existence?" he asked, raising his fiery blue arm to the sky.

It was then that Hades saw my approach, glancing past Zeus. At first, he looked as though he was seeing the impossible. I had seen that look before, on Oz's face when he realized what I was. The impossible was not new to me.

I embodied it.

The demoralized expression on his face hardened into one of determination.

"The Underworld will never be yours," Hades said calmly, his singed and broken body motionless but defiant. He would not show cowardice in the face of death—a trait that I had learned from him over the years.

"We shall see about that," Zeus said coldly, leaning into his brother's face. "Let it be known that the mighty Zeus has returned . . ."

"It will never be yours," I heard a voice mutter, affirming Hades' words. It was threateningly low and menacing. I did not recognize it at first, though I should have.

It was my own.

Zeus wheeled around to see me. The smile he had worn earlier when he blasted me to near death—the one that held the centuries' worth of hatred, jealousy, and madness that consumed him—fell from his countenance. All that was left in its wake was disbelief.

He screamed in frustration, raising the fiery appendage meant for my father toward me, ready to try to kill me again. I, like my father, remained defiant, holding steadfast. It served only to further infuriate him.

A blinding flash released from the palm of his hand was aimed yet again at my chest. But this time when it struck me, I did not move. It did not burn. It did not hurt.

Instead, a cold calm overcame me. My mind cleared. My gaze sharpened. My glowing appendages rose slowly and aimed themselves at the reanimated god.

To know that one so mighty was about to truly fall seemed unfathomable to him, judging by his countenance. The disbelief in his eyes was all-consuming.

"Khara," Hades said softly, struggling to come stand beside me. I did not need to turn and face him to know that he was concerned. He had not known me to be capable of wielding lightning. I, too, was ignorant of the ability. My powers were ever evolving.

"Worry not, Father," I replied, my voice distant and detached. "Your kingdom will soon be restored." I felt my neck crook to the side while the pressure in my arms started to build. It became warm and uncomfortable, itching to be released. Staving off the desire a little longer, I smiled wickedly at Zeus. "You offered my father the opportunity to say his final words. I will extend no such courtesy to you."

Obeying the power's call, I released it as lightning shot forth from my arms, striking Zeus in the chest. It continued to flow from me for longer than it had from him, and his body awkwardly danced in response to the torture. The pain he felt was excruciating indeed, given his shrill cries. I, however, felt nothing at all.

Neither pain nor emotion plagued me.

When the charge had fully emptied from me, I walked over to where Zeus lay, his smoking body motionless. His dull eyes staring up at the sky. At the home he would never see again. His soul was now forever bound to the Underworld, and this time there would be no escaping it.

"Heavy is the crown," I whispered to his cooling remains. "There is a price to pay for attempting to destroy my family. Rest assured that others will soon learn this truth as well."

"Khara," Hades called from behind me. "How? How did you do this?"

"I know not, Father," I replied, turning to face him.

"I don't know either, new girl. But you really are a never-ending source of interest to me," Oz drawled, seemingly materializing out of nowhere. Not far behind him were my brothers. "Nuking Zeus—I did *not* see that coming."

"She is a vessel," Pierson said quietly, approaching with a certain reverence I had not known him capable of. "Don't you see? It all makes sense now. She harbors the powers of others and then releases them. That is her weapon, though she seems unable to control it entirely."

"What are you saying?" Hades asked my analytical sibling.

"I am saying that whatever power is used against her she retains as her own until she is able to use it against her attacker. Perhaps against anyone. That is what needs to be ascertained."

"She used it against Oz, albeit unknowingly, but still," Kierson said, reminding me again that I was to blame for Oz's status as a Dark One.

"I do not believe that was entirely the same thing, Kierson. It seems our sister has an arsenal of abilities, not all of which have likely surfaced yet."

"So what happened to Oz, then?" Kierson asked.

"I think that when it comes to souls, there is a depth to her that I don't fully understand," he started, eyeing me tightly. "Her angelic traits complicate things. I think there is a part of her meant to help those burdened with darkness, though that is purely speculation. It is just the sense I get from her."

"And I thought I was an army," Casey scoffed, though the remark lacked the heat that his cynicism normally held.

"Fucking with her would appear unwise," Oz interjected, demanding my attention with his formidable presence. "I'll have to remember that next time." His characteristic smirk twisted his expression, reminding me of the Oz I had first encountered. The one I loathed, then learned to appreciate in my own way. In that moment, he was a less complicated being.

Then he unfurled his obsidian wings, and the memory faded.

Shrouding our group in darkness, he stepped toward me, our bodies mere inches apart.

"If you're done showing us all your tricks for now, it's time to go." He took my arm in his hand and closed the distance between us in a second. "See you in hell," he taunted the others as he pushed off, flying us up into the night sky.

"I can fly on my own."

"I'm well aware of that," he replied; yet his hold on my arm was unrelenting.

"Where are you taking me?" I asked. I wanted to struggle against his powerful grip, but my body betrayed me. It was all too happy to be where it was.

"We are going back to the Underworld. Weren't you listening?"

"To whom?"

"To Zeus." He replied in a tone that made his answer seem too obvious to have to state. When I said nothing, he leaned his lips against my ear and breathed heavily against it. "He wanted to rule the Underworld. A lofty aspiration for one unable to escape it, don't you think?"

"He had always reigned on Mount Olympus. Wanting to regain any measure of power is not a surprising revelation about one such as he."

"No, it isn't, but it does beg certain questions."

"Such as?" I asked, trying desperately to focus on the harsh wind assaulting my face rather than the warm being at my back.

"Such as how he escaped in the first place. And why he presumed he would take over in Hades' stead."

"But I enabled his escape," I whispered. My admission was barely a sound.

"Indeed," he rumbled softly. "But was that your intended outcome?"

"No. I was trying to protect my father."

"And who was so keen to get you to expel the worst of the Underworld in the name of protecting Hades?"

His question needed no answer. I then clearly understood what he was not so clearly saying. Persephone had been the one to come to me, appealing to the love I had for Hades. Persephone had been the one to misinform me about the gods. She had used me. She had endangered those I held dearest.

She would pay for her affront.

She would pay dearly indeed.

33

We were intercepted on the far bank of the Acheron by a very distressed nymph, who before that moment had remained unaccounted for. Given her disheveled nature—white-blonde hair blown ragged and clothing in tatters—it seemed apparent that her return to the world above had been hampered by someone or something. Perhaps plural of both.

"Khara!" she shouted from the far side of the river, though her erratic breathing made it hard for her to do so. She was cut and bleeding, quite badly in some areas, and she collapsed forward, her hands holding her knees tightly to keep herself standing.

"What's going on?" Oz rumbled, stalking to the water's edge. He scooped me up and brought me across, putting me down quickly to assess the wounded sprite.

"Khara," she repeated between gasps for breath. "I tried . . . I tried to come back, but—"

"Rest for a moment," I ordered, cutting her off. I needed her explanation to be concise and accurate. In her state, neither of those qualities was guaranteed. "Catch your breath, then tell us what is going on."

"I don't like this," Oz said, tensing by my side. His eyes scanned the wide-open area acutely, searching for an enemy I could neither see nor feel. "Where is Persephone?" When Aery did not answer him immediately, he grabbed her face, forcing it to turn upward to meet his gaze. "If I find out that you had anything to do with this, it will mean your end, little one."

"She isn't here," Aery replied coolly. Much to her credit and the strength I had known her to possess, she showed no fear in the face of Oz's wrath.

"Where. Is. She?"

"Gone. I know not why or how, but she is gone."

"Impossible," Oz spat, tightening his grip on the nymph while he yanked her to her feet, still cupping her chin harshly in his hand. "She must be here, which means you are trying to help her."

"Oz!" I snapped, grabbing his forearm. He did not budge under my grasp. "Release her, now. Let her at least offer her side of the story before you crush her. We will learn nothing if you cannot keep your aggression at bay."

His head swiveled toward me slowly. Nothing else moved. When his eyes met mine, they were glowing brightly, and in them I knew there was little of the Oz I had once known. The darkness was taking over.

We spent a moment in silence, staring at one another. As with Deimos, I could not wither away from his growing hostility. His need to inflict pain. All I could do was remain defiant without further angering him, for Aery's sake as well as my own.

"I don't understand how she managed to leave here," Aery began, interrupting my nonverbal war with the Dark One. "But she did. She shouldn't be able to. . . . I get that. But when everything went crazy, and all the veils fell, I looked everywhere for her—to make sure she was okay. I found nothing. No sign of her. No trace."

All the veils . . .

"But she is bound to the Underworld," Oz corrected, feigning patience when it was clear that he had none left. "And because of that binding, she cannot leave."

"I know. When Khara left, it was as though things were back to how they'd been in the past, when Persephone was unable to go, but . . . then she did."

"Perhaps someone helped her," I offered. "Where is Father's army?"

"Slain."

Her reply gave me pause.

"All of them?"

"All that I saw when I escaped the Great Hall."

"My brothers," I asked urgently. "What of them? Those in the Elysian Fields?"

"I don't know," she whispered, her eyes full of unspoken apology.

"Where is Deimos?" Oz asked, directing her attention back to him, his grip on her face lessening slightly. Just enough for her features to twist in confusion at his question.

"He is above. With Hades. He accompanied him when he left."

"He *was* above," Oz corrected. "But he dematerialized when he was struck directly by Zeus' lightning. And you and I both know where he goes when magic overcomes his earthly form, don't we, Aery?"

She paled.

"He comes here," she whispered. Her expression turned to a mixture of disbelief and understanding. My own mirrored hers until my mind caught up to Oz's accusation.

"You think he aided her somehow?" I asked, my tone laced with incredulity. "But if that were possible, why would she have not done so long ago? Why now? What has changed?"

"That, new girl," Oz muttered under his breath, "is what we're going to find out." He turned his once-again dark eyes to Aery, releasing her fully to stand before him. "You are going to pull yourself together and fly to Detroit immediately. You will track down the brothers there, and if they have left, you will not return until you have found either them or Hades. Am I clear?" She nodded her head. "Tell them what is happening here, but do not tell them that Persephone is missing. Leave that detail out. For now."

"Why?" she asked, rubbing her chin lightly with the back of her hand.

"Because we do not know who we can trust. The fewer players involved in this, the better," he said, narrowing his eyes at her. "And if something that has been said here in confidence amongst us is somehow leaked . . ."

"Then I am dead," she said matter-of-factly.

He nodded, his wicked smile stretched widely across his face.

"Others must surely know she is gone," I argued, knowing that her absence amid the chaos could not have gone unseen by all.

"True. But can any of those beings leave the Underworld of their own accord?" No. They could not. My silence served as my reply. "So you see, the matter will be contained for now."

"Are you suggesting we leave here with the Underworld in total upheaval?"

"Yes. That is precisely what I am suggesting."

"Khara," Aery implored. "Everyone here—those that served your father for centuries—they'll all be killed eventually. The swarm of souls is strengthening. I've never seen anything like it. They move as one unit, seeking and destroying. Those that cannot escape are bound to die an excruciating death."

"Then that is their fate," Oz said dismissively, turning on his heel to leave.

But her words tugged fiercely at something in my mind. Something I remembered from just before I passed out in front of the opened veil of the Oudeis. The souls then had appeared sentient, working together to enter me. But they had not seemed that way on the shore of the Acheron when I accidentally released them. There, they had been a swirling, chaotic mass. It was an observation that I could not shake.

It seemed an unlikely coincidence.

"Where is Hecate?" I asked, barely recognizing the menace in my tone.

"I . . . I don't know," Aery replied. "I haven't seen her. It's been a melee down here. It hasn't been conducive to seeking people out."

Oz, having heard my question while he retreated, stopped short. The wheels in his mind turned rapidly. I could see it in his expression.

"Perhaps we will find her not far from Persephone. Those two are thick as thieves."

Before I could respond, a shrill echo grew in the distance. The dead were approaching.

"Time to go, new girl," Oz called, storming toward me. He snatched me up in his grasp just as I saw the wall of ghostly souls approaching in the distance.

"I can stop them," I whispered aloud, mesmerized by their swirling mass.

"Next time," Oz bit out, pulling me against him tightly while he took to the sky to cross the Acheron. The wails of the dead crescendoed the second we reached the other side. Their bodies crashed upon the opposite shoreline only to hit an invisible barrier, bouncing like flies off a window. They could not leave. Comforting though it was, I could not help but feel as though I was abandoning my father's post. The Underworld needed a leader—someone to uphold the order and maintain the magic it required. That void needed to be filled.

I am the princess of the damned, I thought. *I can rule in Hades' stead.* Dark, unfamiliar thoughts ran rampant through my mind while Oz pulled me away from the cries of the condemned. They were calling to me—calling to the darkness within me—wordlessly begging me to return.

And return I would, once I found the one responsible for all this chaos.

The one responsible for my father's near-death.

Persephone could run, but she could not hide.

EPILOGUE

My quest to find Persephone proved more challenging than I could ever have imagined. In my frustration, I returned to the Victorian, under Oz's supervision, of course, to rendezvous with my father. He and the brothers had been hunting the escaped souls with moderate success. The weapons Deimos had provided were indeed working in their hands, but the brothers were greatly outnumbered. Undoing the deed I had been manipulated into doing would prove no easy task.

Once in Detroit, I found myself drawn to the rooftop where Oz had called forth my wings. The rooftop he had promptly thrown me off. The apology I remembered from my dream rang through my mind when I looked over the ledge. *I'm sorry . . .* Sorry for what, I was still unsure.

My father came to find me up there, staring off into the distant sunset. He said nothing, just stood beside me, watching the orange-red glow as it nestled down deeper behind the horizon. It looked like the Underworld.

His former kingdom.

After Oz and I had told him that his home had been overrun by those condemned to it, Hades had not returned. Instead, he remained behind to help slay those that terrorized the world above. There was a distinct sadness in his eyes when they reflected the dying sunlight in the distance. His decision to abandon his home did not sit well with him.

Nor did it sit well with me.

Something was not right about his decision. The boys, though out-numbered, were more than capable of eradicating those that remained above. They had proven as much. They did not require Hades' assistance in the matter. And yet he stayed, though it was so clear that he was needed below. The question of why he did so nagged at me until I could no longer suppress it, the word flying out of my mouth into the darkness that settled around us on the rooftop. "*Why?*" That one word, so small—so innocuous—managed to tear through layers of mystery and deceit and betrayal in a single utterance.

Hades looked down at me with a sorrowful expression. He maintained his silence. But there was an apology in it, much like the one Oz had offered when he watched me fall to my would-be death. There was a story there to be told. Seeing his reluctance to tell it written on his countenance, I ran through all the conceivable reasons that seemed probable, reasons that could satisfy that one tiny inquiry.

After some time, I settled on only one.

Staring at him, disbelief emanating from me, I disclosed my conclusion. His expression fell further. He did not reply, but his emotional devolution proved answer enough. I was right. And the truth was impossible to believe.

Hades, King of the Dead, Keeper of Souls, could not return to the Underworld.

ACKNOWLEDGMENTS

I'm going to keep these short and sweet as always. I have an amazing group of people that I have amassed over time—my team, if you will—and they do everything they can to aid me in my literary journey. My beta readers, Kristy, Virginia, and Cristina, are incredibly helpful (and painfully honest). They make sure that the story is buttoned up tightly. My editor, Jennifer Ryan, makes sure that my ideas flow seamlessly and follow some semblance of proper grammar. My husband, Bryan, juggles all he can to make sure I have some time to write these crazy stories in my head, of which there are many. And last but not least, my alpha reader/amazing friend/voice of reason, Shannon, who helps keep me on track, sorts out the ideas in my head, and reads the jumbled nonsense I email her to help me develop my stories to some level of perfection. I literally could not do this without all of you. Thanks.

ABOUT THE AUTHOR

Copyright 2014 Dannielle Damm

Amber Lynn Natusch is the author of the bestselling Caged, as well as the Light and Shadow series with Shannon Morton. She was born and raised in Winnipeg, and speaks sarcasm fluently because of her Canadian roots. She loves to dance and sing in her kitchen—much to the detriment of those near her—but spends most of her time running a chiropractic practice with her husband, raising two small children, and attempting to write when she can lock herself in the bathroom for ten minutes of peace and quiet. She has many hidden talents, most of which should not be mentioned but include putting her foot in her mouth, acting inappropriately when nervous, swearing like a sailor when provoked, and not listening when she should. She's obsessed with home renovation shows, should never be caffeinated, and loves snow. Amber has a deep-seated fear of clowns and deep water . . . especially clowns swimming in deep water.